The Dead Return

by

DT Mularkey

Drake's Key

Cover Art by *Teddi Black*

The Wild Rose Press, Inc.
PO Box 708
Adams Basin, NY 14410-0708
Visit us at www.thewildrosepress.com

Publishing History
First Edition, 2025
Trade Paperback ISBN 978-1-5092-6207-6
Digital ISBN 978-1-5092-6208-3

Drake's Key
Published in the United States of America

Acknowledgements

Many thanks to my hard-working writer's group the McSherry Writers in McAlester, OK. These ladies have listened to every word in this book. They've kept me honest, told me when I bored them, and laughed in appropriate places. They have encouraged me at every turn.

I am grateful to The Wild Rose Press for publishing my previous Drake's book, The Seven Year Glitch. My editor Ally Robertson taught me valuable lessons I needed as a writer of novels. As I like to say, there's no dialogue in textbooks, so her help was invaluable.

Finally, to my partner Jerry who listens to me as I read my work over and over. I owe you big time.

Chapter 1

Rosalie

"Sit, Mom. I've got something to tell you, something important." Allie squirmed on her chair.

Uh oh. I stood at the sink and peeled apples for a pie. I rinsed my hands and grabbed a dishtowel. "Okay, I'm sitting. What's this big news?"

She looked in my eyes, an old trick of hers to catch my reaction. "I found Dad."

Impossible. I knew Skipper Warren was dead. I'd looked. His folks had looked. The bar association in a dozen states had looked. He fell off the edge of the planet twenty-five years ago. She was wrong. "No you didn't. He's not alive, honey." I didn't want her to be disappointed again. I took her hand in mine.

"No, Mom. I did it. I found Skipper Warren. He's still alive and I'm—"

"Stop this! I accepted it years ago. It's time you did too," I barked.

She pulled her hand away, fished a paper from her purse and laid it on the table. "I have proof. Look, this is my DNA test done last week. Notice the date—April twenty-second—is last week. This man is one hundred percent my father."

"A DNA test?" I picked up the report and scanned it. I recognized the name of the lab, and so far, their work seemed correct. *No process is perfect.*

"It's a test that compares two people's DNA—"

I cut her off. "I know what a DNA test is. What kind of a nurse do you think I am?" I read and re-read the report. My stomach twisted into a knot. *No! No, this needs to stop.*

I stormed off to my room wrestling with demons I thought I'd vanquished years ago; I learned to sleep in a bed of my own making, and this happens. Now my daughter wanted to pull back the covers and expose ugly little bedbug secrets that bite you in the butt, ones that she didn't know existed.

****

Allie sat at the table when I walked into the kitchen the next morning. An apple pie sat on the stove. Allie hated to leave a job unfinished as much as I did. There was a fresh pot of coffee, and its aroma drew me near. I poured a cup and slid a slice of pie on a saucer. To delay the inevitable, I got the vanilla ice cream out of the freezer and added a scoop to the pie. Then, and only then, I joined Allie at the table. "Good morning," I said, but I did not look her way as I took my first bite of breakfast.

She nursed a cup of coffee. "Good morning to you too, and may I add that you look like hell this fine morning." My beautiful curly-haired Allie. Straight to the point even if it included a thorn. I taught her that. I ate until my pie was gone. Delicious. My recipe, but she added something else I couldn't quite put my finger on. Something I never used. Something that made it better.

"I prefer that you not pursue this, Allie," I said, exhausted from a lack of sleep.

"I know, Mom." She refilled our cups but avoided my kiss on the cheek I loved so much.

I avoided her eyes. "There are things that you don't

know that…that could hurt him."

She gave me a knowing smile. "Him? Oh, you mean *Dad* might have a family, or that *Dad* might reject me, and by association, reject you?"

Straight to the point. *Crap. I hate it when she's right.* "Yes. Even if it turns out with your imagined happy ending—whatever that might be—it's going to get ugly first. For me, for him, and for you caught in between." *Real ugly, and she might be a casualty.*

There was a long silence after which she hit me with her best shot. "You need to *know*, Mom. As much as I do, you need to. You've kept him alive for me. Why? Why if not to prepare *me* for finding *him*?"

She waited as I mulled this over. I never should have let her take those psychology classes. *Was she right?* I always left room for doubt, so maybe…maybe she was.

"How did you locate his DNA?" Simple question. *Just how did she find him?*

"I loaded my DNA profile into a national database that the US Marshal's service has access to. I know, it was a longshot. I got a hit within half an hour." She finished her coffee.

He's alive? "So he's a criminal?" That gave me reason for pause. *I never expected that.*

"No. Well yes, but no. It's really complicated. I can explain it to you on the way there." She took my plate and licked off the melting ice cream.

Gee, thanks, kiddo. I was saving that ice cream for last. "There? Are we going on a trip?" *Whoops, what did I just do?*

"I arranged for you to go with me as a paid nurse next week. I'll be undercover for a few days, but if everything goes according to plan, we'll all meet up at his island."

I know personally about "plans" and how they can suddenly go off the rails. "All right, but…Allie, this is the last time. The *very* last time. Promise me."

He was a criminal and owned an island. Yippee, Skippy. *I could hardly wait to get this hopeless obsession over with.*

****

I parked my fanny in Allie's Miami apartment while she went undercover at Drake's Key Resort. She held a briefing before she left. "Okay, Mom. Hold your questions and comments until I finish. Skipper Warren owns this expensive resort and island. He also owns this machine called the Gizmo that lets two people exchange bodies."

I rolled my eyes. I put my hand on her forehead and checked for a fever. She pushed my hand away. "Seven years ago my dad and a man named Dexter Drake changed bodies when they opened the resort. We don't know why. However, every summer the resort shuts down for hurricane season." I checked her pulse. *A little high, but she's excited.*

"Last summer, Dexter Drake was arrested after the Preakness—you know the horse race near the end of May in Baltimore. He was accused of beating a bookie about a bet. In the state of Maryland, DNA samples are taken when an arrest is made for certain types of crimes, and that was one of them.

"Now if charges are dropped the person can request the DNA be erased from the database, but that didn't happen. Maybe Dexter forgot. Maybe he left it there on purpose. Anyways, when I ran my DNA against the database, my match hit my dad's DNA but under the name of Dexter Drake. Now I admit that threw me for a loop."

"The Gizmo?" I asked.

"Yes, but you know me. I came across a rock-solid lead after so many years. I contacted the police department that arrested Drake. His mug shot from that arrest was a photo of Skipper Warren. Older, of course, but I'd have recognized him anywhere."

"May I see it? The mug shot?" I was afraid to look. *What if I didn't recognize him?*

Allie nodded. I raised my hand, but she ignored it. "I'm on a roll, Mom. Dexter Drake has a record."

My brain was upside down. Who beat the bookie: the man or the brain in the man? This was stupid even to me. I felt my own forehead just in case I was the one with a fever.

"Mom, did you know my dad's full legal name?" She paused with her lips pressed together.

"Silly question. Of course. It's Skipper Warren." I smirked.

She shook her head. "I thought so too, but it's not Skipper; it's Captain. News to me that Skipper is just another way to address the captain of a ship, but there it was on his birth certificate: Captain Rutledge Warren."

"Huh. How did I not know his name?" I felt slightly—I don't know—slightly stupid again.

"To make things more complicated, he quit using Skipper in the Army. He went by Ledger from Rutledge, I suspect. When he passed the bar in New York he registered as C. Rutledge Warren." She stopped to catch her breath.

"New York? We never thought to look in New York. That's a mighty long distance from Oklahoma, baby girl."

"It is, and he changed his social security number. Yes, it is a far piece as Momsie used to say. FYI, C. Rutledge Warren does not have a record."

"So why are you going to his island?" *This better be good.*

"We're arresting an international trafficker who will be a guest there. I'm not promising anything, but there's a chance I may be able to arrange a meeting between you and Skipper Warren. For sure I'll be able to speak to him after the arrest. There's also a chance he may leave before I can arrange a meeting. Are you in for that? Even if it's not a sure thing?"

Was this a hare-brained scheme or an honest to goodness longshot? I considered my options. "Yes, regardless of the outcome, as long as we don't do whatever this is *ever* again. Deal?"

We shook on it. "Deal." Then we hugged. I got my kiss on the cheek.

How could I believe Allie would ever find him? *More importantly, what do I wear to a legal kidnapping?*

****

Drake's was a chic resort for the richest folks on Earth, and I was dressed in my most dazzling nurses' scrubs. I didn't mind because the plan said I wouldn't be getting off the plane. *Super-duper.* I was still unclear on the deal with Skipper.

I boarded the US Marshals' plane in Miami. A forward compartment was set up as a small nurses' station. The only other passenger gave me a quick tour. Señor something-or-another would be confined to a small, reinforced room in the back, or the "aft" as he told me, and wearing handcuffs and leg chains. He'd be under the effects of a sedative administered via whiskey, which at once presented a problem for me. I should know how much and what sedative he was given before I administered any more.

The other passenger told me, "Rosalie, if he still resists arrest and is a danger to the Marshals or the crew—and of course *you*—it's your job to put him down, legally of course."

My job? This free trip was coming at a higher price than I expected.

We landed at an out-of-the-way cargo airport on Drake's Key about 11 p.m. Saturday. I paced from one end of the plane to the other dozens of times, twelve steps each way. I counted the sutures, I counted the plasma and the O-neg blood packs in the fridge, I counted every last adhesive bandage twice. I peed three times in an hour. No, I wasn't nervous; not much I wasn't.

I never expected to see Skipper again. Now I worried that I wouldn't. *This was not me. Get it together, Rosalie, or Allie won't take you out to play anymore.*

A dark limo pulled up on the runway. The man in the plane opened the door, let down the stairs, and stepped back. I peeked out a window as a dark-haired man was hustled up the stairs and into the plane. I guesstimated his weight at 170 pounds. He was seated and secured in the aft compartment, his seatbelt his only restraint other than the chains. *Yikes!* He was still swearing in Spanish and yanked on his restraints.

I double checked the tranquilizer recommendations and his weight. Not too much, not too little, only the Goldilocks amount that was just right for someone who farmed and sold infants. He slept like a baby after my little nightcap.

When they were done, the two men sat in front of the locked door to the cabin with the prisoner. A few minutes later, the older man answered his phone.

"Yes, Mr. Bennett. Mr. Fernandez is tucked in tight." He nodded at me as he spoke. "Nothing we, or I should say the nurse, couldn't handle." He winked at me. "Yes, sir, we do have room for another passenger. Who is it?" He looked over at me and smiled. "That's a surprise. Mr. Warren himself. Yes, sir. We are ready to go as soon as you are on board."

Sooo… it seems Rosalie's best-case scenario was happening after all. The resort owner Mr. Skipper Warren would be catching a ride to Miami with us. I had no idea what to do or what to say to a ghost. I kept myself busy as I heard people come onboard. I heard Allie's voice, and then I heard *him* talk to the two men in the back. I pretended to count swabs until I heard Skipper's voice behind me.

"Excuse me, nurse. Would you look at this cut?"

I turned around, took his hand in mine, and replied, "Certainly, sir. Let me see that." *Scintillating conversation, Rosalie.*

He said, "A promise ring? I haven't seen one of those in a while."

Oddly enough, I'd put it back on before we left home. *Why?* "Yes, sir. I refused to give mine up. Mom bought another to send to you, Skip," I said simply.

When our eyes met, I knew we still had unfinished business, with a daughter thrown in for good luck.

Chapter 2

Skipper AKA Ledger

"Mr. Warren, are you comfortable?" the Marshal asked me.

"Yes, thank you." I sat by my daughter Allie as I held her hand and across the aisle sat Rosalie. I evaluated the risk I brought to any relationship with both of these women. Having found them, or more correctly, having been found by them, could I let them go? Even this very meeting seemed to be a risk for all of us. *Was this meet-up just to acknowledge that we all existed and are related, or do we try to find a way to build a family, a family that was inadvertently put on hold twenty-five years ago?*

I leaned towards Rosalie and whispered, "I don't understand. When did you find out our dads were brothers? How is it you are alive?"

"I know. It's complicated. We'll talk later..." she said as she looked towards the aft end of the plane, "...in private."

My daughter, on the other hand, wanted to talk now. She pulled a small photo album out of her carryon and off I went on an emotional carnival ride. Up and down, around, and around. Whee!

"Let's start with my first year. Okay, Dad?" She had her finger inside the album cover.

"Sure." I stared at the album marked *Year One* and

tried to recall what year that was exactly. *I failed.*

Allie opened the album to the first page. It wasn't a picture of her but of Rosalie, my Rosalie as I remembered her for so long. It was surreal looking at that photo and knowing I was sitting across the aisle from her, but not *her*. Her pregnant belly in the photo was not anything I ever imagined. "Here's Mom and me on the day I was born, just before Poppy took us to the hospital." She pointed to the bulge in Rosalie's shirt as she laughed.

I was overwhelmed realizing that I didn't know anything about how hard it must have been to be seventeen, pregnant, and alone. I used to make fun of those girls who left high school because they "got knocked up" and of the boys who did it and then abandoned them. *Now I knew that was us. Rosalie and me.*

I shook my head as Allie moved from picture to picture. I started to feel dizzy and as if I were running into walls, so I asked which way to the rest room and excused myself. I wondered if Allie was telling Rosalie about the attempt on my life. Or how she and Marshal Bennet caught me making a run for my own plane before offering me a ride on theirs. I wondered what Rosalie thought about all of that. We had three hours until we landed. *Let's see how far we get by then.*

I sat down again between my ladies. "Allie, could we go back to the beginning and take it slower? Please." My mind kept wandering from the photos to other things. Was my former general manager Dex still alive and out to kill me? How could I have had a daughter and not known it? What outstanding threats against my life were left to *slice* and *dice* my life to pieces? And the Gizmo, what do I do about it?

When I found myself escaping from my own island with Rosalie and our daughter Allie, I thought my life was suddenly going to be what it *should* have been. We would pick up where our lives together ended: me in the Army off saving the world, and Rosalie finishing high school. I envisioned Rosalie going to class, living at home helping her father the Reverend Smith, baking brownies for the veterans' home, and adoring me from afar. Now, after twenty-five years all wrongs would be made right. *Yeah. This was going to be a piece of cake—not.*

****

The US Marshals dropped Allie, Rosalie, and me off in Miami. Allie promised to catch up with us in a few weeks. "I love you both," she said, "but remember you are complete strangers in more ways than one." She hugged and kissed us both and drove off to her apartment. I met my daughter less than twelve hours ago. *Already she was giving me orders.*

It was decades since I was alone with Rosalie. I said, "What now?"

"We talk. We talk until we are done or dead. Your choice," she answered as she picked up her luggage. *She looked at me as if the ball were in my court.*

All right. I can do that. "Your place or mine?" Mine, it turned out. My private plane was waiting in Miami thanks to my assistant Peaches, and off we went to my New York City apartment. My driver June picked us up in my limo at my private New Jersey airport. Rosalie fell asleep on my shoulder in the car.

Peaches alerted my housekeeper Estafania, so the fridge was stocked, the fireplace ablaze, and she'd discreetly left to visit her daughter in Westchester. June, whose apartment was on a separate floor, could have the limo or the Range Rover at the front door in five minutes.

"Is there somewhere I can shower, Skipper?"

"Sure, my shower is straight back and to the left."

She hesitated. "Is there a guest room? I'd be more comfortable in my own…"

Why did I assume she'd be in my room? What must she think that I even suggested it? I led her down the hall to my farthest guest room and opened the door. She poked her head in and looked around. "Thanks, this will be just fine. I won't be too long." Rosalie closed the door behind her.

Peaches called earlier and left a message. "Boss, nobody has seen Dex since last night. Should we just cover for him and go on?"

If I guessed correctly yesterday that my Drake's general manager was trying to kill me, and his off-the-books clients from last night had a score to settle, he was dead. I called Peaches back. "Peaches, you know that Dex and I traded bodies again in the Gizmo, right?"

"Yes, Boss. Vic said no one has seen the new Dex since he did the two walk-ins last night. Vic said he needs to talk to you ASAP." *Something was up.*

There was a standard procedure we worked out over the last seven years. "Have all the guests left?" *Getting our rich clients off our hands was our top priority.*

"Yes, but the Feds are confiscating the *Canopus* from our cargo port, and they took the owner into custody. All the other private ships are gone."

Oh yeah. My guest's yacht with the underwater pods on the hull. "Good to know. Has housekeeping started the deep clean?"

"No. I think we should wait a bit. Let's just do the rooms for the guests coming in two weeks. The weatherman says this will be a bad season. We already got a tropical storm warning. I think we should stock in extra water, canned food, gasoline, and medical supplies. Remember we couldn't get any help last year because of the bad water between here and St. Thomas?"

"Yes. I remember. Good idea. Get some extra medical stuff in case we get some late flu cases. Didn't we have a resident die last year because we didn't have something he needed?"

"Yes. I know what you mean. Meanwhile, your summer manager Rex got here today to prepare for the short season, and Scott is arranging a summer soccer camp for the children. Bless you, Boss."

"Don't thank me, Peaches. It was Scott's idea. Be sure Doc gives everyone their flu shot if I don't make it back anytime soon. Have we—" I jumped when I saw Rosalie standing by the fireplace watching me.

Rosalie signaled me to go on with my phone conversation.

"Uhm…have we…" I checked my watch. It was already after 7 p.m. New York time. "Never mind. Yes, just go through the standard procedures. We'll talk tomorrow." I walked over to Rosalie. This was our first private moment since I left for the Army. She put her arms gently around my neck as my arms encircled her waist. She smelled divine, the same perfume as I remembered. I turned my face towards her and took in her astonishing blue eyes.

"What are you waiting for, Skip?" I saw an invitation in those eyes.

"You. A part of me has always been waiting for

you."

She smiled her sweet smile. Her lips brushed mine, soft as a baby's breath: tentative, warm, firm, delicious.

My kiss quickly escalated into high-school-boy lust. She pulled back and asked, "What kind of a girl do you think I am?"

I was caught off guard. Again. A proverbial hand slapped the back of my head. I've been thinking about the past so much on the flights home *that I didn't take a single minute to consider what might come next.* "Well, I thought—"

She took a step backwards. "Well, *I'll* tell you. I'm not the kind of *woman* who can think about the rest of her life on an empty stomach. Do they serve a good ribeye steak here in the big city?"

Why was she pulling away after that kiss? How did we pivot to food all of a sudden? We just got here, and she wants to go out? My head was spinning.

"Uh, sure. Steak?" I hadn't been out to a nonbusiness meal in years.

"Ribeye. With a baked potato and salad with blue cheese," she recited in all seriousness.

I saw she dressed in a skirt and sweater and had earrings on. My usual hangouts had a dress code, and she was probably wearing everything that was in her overnight bag. I rang my driver. "June, ready in five. Not the limo."

"Rosalie, let me change my…never mind. I just need to…" and I went to wash up. I remembered a great place for steaks from my earlier life. And no one goes to it on a Sunday night. Perfect! I ditched my tie and put on an old sports jacket, meaning last year's Gucci.

As we descended in the elevator, I started to snicker.

"What's so funny, Mr. Warren?" she said in a playful voice as she leaned back on the polished brass elevator wall.

"Blue cheese, that's what. I haven't heard that since I left home. Does Quincy's still serve that apple pie with the crumb topping?"

She shrugged. "How would I know? I moved to Texas fifteen years ago, but I still like blue cheese."

Texas? The elevator opened. June wore his casual jacket as he held the backseat door open for Rosalie.

"June, this is Miss Smith. Rosalie, this is my driver June."

"Good evening, Miss Smith." *I didn't appreciate June's slight smirk.*

Rosalie stopped and turned to June, her hand out. "Howdy, June. I am very pleased to meet you. I apologize for earlier, but I was exhausted. Just call me Rosalie."

June had a panicked look in his eyes as he looked at me. I wasn't in much better shape, so I just shrugged.

June took her hand, "Miss Smith, nice to meet you. Please be careful getting into the car."

He shined a flashlight into the car's interior so she could see where to step.

"Thank you, June. And it's Rosalie." She settled in and fastened her seat belt.

Once the Range Rover was on the street, I asked June, "Do you know the Stock Yards Steakhouse in Midtown?"

He looked at me in the rear-view mirror. "Uhm, is that the steak place that has the statue of the big cow with the horns out front?"

Rosalie giggled. I was pretty sure it was because she

knew the difference between a cow and a steer, and city-boy June obviously did not. We used to joke about "Yankees" in high school. *I'd forgotten the statue.*

"Yes, that's it. That's where I—where we want to go." I held her hand. It was warm. I'd forgotten that too.

"Sure, Boss, but it's called the Beef Market Steak House now. It's just a couple of blocks away. We'll be there in a New York minute."

Rosalie chuckled. "What's that, June? A New York minute, I mean."

The Rover slowed approaching a red light. "Watch this. See how long it takes that car behind us to honk after the light turns green." We waited, we listened, and then we laughed.

"I counted less than two seconds," she sang out. "My grandma used to say, 'in two shakes of a lamb's tail.' I believe they're about the same, don't you?"

I always loved her laugh.

June joined in. "I believe you're right. And here we are." He pulled up to the curb, jumped out, and opened Rosalie's door. "Enjoy your steak, miss. This restaurant is known for its maracuja dessert and exotic things like that."

"I *love* things like that. Say that again, and what does it mean?" She leaned in to listen.

"Maracuja. It's passionfruit custard from Brazil. Great if you like the taste of grapefruit. Sir, bon appétit."

Rosalie took my arm as we walked in the restaurant, and back twenty-five years in time.

We danced around the topic of our parents since, apparently, I was still hot under the collar about them. We kept to the safe zone of our one real date, our one year and a half of sneaking around behind our parents' backs, and our fond memories of high school. Mine were fewer than hers. "Honestly, I don't remember being in that class. Who was the teacher?"

"Mr. Garbutt. You nicknamed him Bobby the Butt because he always left class early to smoke a cigarette…Now this is a ribeye. I like this place. Here." She cut a piece off her steak and placed it on my plate.

"Did I? I don't remember graduating second in my class. Who was first?" I took her offering. *This steak is better than I remembered.*

"Amy Burkleshirt. Her mom taught English Lit."

I strained to recall a face. "Mrs. Burkleshirt? Was she the English teacher who made all her own clothes?"

"Yes, and she always used the same paper dress pattern! I'm glad she didn't teach home economics, or all the girls would have been wearing that same dress in different colors."

I excused myself to make a quick call to Vic at Drake's. Part of the décor of this restaurant included a wall of non-working old-fashioned phone booths. I remembered when those phones used to work. I could make a call, and no one could overhear my conversation. I was glad they figured out a way to still use them.

Things were dicey last week at Drake's. I randomly put my finger in the decorative phone dial at number 3 and pulled the dial counterclockwise until I hit the finger stop: zzzt. I pulled my finger out and waited: click-click-click-These phones made the same sound even if there was no real connection. The sound effect as I dialed, released, and the dial rolled back in place was soothing: zzzt-click-click-click-

Vic wasn't answering. zzzt-click-click-click- I wondered where he— My cellphone rang and startled

me. "Vic, what's up?"

"Remember Mr. Velasco and Mr. Lau? Both were guests two years ago."

"Velasco? Was he the guy who tried to corner the Asian stock markets in palm oil?"

"Yes. Lau was the coconut king from—"

"Him I remember. His hair always smelled like a piña colada." zzzt-click-click-click-

"That's him. Both of them were here with Dex after you left and after he did the two walk-in transfers, well one walk-in."

What? That couldn't be right. Only one walk-in meant that Dex could still be alive and a threat to my life and now even to Rosalie and Allie. "Why just the one transfer?" I felt warm as sweat popped out on my neck.

"The guy's wife reconciled with him at the last minute. He forfeited the fee and left. Anyways, after Lau and Velasco traded bodies in the Gizmo, they attacked Dex and took him with them. No one has seen any of them since."

I'd overheard a conversation earlier that night between Velasco and Lau. It seemed they were unhappy with the increase in price for the services of the Gizmo and planned a little surprise for Dex. But if they *did* get transferred, they might have been happy just roughing him up. *Truthfully, so would I.*

Chapter 3

Ledger AKA Boss
I asked Vic about the Gizmo. "Do you remember the professor's name?"

"No, Boss."

"Didn't you end up in his clothes?" *I've been there. That's how it works.*

"Yes, but I wanted my pocket stuff back, so we traded. All that was in his were keys that he gave to Dex when he lost the poker game, and a skinny wallet. Not even a comb. I left to get a haircut."

"I heard he died at the game. Do you know if anyone, uh, checked for ID or called the cops?" Not likely given the illegal nature of Dex's poker marathons.

"No. Luscious said everyone just disappeared."

"Luscious?"

"The skinny girl who helped Dex at his games. The waitress."

"Oh, yeah. How about the address where you got the Gizmo?"

"No, but I could probably find the building if the neighborhood is still standing. Didn't the city do some urban renewal projects down there a few years ago?"

"Yes, they did." The Hudson Haven project. One of my companies did the demolition and another did the construction.

"Okay. Back to Dex. How do you know all of this

about Lau and Velasco?"

"You can thank your chief engineer."

"Chet? He saw this happen?" I dialed the old phone again, but a higher number: zzzzzt-click-click-click-click-click-

"In a way. After Twitchell sabotaged the Gizmo, Chet installed cameras in the Transfer Room."

I thought back to the Transfer Room. "I didn't see any cameras." I didn't pay attention at the time. Transferring back into your own body does that to a person.

"Good. You weren't supposed to. Fiber optics are very discreet. One more thing. That meter that has Roman numerals on it?"

Since when was Vic noticing the meter? "What about it?"

"It's all blanks now."

Blanks? "Not zeroes?"

"Boss," Vic sighed, "the Romans didn't have the number zero," and he hung up. zzzzzzt-click-click-click-click-click-click.

My Cicero spouting security chief just schooled me in Latin 101. I realized I needed to do some schooling of my own. How could I find someone who knew how to fix the Gizmo? There was a loud noise. I jumped, hitting my head on the payphone. It was Rosalie knocking on the glass. I pushed the door open and explained, "I needed to call Drake's," as an apology. "It's the end of the—"

"No need to apologize, Skip. I know you're a busy guy. You missed the maracuja. It was fabulous. The bill is paid, so let's go. I'm tired." She looked a little put out.

"June usually—"

"I know. I paid his bill. He says thanks for the great steak. You can use Zelle to get the money to me later."

Who was this woman? Not my high school girlfriend by a longshot. What was this mara-something I missed? *And who the hell was Zelle?*

Rosalie took my arm and led me out to where June waited with the Range Rover. June opened and held Rosalie's door. I climbed in the other side. The car moved forward, but I wasn't looking where we were going. *I'm not in control of this moment.* My head hurt from banging into the payphone. I was going wherever June was going. He didn't ask me as she already told him to "please take us home." I never said please and thank you to my staff. They'd think it was quaint.

June and Rosalie chatted like they were old friends. She told him, "That dessert was great! I got the recipe from the chef." She'd write it down for him so his wife can make it. "Easy-peasy," she said. "How do you like this Rover?"

June said he liked the car but had trouble remembering the Brits call the trunk a "boot" and the hood a "bonnet," but other than that, he liked it just fine.

They did that counting thing at the stoplight again and laughed. I thought I heard her ask about shopping and the rest was a blur. I started breathing hard. *What is happening? Was this an out-of-body experience? Had I been drugged? Even worse, had I been poisoned? Is this how it ends for me?* My hands were shaking. *Or is this what a panic attack feels like?*

****

I woke up alone in my apartment. The sun was full up. I heard a loud sound from the kitchen. I grabbed my shiv and taser and creeped down the hall barefoot. No one has ever made it into my apartment uninvited. Whoever was here to kill me was incompetent or new to the job. I wasn't going down without a fight. I inched along the wall and turned fast into the kitchen. A woman! I'd never had a woman try to kill me. *A killer is a killer.* She turned around.

"Good morning, Skip. Sorry for the noise. I was looking for a notepad and pen to leave you a message."

Rosalie? I thought I just dreamed that part about her.

"Well, well, well, Mr. Silk Pajamas. You always bring a knife to breakfast?" She looked me up and down. "Want a cup of coffee?"

This had never happened before. My face felt hot. I shoved my weapons into my pockets. "Yes, I do. The coffee, I mean. Let me just get dressed." I hurried back to my room and threw on a suit and tie. "What are we going to do today," I asked Rosalie as I walked into the kitchen.

"I'm on my way out. June is dropping me off for some shopping. How about lunch? I left my card on the counter with my cell number. Call me." She picked up her purse and all but ran out of the apartment.

I heard the door slam, and I was alone, but I had stuff to do. I grabbed the coffee she left for me, and my jaw dropped. She made biscuits. Still warm. There was butter and blackberry jam—my favorite—on the counter. I snagged my phone and settled down to a meal of real southern buttermilk biscuits like mama made, as I speed dialed my favorite private eye.

Earl Chester duBois and I went back a long way, back to when I worked for the Family, back to when we were in Bosnia when he saved my life. He knew *some* of my history, but I didn't give him any freebies.

I kept a respectable sized retainer in Earl's pocket in case I needed someone like him in any of my East Coast business affairs. I kept him on retainer so I knew I had someone I could trust. It gave me a way to be sure he went to the VA hospital when that particular day rolled around every year, and he started ducking for cover. *Come on, Earl. Pick up!*

With my Gizmo situation uncertain, I didn't know if I could use it again, or if we would need to polish it up as a historical casino artifact. I needed to find someone who might know about it, or I'd lose my top attraction. I heard someone pick up, but they didn't speak. I heard a groan and a rumble, "This better be good or I'll rip your throat out." Then he waited... and wheezed.

"Earl, this is Ledger. You still got some of my money in your pocket?" I heard the sound of a cap unscrewed from a bottle. "That better be mouthwash I hear." I heard a gulp, then a glug followed by a gargle. Then another gulp.

"Yes, Ledger, it is," he lied. I liked Earl because I could tell when he was lying, and he knew it. "Brush your teeth and wash that ugly face of yours. I got a job for you. The usual place in thirty minutes." It felt good to be back in control again.

****

After Skip left the kitchen to get dressed, I called June to pick me up in the Range Rover. I had some serious shopping to do. There I was in the Big Apple, but I was the one that needed some polishing up. I left Skip my card expecting to have lunch together when he returned.

"Miss Smith, I don't think my boss will like it if he finds out you sat up front."

"No? Then maybe I should drive, and you can tell me where to turn." I saw that sudden look of panic, maybe even fear, that I was going for on June's face.

"Uh, no, no way." He looked left and right as if we were being watched.

"Why thank you, June. I'd love to sit up front where I can see more of New York than just the back of your head."

"Where to, Miss Smith?" His voice was flat, and his eyes looked straight forward.

I handed him my handwritten recipe for maracuja. "This is for your missus."

His eyes grew big. He put the recipe in his pocket. "Thanks." His voice was warmer.

"Macy's Department Store," I said. I couldn't decide which department to hit first.

"Macy's it is. It doesn't open until 11 a.m., but it stays open until nine tonight. Have you ever been to New York before?" He gave me some side eye as he did a quick head check at the intersection.

"Yes, but it's been some time." *Shoot. That put a crimp in my big city shopping spree.*

"How about my tour of Central Park and Manhattan, or what we can see until then. I'll have you at Macy's front door at eleven on the dot. Boy Scout's honor." June gave a two-finger salute.

I laughed. "Are you sure Mr. Warren won't need you?"

He shook his head. "I arranged for a backup driver, and we have a limo for him. He's good, so no worries."

"Well, scout, the tour sounds lovely. Thank you." A tour gave me time to decide what I needed since I wasn't sure how long I'd be here. *How would Skip and I cover twenty-five years and be honest about it?*

"We're in Manhattan, the smallest borough of the five in New York City. I'll start by going up the Franklin Roosevelt Drive by the East River. It's famous as a place to dump bodies. So many bodies show up in April that the cops call it the 'spring harvest.' " As he turned into a new street, June said, "Can I ask you a personal question, just between us?" He pointed towards the river on our right side. "Across the river is Queens, the biggest borough. If you were staying longer, I could give you a tour of it."

Skip said to trust no one. "Sure, why not?" I turned and looked at him, but his eyes were on the traffic. *I wonder what he's curious about.*

"Your name isn't really 'Smith' is it?" That was more of a statement, not a question but I played along.

"Honestly, no…" and June smirked, "…and yes," and thus endeth the smirk. "Mr. Warren and I are high school friends. My name was Smith back then."

"But you got married since then?" I raised my hand. "So you are Mrs. who now?" He almost looked sincere. "Oh, that's the UN building ahead." He waved to the front of our car.

"I'm a widow, so until I'm ready to tell Mr. Warren, I am Miss Smith, if you don't mind." *Yep, all the flags, looks just like the UN pictures in the magazines.*

"Sure thing. I figured a lady as smart and cool as you must'a been married. Sorry about your husband though. That's a tough break."

"Thanks. I miss him still."

He made a turn. "I'm gonna circle Central Park. It's the oldest public park in the country. It's 840 acres. I'm guessing from your accent that you gotta better idea than me how big an acre is."

I double checked my seat belt as my guide drove pointing left, then right, then back while giving me random names and dates in his rapid-fire Yankee accent.

****

Earl was smoking when I spotted him as he paced in front of the 7th Regiment Memorial. His black skin had an ashen look to it. His eyes were rheumy and swollen. His rough beard told me he hadn't shaved in days. We did the handshake and chest bump guys do. To him I was still his Army buddy who made a little money; good for me, and I looked great. To me, he's in trouble and fading fast.

We moved out to the sidewalk and sat on an open bench. We did the small talk before business. "Got an appointment at the VA yet? It's getting close." Earl looked much older than when I last saw him six months ago just before Christmas.

"Yeah. But thanks for remembering. I'll expect your call like always…Ledger, I keep asking how come I freak out on the day of the massacre, but you don't. Why do *you* think it is?"

"Honestly, I don't know. PTSD hits everyone differently. But if they were my women folk, I'd have gone crazy too." *I didn't have the nightmares as much, but they were still as vivid.*

We sat silently and watched traffic go by. The sun filtered through the trees. Birds chirped. We were as far away as we could get from a memory that lacerated our psyches. Earl spoke up in that satin voice of his, now raspy from too much liquor and too many smokes. "What can I do for you, my man?" He had that same infectious grin.

I passed a photo of Vic I took when I started Drake's Key seven years ago. "Earl, this man is a mystery to me. He works for me, but I didn't know him before then. He might be a scientist or a college professor. He may not even be from this city, but I think he's American. Find out what you can. Find out where he worked, say eight or nine years ago."

"That's slim pickings for information, Corporal. Got anything else? Got a name at least?"

I rubbed my chin as a couple of facts coalesced in my brain. "He played poker…He was looking for a big score here about eight years ago and he played poker with Dexter Drake once…He might have been an engineer. There was a lab or storage room down where the Hudson Haven Center is now…Sorry, that's all I got."

"He works for you, but you don't know his name?" I recognized Earl's skeptical look. My phone alarm beeped. "Yeah. Hey, I may or may not be here long. Here's some expense money in advance." I discreetly passed him ten thousand dollars in cash and a loaded debit card. "Call any time." This time I gave him a sincere man-hug. I saw the shadow of death in his eyes. He pulled me back from that years ago; I was failing him at returning the favor. My backup driver picked me up and I went to my office for a full day of meetings. I completely forgot about lunch with Rosalie.

****

I got stood up by Skip, so I decided to make this a full day of shopping. I started at the world-famous Macy's Department Store in Manhattan, their flagship location. As promised, June put me at the front door when they opened. I downloaded the Macy's app, so I knew where to find the items I needed, and more of those that I didn't but bought anyway. I bought a new suitcase to hold it all.

"You must be heading out for a wonderful vacation, miss," the salesclerk commented as I handed her my driver license.

"No, this is for here. I guess I didn't pack as much as I should have." *But then I didn't expect to come to New York, did I?*

"Here's your ID. You *are* a long way from Texas. Not many cowboy hats here, I'm afraid. Please sign." She handed me my charge slip and a ballpoint.

"Ouch," I said under my breath as I scribbled my name.

"What was that?' she asked looking behind me.

"Just my credit card crying 'uncle.'"

She cracked a smile and compared the signature on my card to what I just wrote. "Thank you, Miss A,…bat…song? Is that correct?" She wrapped my new nightie in tissue paper.

"Close." I repeated my name. "Abatsong. All one word. Thank you for your patience." I snatched up my armload of bags, grabbed the handle on my wheelie suitcase, and headed for the ladies lounge looking for a place to sit and catch my breath.

After powdering my nose, as they used to say in the South, I spotted an overstuffed armchair with a footstool. Just what I needed. I piled my goodie bags by the chair, put my aching feet up, and caught my breath. I dialed Allie but hung up before the first ring. I recognized two women I didn't want to see as they came in. I ducked and texted June to pick me up ASAP. I scooped up my bags and suitcase, but as I turned, I heard my name called.

"Roh-zah-lee? I never expected to see you in New York. In fact, I think *you* are dead." That same snide voice I knew all too well, but I did know she couldn't hurt me here in my own country. Her companion corrected her tense. I suspected she meant what she said the first time.

"Of course, in fact I *thought* you were dead." Her smile brought a chill to the over-air-conditioned room. "My French finishing school did not emphasize English so I may be lacking in finessing the tenses." She looked to her right as she spoke, and I knew she was lying.

"Perhaps your parents should ask for a refund from the school," I offered as I secured a slipping bag. I knew that the "lady" spoke better English than I did. I mimicked her insulting pronunciation. "Mee-ree-ham, have you been barred from Bergdorf's again or do they not have a size to fit you any longer?" *That felt good but I needed to leave.* Her smile seemed permanently frozen. *Too much Botox and filler?*

"Are you waiting for your husband? Oh, I forgot. He *is* dead," she snarled ever so politely.

29

Chapter 4

Rosalie
This was a waste of time and breathable air.
"Charming as always, Mee-ree-ham." I turned and walked at a slow pace turning my head back and forth as if browsing. Suddenly, I flinched. There was a tap on my shoulder, and I snapped my head around.

Madame Miriam's henchman hand maiden handed me a bag. "You missed this. Sorry she is so rude, miss."

I made a beeline for the elevator I thought took me to June in the shortest amount of time. He was waiting as I speed-walked to the Range Rover. June took my bags and put them in the back as I wheeled the suitcase around to stow in the passenger side backseat. Wham! I was slammed against the Rover. I took a long look down the road at the black SUV with license plates MMD2 something-something as it sped away. I clawed at the door handle. The excruciating pain in my right leg told me I was in trouble.

June popped up out of the back of the Rover and swore at the speeder. Then he saw me. He shouted, "Miss Smith, you're hurt!" and rushed to me.

I suppose my grimace and white knuckles gave me away. "Call an ambulance and the police. I think my leg is broken." I directed him to help me lay down in the back seat while moving my leg as little as possible. When I asked him to put something, anything, under my head to keep it elevated, he quickly used a clean blanket from the trunk.

The police arrived almost at once, but I attributed it to us exceeding the parking time in a loading zone. The ambulance came and EMTs put me on a gurney, did what they do so well, and stabilized my leg. The EMTs and June saved me from going into shock. "Don't call Mr. Warren. Follow the ambulance. I'll need you to take me home later." He did as I asked.

What's the going New York tip when your driver saves your life?

We got back to the apartment after dark. I was the one surprised when June produced a wheelchair for me. "My wife's, Miss Smith," he said. His explanation was enough for me for now. He made me comfortable and then brought up my shopping loot for the day.

Estafania's dinner waited in the oven, and I listened for a front door key. It was after 10 p.m. when I heard Skipper come in, hang up something in the coat closet, and walk down the hall. I'd taken all the pain killers modern medicine allowed, so I was mouthy and unfocused.

"I am *so* sorry, but I completely forgot about lunch. I'll—" That's when he saw my cast propped up on a footstool. He came around and sat near me. "What…what happened?"

"I neglected to tell you I was trying out for the Rangers hockey team today, but I forgot I don't know how to ice skate so—"

"Shut up! I leave you for one day and this…" he yelled as he waved his hand at my cast…

"Broken leg," I threw in as offhand information.

"…broken leg happens?" he sputtered. For some

odd reason I felt protected and started to cry. He stopped and moved closer to me. His arm went around my shoulders, and I sobbed because I was being reprimanded. He took a handkerchief from his pocket, and I destroyed it.

I doubted Estafania would even touch this snot rag tomorrow but we both calmed down. "It's going to be okay. I'll hire a private nurse," he murmured in a comforting voice.

I shook my head. "That's not why I'm crying." I wiped snot from my face.

With a gentle hand he guided my head down to his shoulder. "Well, then, what is it?"

I wiped the last tear from my face and said, "It was deliberate. Someone I know was trying to kill me."

Skip was quiet for a very long time. "I am worried about that too, that someone might harm you or Allie because of me."

I had to know. "Are you *that* kind of a guy?" Allie only told me he was wealthy.

"Some people would say 'yes.' You know that the Marshals gave me a ride because of a death threat, don't you? It wasn't my first and probably not my last. Is this a deal breaker?" He continued holding me close.

I thought about what a deal breaker might be as Skip put food on a plate and picked up two forks. I was having trouble reconciling the Skip I knew and loved with Ledger, the man he had become. We sat on the couch eating and watching the fire snap, crackle, and pop. I came to talk, so I opened my own history a crack, and let him take a peek. "Skip, I was married when Allie was ten. He was a great husband and stepdad."

"Was married is past tense." He speared a piece of

watermelon and fed it to me.

I took the bite and replied, "Yes, it is, and so is he. He was killed five years ago in a deliberate car bombing. I escaped with burns on my back. Allie wasn't with us, thank god."

"That must have been horrible." He ran his fingers through my short curly hair, like he used to so many years ago.

I felt myself softening towards him. *Damn! I didn't want him to pity me.* "Yes, it was. Damon was the finest man I'd ever met but some people objected to his work and to me. I say this because I'm not sure this 'suspicious accident' wasn't meant for me, with no connection to you."

"You're tired. I'm tired. This sounds too serious to finish tonight." He put the plate on the coffee table. In one fell swoop he scooped me up into his very capable arms. "You are going to bed."

"But I—" I mumbled, but I didn't object.

"No buts about it." Skip started down the hall.

We were just short of my room, when I said, "But I have to pee, and I need my crutches." He looked at where I pointed for my functional and very ugly hospital-issue crutches laying on the floor. Skip managed to get me into the bathroom, fetch my crutches, and then the fun began. I insisted on brushing my teeth which was hilarious to me. "I'll pay for the dry-cleaning to get the thoothpaste from your thie," I lisped. *Skip was patient, as always.*

"Not to worry. I've got another tie just like it. I haven't done this in a while. Do I take them off completely?" My skirt and panties hit the floor. He turned away, kind of sweet I thought, to give me a small semblance of privacy. Skip found my flannel nightie in a shopping bag. I heard a snort as he removed the tags. "Pure sex, babe. This would drive any man into a frenzy." He helped me pull my sweater off, averting his eyes, removed my bra with just a tad too much expertise, and slid the gown over my arms. He pulled the covers up.

"Well this is sure different than the last time you took my clothes off," I mumbled as the meds kicked into high gear. I thought his smile might be a smirk, but I let it pass. I said, "I wrote in my diary 'tonight *pasionis aestu.*' I'll never forget it. That was the night that we made Allie."

"Is that 'an act of passion'? Why write it in Latin?" he asked while tucking in my blanket.

"How do you know that's Latin? Besides, I was a seventeen-year-old girl in my third year of high school Latin. It was the only foreign language I knew that my folks didn't. No Internet, remember?" I snuggled down under my covers. "No nighty-night kiss?"

He chuckled, ruffled my hair again, and placed a light peck on my forehead. "Say, you don't know a guy named Vic who looks like Einstein, but speaks Latin like Cicero do you?"

I shook my head as I closed my eyes.

"Well you're about to," he whispered in my ear.

****

The next morning I sat Rosalie at the dining room table and started coffee. I heated a couple of her leftover biscuits after I split them, buttered each half, and laid down thin slices of cheddar cheese. A dash of salt and pepper and into the oven they went. "Just like my mom used to make," I bragged.

"Yes, delicious. I seldom make these anymore."

Rosalie's crutches clattered to the floor.

She seemed more coherent this morning so I thought I should just hit the next issue head on.

"Rosalie, I think we should go to Drake's for a few weeks. We can talk. It will be much more private, and safer, I have a doctor, and…and closer to Allie."

I was scrambling for more ammunition when she said, "I'll need more clothes, but I can shop from here. Do you have a computer I can use?"

"Uh, yes. Use my account for shopping. They'll deliver today." I opened my second computer and showed her where my Nordstrom's and Neiman Marcus credit cards were located.

"Thanks. When do we go, to the island, I mean?" She was doodling on the back of an envelope, probably a shopping list.

The timer rang and I slid perfectly warmed biscuits with melted cheese onto two plates, sliced a banana, poured two cups of coffee, and served up breakfast. As I savored our quiet meal, I mentally listed the things I had to do here in New York in person: check in with Earl to find out who the professor was who built the Gizmo; hold Earl's hand through our yearly PTSD flashback; find out what George Hong knew about assassins Xin might have sent my way; review the sale of a four billion dollar company I currently owned; and, take Rosalie to a checkup for her broken leg. I thought it better to not fly at night. Except for Rosalie, my day as usual.

"Day after tomorrow. Early." I wanted to get her away from New York as fast as humanly possible.

"Roger that. Anything else?" She took a second biscuit and examined it closely.

"Passport?" *Is she criticizing my cooking?*

"In my purse." She glanced over and said, "Good job."

"Meds? Need any refills?" I know my doctor at Drake's has a well-stocked medicine supply. *Just in case.*

"Ditto and no." She seemed anxious to see me leave.

I finished up my last biscuit and coffee and stood. "Okay. Don't let any old ladies with a basket of apples in, and for God's sake don't take any free samples." I joked, but I was edging towards paranoia. I was afraid Allie wouldn't talk to me again if her mom died on my watch, or something like that.

"How do you feel about wolves in nightgowns?" she said with a toothy grin. She's tough and I liked that. *I always have.*

Estafania let the private nurse in. I left orders Rosalie was not to leave my apartment. "Whatever you need, just let Estafania know. I've got a full day of meetings, but I'll swing by at 1:00 for lunch, I promise. I'll get the best Chinese food in Manhattan. What do you like?"

"Chinese in New York. Yummy. I see dumplings, pan fried. Pepper beef, a side of stir-fried al dente broccoli. And an order of Chinese barbecue pork. What are you having?"

She has some *appetite.* "I'll decide when I see the specials of the day. Any rice?"

Her head shook. "And no fortune cookies or soup. Green tea ice cream if they have it."

I peeked into her room as I left. It's going to take all day just to open those bags. That will keep her busy. The elevator ride down seemed empty without Rosalie. *Odd, but I chuckled again at her ribeye and blue cheese request.*

June opened the Rover door. "Good morning, Boss. Looks like a high of eighty degrees today and a chance of rain." He handed me a small umbrella that I slipped into my briefcase.

"Thanks, June, and thanks for helping Miss Smith yesterday. I appreciate it, oh, and the tour, great idea." I watched his eyes in the rear-view mirror. His eyebrows furrowed up.

"You're welcome...She's a funny lady. Where to?"

"Chinatown, the Hong Building."

"Yessir," June replied and gently accelerated into the perpetual morning rush hour traffic that was in no particular hurry to get anywhere. No chatter or laughter today. Strictly business. My first order of business was Rosalie. I called a nearby medical supply company I knew of. Crutches were so twentieth century.

George Hong knew everyone in Chinatown and Manhattan for that matter. I needed a reading on a threat I received three days ago, but it wasn't in a fortune cookie.

****

Less than half an hour after Skip left, I received the delivery of a cool knee scooter. The muscles in contact with my crutches were already sore. Since I could bend my knee, this scooter freed me from crutch torture. Yea!

"Miss Smith, this came with the scooter." Estafania handed me a cupholder.

Bonus! I cleaned up, dressed, and sat at Ledger's desk. I'm not used to his name yet, but it didn't stop me from typing it in as I shopped for everything I needed for an extended stay in paradise. At least this time, I'll get off the plane.

****

"George. Thanks for seeing me on short notice." I shook the hand of the most important man in New York, at least to me, and today in particular. "How is your son doing?"

"Kind of you to ask, Ledger. Very well, thank you. That school you recommended has made such a difference in his life and ours." His smile was sincere.

I suddenly realized the importance of a young child to a caring parent. *Was it too late for me?* Hope House was the top school of its kind in the city. I own it, so I know. It was a school for students with Down's syndrome. I started it for my entertainment manager Max at Drake's who's from New York. Of course George Hong doesn't know this, but Max's youngest is a boarding student there. The school has been helpful to me over the last few years for high profile families. "That's great to hear." I sat patiently, conscious of protocol in this meeting.

George's assistant set cups of green tea in front of us.

"*Kanpai,*" I offered as a toast.

He face wore a bemused smile. "That's Japanese, but close enough." We clinked cups.

Japanese? Right.

George offered the Chinese version of the toast, but I couldn't hear the difference. I moved on. "George, take a look at this," I said as I passed the business card that an unhappy winner at Drake's threw on my desk just two days ago, or was it three?

George turned the card over. "Did Xin say anything at the time?"

I focused on the meeting last week in my casino

office. "He said 'Now death is in your cards,' as best I remember."

"His calligraphy is impeccable, but what else would one expect. What did you do to piss him off?" he asked as his smile dried up.

I straightened in my chair and flashed a smirk of satisfaction. We're not particularly friends, but I trust George. "I fined him five-million-dollars from his winnings as a security fee. He seriously threatened one of my employees. I suspect it would have been more violent if my security people didn't step in. And I banned him from the island." I had to made a serious point to other guests who might try me on for size.

George smiled that lopsided smile again I've known since law school. "Well that explains the five-million-dollar bounty he's put on you."

My head and shoulders jerked back. *Now, that's a sore loser.* "Poetic, isn't it? Dead *or* alive?" I asked out of curiosity.

George stopped smiling. "Xin never takes prisoners, Ledger."

Yet another reason I need to get out of town. "Have you heard of him doing this before, George? Does he have a standard MO?" *I needed to know what to watch for.*

"As far as I know, he never gets his hands dirty. He'll send one or two assassins to the island—scene of the insult—and they will get on even if it is a private island, and soon. They might even be there now."

****

After I left Hong's office I made a call from the lobby to my head of security at Drake's.

"Yeah, Boss." Vic's not much on social conventions

like "hello" and "goodbye."

"How's the weather in the islands. Much rain yet?"

"Not yet. We've got temporary workers cleaning up the grounds. Anything in particular?"

"Yes. I don't have a general manager under contract. Want the job?" There was a pause at the other end of the line, but I waited. *Temporary workers, huh.* The last guy on the island who said that was his job concealed a garotte in his pocket and got his hand seriously sliced by a deep sea salvor.

Vic says, "No, I'm not a meet, greet, and schmooze kind of guy."

True statement. "Fair enough. Got a recommendation from within our current staff?" I had an idea already.

"Yes. I recommend Singh or Bad. I like both of them, but I think Singh has the edge. He cuts quite the figure in his turban and beard, and he's tall, and he won't take any nonsense. He's diplomatic and sharp."

Good assessment. I pictured Singh in my head. He *was* imposing. Now "Bad" Bahadur doesn't come to my chin, but in a fight, I'd pick that 5'3" Ghurka, and his seventeen-inch khukuri knife to be on my team any day of the week and twice on Sunday. "We are coming back to Drake's day after tomorrow." *Not a day too soon for me.*

Chapter 5

Boss

"Vic, arrange one—no make that two of the extra guest rooms off my suite. Tell the doc he's got a new patient. Give Singh a ping to see if he's interested. I'll see him when I get back. Wasn't he Dex's right-hand man?" I was relieved to get Dex's replacement underway.

"Yes, he was. He knows the ropes and he'll do a bang-up job. Mind if I promote Bad to my second in command?"

"Good idea. While you are at it, have Bad snoop around to see if any suspicious guys are asking questions about me. Xin may have sent over a couple of ninjas to take me out."

"Sure thing. By the way, Boss, ninjas are Japanese," he said as he hung up.

Japanese? Right.

June held the Range Rover door for me.

"Is there a florist shop on the way to pick up Chinese takeout? The usual of course."

"Yes, sir," he said and closed the door behind me. We headed towards Chen's Chop-Shop. I called and ordered from the menu June kept in the glovebox. As June pulled up to the curb, I saw I was a little short of Chen's restaurant. When I got out, I was two doors down and smack in front of the White Lotus Pearl Florists.

June knew his way around Manhattan, for sure. "Will this do?" I didn't answer because I knew that he knew it met or exceeded my request.

I picked up two bouquets and all the food because an empty car will be towed in a second. June dropped me at my elevator. I passed a bouquet to June. "Did you forget today is your anniversary?" He looked panic stricken. "Give Ginger a 'congratulations' from me." I handed him a bag of food. "Lunch for two. See you in ninety minutes. *Bon appétit.*" *I'm damn sure that's not Japanese!*

****

June was waiting by the elevator. He stopped me before I got in. "Ginger says thank you. Man to man, you saved my bacon. I appreciate that. Now where to?" he said with a smile.

The cup holder held a hot cup of coffee. *That's a first.* "The office," I said. I reviewed my mental list as I sipped the hot java I lived on. *What's left?* Call Earl later tonight about the professor, and tomorrow for sure for the yearly Bosnia nightmare. I set my alarm for his morning call. Tomorrow was Rosalie's checkup, and I was not subbing that job out. That left my big deal that I'm heading to now. I called up a picture on my phone Marshal Bennett took of me, Rosalie, and Allie on the plane. We looked like a happy family but...Allie was right. We were strangers. What I need now was...patience, lots, and lots of patience.

Rosalie sat in the kitchen addressing a postcard. "Got any stamps, Boss man?"

I looked at Estafania, who pointed to a drawer in the credenza.

Rosalie said, "Sit down. Dinner is ready," as she

waved to my housekeeper.

I went to wash up, shucked my tie and jacket, and kicked off my shoes. Dinner was on the table when I sat down. It felt different sitting at my table with another person sharing a meal I didn't order or take out. I was spooning cheesy potatoes on to my plate when she said, "This feels weird. I'm used to eating with Elsie but she's not much of a conversationalist. Sometimes Bonnie from next door. But with you—weird…but in a good way—I think."

"I agree, in a good way." *Since when does Estafania cook cheesy potatoes?* They were delicious, just like my mom's. As we ate, I mentally reviewed how to keep Rosalie safe from people I knew about. I had no idea how to start on the people I didn't know about, like who was responsible for her broken leg? And oddly enough, to whom was she sending a postcard?

Afterwards, I went to my home office which Rosalie had commandeered. I called Earl. The phone rang five times. As I started to hang up, he answered.

"What's up, big man? Are you busy?" Earl was an enigma to me in most ways. I focused on what I did know.

"Nah, not tonight. But I got a line on your man with the fluffy white hair. Professor Heinrich Albert Schwartz. Got kicked out of Stanford eight, nine years ago. There was a kerfuffle over conducting unauthorized, and probably unethical, experiments with human subjects. The thing is he has entirely dropped off the face of the planet as far as research goes. I can't find a single reference to this guy anywhere after about eight years ago."

That would have been about the time the professor

and Vic transferred bodies.

"And this guy works for you, Ledger?" I caught a whiff of alarm in his unspoken concern.

"What was his field?" *Human experiments? I never thought about that part.*

"Seems to be a new area of research involving physics and—let me check my notes—and neuroscience. He was funded for a while by DARPA."

"Who is DARPA? It doesn't ring a bell." I took notes as Earl talked. It might give me a lead to a co-researcher.

"That's the Defense Advanced Research Projects Agency. It's run by the Defense Department." *Ding!* Now the bell rang. A research juggernaut with deep pockets. I hoped the Gizmo wasn't some kind of stolen classified work. I owned several defense companies. This could cost me plenty, maybe even jail time.

"Were there any other researchers on the project?" *Just one name, Earl, please.*

"I haven't gotten that far yet. Any published stuff might be classified. I'll look for any grad students who might have been on board. I'm betting any college records about a dismissal are not public, but I might find someone who knew about it off the record."

I relaxed. "You're a good detective. I wouldn't have thought about looking for college gossip on the guy, but I suppose it's always out there." I changed the subject. "What time are you due at the VA tomorrow?"

"Nine sharp. You sending the doughnuts and coffee, Corporal?" Earl still had a decided sweet tooth.

"Already on order, buddy. I'll call you—" I'd forgotten to close the door, and Rosalie scooted in.

"Skip, do I have to—oops. Sorry." She tried to back

44

up her scooter and got stuck on a throw rug.

Earl asked in his silky teasing voice, "And who is *that,* my man? She sounds pretty friendly." I heard his slow deep laugh erupting from his gut.

"Earl, gotta go. Call you tomorrow. Be safe." As I hung up, I said, "Rosalie, stop. Let me help you with that." Taking hold of the scooter with one hand, I put my other arm around Rosalie to steady her. I stepped on the rug to keep it nailed down as I lifted the scooter off. As I set it down again, Rosalie started to sink and I instinctively pulled her closer and wrapped my other arm around, just to be safe.

"Always the gentleman, I see," but she didn't pull away.

There is something I've been wondering about, something I needed to know, so I leaned in closer and slowly kissed the love of my past life. She didn't recoil or push me away. She relaxed and fully participated. Three times. I felt my heart beating again and heat rising.

She leaned back and said, "I needed to know, didn't you?"

****

I turned into the kitchen and saw Rosalie beat me to it. "Good morning," I said. "Ready for your checkup?"

I smelled coffee, glorious coffee. I picked up a clean cup by the coffeepot. Then I noticed a hot pot on the stove. I lifted the lid—something my mother sternly disapproved of. *Bloated oaties.* "I didn't know there was oatmeal."

"There wasn't, but you said, 'Just tell Estafania,' so I did." She put a big spoonful in her mouth and grinned like granny was here and cooking all her favorites.

I spooned the hot cereal into a bowl near the pot. On

the counter sat a container of brown sugar, the butter dish, and maple syrup. "You went whole hog on this. Did you get—" and then I spotted the dried cranberries. "Never mind." *This looked good.* I hated overcooked oatmeal the consistency of snot. I put my cup and bowl on the table, sat down, and took a bite. Just…the way… I liked it.

"I explained to Estafania the aversion you have to overcooked oatmeal. I think she's got the hang of it." We chatted a few minutes longer when she stood, picked up her bowl, and scootered to the sink. "I'll be by the door in fifteen."

The oatmeal was so good I didn't even look at my phone. I quick mixed up a second bowl and wolfed it down. When I got to the door, Rosalie was waiting as promised. Something from dinner last night hit me. "Did you tell Estafania how to make my mom's cheesy potatoes? She's never made them before."

"I guess every housewife in the South knows how to make those. I just offered her a recipe she's never heard of that we liked when we were kids. She doesn't cook potatoes much, she told me."

"Oh, I see. Thanks. They were good. Reminded me of hom…." I didn't finish the sentence. It's been a long time since I'd thought of Oklahoma as "home."

Rosalie smiled, but we didn't talk much past the weather forecast. When the elevator door opened, June was waiting with a wheelchair. "Thanks so much, June. I needed to sit down for a moment. And a ton of thank yous for putting me in the car so gently until the ambulance came. How was the anniversary dinner?" She seemed truly interested in his answer. She'd been sitting all morning, so I knew she said it to please him.

"Delicious. She loves the flowers. Thank you, kind lady."

Kind lady? Yes, she was kind. In this instant I remembered her kindness as a characteristic I didn't always find in a lot of girls back then. The same old Rosalie.

"Peonies smell better than roses. When Skip mentioned your anniversary at breakfast, I thought of them." The elevator stopped. Rosalie stood and June hurried to open her car door. He suggested she sit on the passenger side, then that she should sit sideways and push back into the car while he supported her leg. When Rosalie's leg was clear of the door, he helped her pivot and set her cast down gently. "June, you've done that before. That was a perfect landing."

He smiled from ear to ear.

I got in and handed her the purse I was holding, feeling both helpless and foolish. I assumed we will reverse the process at the hospital, but I knew the routine now. As we drove to the hospital, I asked her, "What was it you wanted to ask me last night when you came into my office?"

"Last night…oh, that. Can I bring my hunga munga to the island? It was a special wedding present from my father-in-law, a family heirloom. I have written permission to import it and to export it, but I would never—"

"Sure, sure. Bring it if it makes you happy," I said, brushing her off. *What could a huggie muggie be that I should worry?*

After I checked Rosalie in for her follow-on appointment for her broken leg, I texted her where I was headed: the hospital chapel. Hoping it was empty, I entered the small chamber with a simulated stained-glass window of nondenominational design, checked my watch, and called Earl.

"Right on time. Anything going on where you're at?" I heard him whispering into his phone. *He's back there in Bosnia, somewhere in a foxhole built of his own hideous recollections.*

"Roger that, buddy. Nothing moving. Nothing making noise. You hungry, man? Need a cup of coffee?" My chest constricted and squeezed the air from my lungs. I breathed in shallow gasps. I had one foot in that foxhole with him.

"I could sure use that. What' cha got?"

I knew that thousand-yard look he had in his eyes. "Earl, man. See any friendlies around?" I hoped he was sitting down. He's a big guy and he's intimidating when he's hallucinating.

"I see…I see a few…a few old guys. I think…I know that guy across from me. It's the Lieutenant. Ledger…" He was coming around. "Ledger, that you, man?" My chest loosened. I gasped in air, filling my lungs.

"Yeah, buddy. Look around, Earl. See any coffee, any doughnuts?" There was a long pause. "Yeah, I see them. I see Johnny. He's bringing me a cup…Did you order my favorites, the chocolate glazed?"

I smiled, grateful he made it again, grateful that we both did, and rubbed my forehead. He was okay—okay for today.

"Hey, Ledger?" His voice evened out.

"Right here, Earl," I said, relaxing from his voice.

"I got something else on Dr. Schwartz. He employed a grad student named Ricky Mixon. The dude's in New

York, man. Write this down. Ready?"

I grabbed a pen and my pocket notebook. "Ready."

"Dr. Ricky Howser Mixon, M. D., Ph.D. Stanford, now a research and teaching professor at SUNY Downstate Health Science University, some kind of Neurodynamics Laboratory. I got no idea what he does though."

I hoped this was a solid lead. "Thanks, man. This might be a lifesaver." Dr. Mixon might have an idea about Mr. Lau's sudden mysterious illness. "Have another doughnut, Earl, and when you leave use some of that money for a steak on me." *He's good for another year.* I stood up and turned to leave.

Rosalie was standing at the door. Her face was somber. "Where to next?" she said as she handed me a cup of coffee from her scooter cup holder.

"Brooklyn." I took a long draw on the coffee.

"Are the Dodgers back in town?"

"No." I choked while hiding my smirk. Poor kid never did know a lick about baseball.

On the ride to Brooklyn I looked up Dr. Mixon. She, not a he, was studying "brain oscillations." I knew what each of those words meant independently but not together. I hoped she would dumb it down so I could ask the right questions about the Gizmo. I made an appointment for 11:00 a.m.

After two wrong turns and a floor change, we found Dr. Mixon's office. I knocked and in a few seconds the door opened. Dr. Mixon looked familiar, but I did not place her face.

"Mr. Warren?" Her voice was clinical. She waved at two chairs in front of her desk. Rosalie scooted in. I helped her to a seat. I moved to the chair closer to Dr.

Mixon's desk. "I got a call from the Provost's office asking me to accommodate you with this meeting," she said with a scowl. " Let's make this short. What *exactly* is it you want?" She eyeballed Rosalie who cocked her head slightly.

I can make it short. I started with, "Dr. Heinrich Albert Schwartz."

Her head snapped to me. "I haven't seen him in years. Not since he got dismissed from Stanford. I was forced to find a new advisor and change my major. *He's* the reason it took me so long to graduate." I sensed a bit of panic from her snarky voice and red face.

"I can't find any published work under his name or yours for that time frame. Since DARPA funded the research, I assumed it was classified. Is that the case?" She bobbed her head.

I continued, knowing I was in way over my head. "Your current research, is it related to your work with Schwartz in any way?" I kept my voice non-threatening or so I thought.

"Yes…and no. Both relate to brain function. I am prohibited from discussing that earlier work obviously. My current work involves oscillations in the brain that may have some relationship to alcoholism. I try to find and track frequencies that may appear more in people who are alcoholics or who may become alcoholics."

I perked up at hearing the word "frequencies." I was a part-time radio operator in Bosnia, so I took a stab in the dark. "Do you think you will be able to predict people who could become alcoholics?"

She shrugged. "That is a part of my personal hope for an outcome."

I dredged up more radio knowledge. "Do you think

you might be able to retune those frequencies to a different frequency in a way that people lose that taste for alcohol and stop drinking?" I knew that was a reach.

"Wouldn't that be wonderful. Perhaps even other types of addiction, but research is an uncharted winding road with many potholes and many forks in it, Mr. Warren."

"Dr. Mixon, I am the current owner of Dr. Schwartz's Gizmo." She paled and her breathing sped up. "I have a bit of a situation on my hands, and I need your help." She relaxed a hair in her chair, but her hands were clenched white. I've discovered that people relax when you ask for help. "I have several questions, and I hope you're the one who can answer them."

She said in a slow voice, "Before we start, my work *never* involved human trials. I was in Europe on a summer internship. I heard about them when I got back, but Schwartz was already gone."

"I'm not here to ask about that." I noticed several diplomas on her wall: Ph.D. and M.D., so she's doctor-doctor. *She's no slouch.*

"How many transfers was the Gizmo set for?"

She pondered her answer, or was it her options? "My understanding was fifty transfers." *She just opened a way in for me.*

Chapter 6

Boss

"Fifty. And when that number was reached, what then?" I listened *very* closely.

"As I understood it, when a new mermaid egg is inserted, the machine automatically resets to fifty. But Schwartz ran four trials before he ran into a glitch, other than not having permission for human trials." She said this as she twitched and stopped looking me in the eye.

Mermaid eggs? *I've never heard this term before.* "What is a mermaid egg? A type of fuel?" I guessed the fuel part. It only made sense. "What does it look like? Do you know what it's made from?" The more she answered, the more questions I had.

"They look like a dark pink fish scale the size of a…of a…" she looked around her desk. "Ah, the Home key on my old iPhone, and I have no idea what they were made of. The professor cooked them up himself, but he did a trial run with a smaller mermaid egg that he thought might last for perhaps half a dozen transfers. He did say that he designed the Gizmo to function until all the fuel was used up, and he made a dozen mermaid eggs."

I couldn't do the math in my head but fifty times twelve is more than I'd ever need at Drake's. *If I find the darn egg things.* "And what was the glitch?"

I glanced at Rosalie. She had the best poker face I'd ever seen.

Dr. Mixon again avoided my eyes. "He lost a student...I heard. He ran this one kid through three times. Three days later the kid's brain literally turned into scrambled eggs. Mr. Warren," she choked out, "no one can live with scrambled eggs for brains. No one." She looked disgusted as she said this last part.

"Why is the fuel called mermaid eggs, do you know?"

She snorted and look like she had just bitten into the most revolting dish on the planet. "Whimsy. He said everyone needed a bit of whimsy in their life. That was his. That and the Roman numerals." *Aha! Now I know why there are Roman numerals on the Gizmo.*

"How and where are the mermaid eggs inserted into the Gizmo?"

Her eyes flared at my question. "That is all covered in the Gizmo manual. You must have that, don't you?" She pursed her lips tightly.

That was in the manual? *I don't think so.* "It's not in the manual that I have, so I guess mine is incomplete," I said waiting for whatever else she had to offer.

"It's in the Addendum after the Index." She was smug and clearly expecting us to leave.

"Dr. Mixon, I assure you there is not an Addendum in the manual. Is there anything else I should know?" I was no further along on fixing the Gizmo than when I walked in. She shook her head. "Then thank you for your time." As I stood to help Rosalie up and onto her scooter, I heard the good doctor unlock and open a file cabinet drawer.

I reached for the office door when Dr. Mixon said, "Mr. Warren. You should take this. I sure as hell don't want it." She stapled one of her business cards to something, then she handed it to me: a manual to the Gizmo.

I thumbed to the Index and then went past. There were extra pages titled "Addendum" that mine didn't have. I looked at her with my eyebrows raised.

"I guess the professor forgot to include the latest revision to the manual," she said sharply with a shrug. "You know how absent-minded we academics are."

****

I helped Rosalie into the Range Rover. I strapped myself in and heard my stomach growl.

She giggled. "That's called 'borborygmus' in case you were wondering, but I could eat."

I remembered stumping each other with weird words in high school. I see she hadn't forgotten. "Well, what do you fancy, Nurse Smith?" I asked. "We called them 'wamblys.' "

"In fact—it's Nurse Abatsong, and I'd love to try some famous New York pizza."

I was taken aback at her name and at a loss for pizzeria names. "June, any ideas?"

He flashed a big grin. "Yes, sir. I know the best pie in Brooklyn, the best in New York. Fasten your seatbelts." He headed in a direction I did not recognize.

"Abatsong? I've never heard that name before. Where's—"

"Cameroon." She fished a wallet from her purse and showed me a group photo. "This was a bush hospital where we introduced better prenatal and postnatal techniques." Her pride shone in her eyes.

"Which one is Damon." *I remembered his name.* She was the only Caucasian in the group, so she was easy to find. She pointed to a handsome man in scrubs next to her. "Oh, the tall one." If she loved this guy, he was someone really special because Rosalie didn't suffer fools gladly. *With the possible exception of me.* "And he was a good stepfather to Allie?" *My daughter, who I wasn't around to raise.*

"The best. Just ask her sometime." Tears inched down her cheeks.

I handed her my handkerchief. "Do you miss him?" I was both surprised and grateful for this turn in our conversation. I was starting to collect pieces of *her* puzzle.

She wiped her eyes as she said, "Yes. It's been five years. I've moved on with my life. But every once in a while..."

I took her hand and held it. "I'm glad you married him. I'm glad Allie grew up with a strong positive man in her life."

"Thank you for that." She squeezed my hand. "But we will have to talk about your mom and dad one of these days."

I changed the subject; today was not the day for my dad. "Grimaldi's. Great choice. If you don't like this pizza, Rosalie, you need a tastebud transplant." I helped her out of the car as June had done.

The lunch crowd was thinning out and we found a free table near the back. "What does everyone want? June, the usual?" He smiled ear to ear.

"I'll eat anything but anchovies or pineapple," Rosalie replied.

"Okay, but save room for tiramisu after," June added as the waiter took our order.

Rosalie stared out the window. "This building is under a big bridge. Is it safe?"

June and I exchanged glances. He said, "Since 1883, Mrs. Abatsong," with a toothsome grin. "That's the world-famous Brooklyn Bridge." He went ahead to give her a discourse on the bridge until our pies thankfully arrived and we dug in.

As I paid the bill, the waiter asked if we wanted to take the rest home. I started to say no when Rosalie cut me off. "Please." She said to June. "I bet your wife will love this as much as I did." June was speechless. He excused himself to retrieve the Rover. At the car, Rosalie handed him the pizza that he stowed in the trunk. As June placed her scooter alongside the pizza, I helped her into the Rover. He got my attention and jerked his head towards the back of the car.

"We're being followed. I swear it's the SUV that hit Rosalie, I mean, Mrs. Abatsong."

"Is there any way you can lose them?" I didn't dare turn and look.

"I'll try. That SUV might be too narrow for some of my 'short cuts.' Can you sit here for couple of minutes?" Before I could answer June walked back into the restaurant.

When I got in, I scooted closer to Rosalie. "June needed to use the men's room," I fibbed.

I restrained myself from looking up the street towards the SUV. I made small talk and explained how this pizzeria was famous, how there were others in other cities, how they partially shut down in the afternoon to clean the coal fired oven, how they only played music sung by— "Here's June."

June came out of the restaurant out of breath and out of patience. He opened his phone to a GPS map. He turned to face us. "Guys, I'm going to try and beat the rush hour. I'm gonna work my way over to Flatbush Avenue and get on the Manhattan Bridge. Be sure your seat belts are tight." He checked his left-side mirror and pulled into traffic. I was lost once we turned onto Water Street. I lost track of the right and left turns. I wondered why June checked the GPS on his phone after each turn because we'd been here before and he knew where we were going. Then it hit me: he planted a tracking device on that SUV like in the movies. Good man, June.

"We're going home, now, Rosalie. You must be tired," I said in a somewhat condescending voice, "and you still need to pack."

She looked shocked. "What? No drive-by shootings? No, road rage confrontations? No psycho taxi drivers? People won't believe I was even here in New York." I couldn't tell if she were smiling or smirking, but I could see she was holding her breath. I assumed she was joking, but I began to think she was savvier than I gave her credit for.

Ping...ping. There were two sounds on my side of the Rover. *Rocks?* As we whizzed by street signs, I finally read "Flatbush Ave," and I knew the Manhattan Bridge was in front of us. "June is taking the scenic way home," I lied to Rosalie, "but you'll have plenty of time." My Range Rover had armor and bulletproof windows. That didn't stop someone from following us.

Once in my building, June stopped in the parking garage and opened my door first. As I stepped out, his eyes dropped to the door panel. Two long dark horizontal streaks decorated and indented the side. June whispered, "I'm guessing he used a silencer. It sounded like rocks hitting the door. Anyone in town who would try this already knows where you live."

"Good point. Anything else." Assassination was why I had bulletproof vehicles.

"She's new," he said jerking his head towards Rosalie. "No one knows where she lives." He leaned in. "The shooter didn't know his way around Brooklyn, or he could have cut us off more than once. Check her for a tracker."

This wasn't like a ride at Disneyland. I better have my planes checked too.

Back at the apartment, Rosalie packed for our trip to Drake's Key, and I returned a call.

"Hello, Mr. Warren. I appreciate you are returning my call yourself. I realize you may not be familiar with me or my name, but I am acquainted with several of your earlier guests."

"And what is the business or pleasure that we will be discussing, Mr. Huang?"

"I wish to play in the Chairs this season."

Okay, business as usual. He was correct. I didn't recognize the name he left with Peaches, but I Googled it in a flash. "Huang, is that Korean, Vietnamese, or Chinese, sir?" I had a choice of several Huangs on the Forbes Millionaires and Billionaires List.

"Chinese. I am the sole owner of Soon and Son, Ltd."

Yes, you are. "I see you are a Canadian citizen," I said and noted it in my Players notebook. I made a quick check on the estimated value of his company. Very respectable was an understatement. His net worth had my attention.

"Yes. My parents immigrated to Canada before I was born."

"Is that why your first name doesn't sound

Chinese?" I asked casually while searching for other information on a second screen.

"No. That's a funny family story. My late aunt was Canadian but not Chinese. I was born with a very full head of black hair. She exclaimed she'd never seen such a 'hairy baby,' and my parents decided to keep it, after changing the spelling."

I imagined a newborn with a giant mop of black hair. His story made me laugh a bit. "Mr. Huang, I was named for someone I never met in my life, so I find that story relatable. Who are your friends that referred you to me?" This was a top concern for me.

"Mr. Lau, who was on Drake's Key last week and Mr. Xin who played in the Chairs. Now please show me the kindness to let me finish before you refuse me."

Lau, who transferred bodies with Velasco again off the books and probably killed Dex just a few days ago. Xin, who has a five-million-dollar bounty on my head. *Nice company you keep, Mr. Huang.* "I'm listening," I said. *Was this a setup?*

"Mr. Warren, these men are most decidedly not my friends. We have a large diaspora of Chinese in Canada, and these men were vising here in the last day or so. It has been impossible to avoid them as we have many friends in common. Sadly, I suspect Mr. Lau may be a very distant cousin."

I had no trouble imaging a large party with dozens of exotic Chinese dishes and Xin and Lau toasting each other. I wondered if Lau came and left on Xin's yacht? That would account for how he managed to stay hidden from my security. They must have flown to Canada from St. Thomas or St. Croix.

"These men have bragged about outwitting some

governments of taxes and some banks as well for several years. I own stock in those banks and do not appreciate their criminal activity.

"Naturally, the story of your Gizmo circulated. It explained the changes in Mr. Lau's physical body and his face the last nine years."

Wait. *Nine years?* Dex and I didn't even know each other nine years ago.

"Did you say, 'nine years ago,' sir?" *This could be significant.*

"Let me think again. Yes. It was nine years ago that he came back from a trip to New York a 'changed man' one could say." *The Gizmo?*

"Did he play poker back then?" A bad feeling started to claw around the pit of my stomach. I searched for an antacid tablet. Peaches always had them—but this wasn't Drake's.

"Why yes. He still does. Always ready for a high stakes gamble, poor man. And I heard just today that he is ill and now hospitalized quite suddenly." I remembered what Dr. Mixon said about three transfers, and I tried to recall something else I once heard about the Gizmo, something much earlier. *I need to talk to Vic.*

"Why have you mentioned Mr. Xin, if he is not a friend?" *This was an odd kind of reference.*

"Because any man that would fine Xin five million dollars and live to tell about is someone I want to meet. I hear he isn't finished with you though, Mr. Warren. You have stirred a viper from his pit, and I say keep up the good work."

His last comment put a positive spin on my opinion of this potential guest at my resort. "Mr. Huang, why do you want to play in the Chairs?" *He didn't sound like my typical Player.*

"I am retiring. My wife passed away two years ago. I refuse to leave my company to my rotten-to-the-core cousin. I am a man who needs a change in life, a big change if you please. And I would like to be number eight."

"Eight it is. I'll be in touch, Mr. Huang. There is a procedure we follow. Please email my office at Drake's Key with your financial contacts. But, before you go, could you do me a personal favor?"

"Most assuredly."

I stepped way out on a limb. "If Mr. Lau's situation changes, would you let me know the details? I have an island full of people to care for. If he is sick from something on the island I need to act." This seemed a believable ploy. A reasonable request for a so-far reasonable man.

"Yes. Of course. You are a man I see who takes his responsibilities seriously. I admire that. Good day."

"Good day to you," I replied and hung up. I texted my original accountant Beryl to expect information from one Mr. Harry Hansan Huang, a potential Player in the Chairs for next season. Although she wasn't a fulltime employee, I had Beryl on a retainer plus expenses to do the forensic background checks and to set up the transfer of asset agreements for the Chairs.

That night the conversation turned to the car-chase nature of our return from Brooklyn and Dr. Mixon. Rosalie brought it up. "Skip, if we are to have an effective and open discussion, you have to be honest with me. I'm committed to that. Are you?"

I smelled a trap. "Yes, I am. Allie said that we—"

"Shut up. Yes, it's *your* turn to shut up. You lied to

me today, and you are lying to me now." Her eyes were squeezed into slits, and she was right.

"What did I—"

"I said 'shut up.' You're insulting me. That car chase here from Brooklyn? What was *that*? You certainly didn't leave without paying the check, so what *was* that?" She tapped the table with her fingers.

I clenched my teeth. What will she do? What will she say? I had no frigging idea.

"And before you lie to me again, know that I know the difference between a rock hitting a bullet-proof car and a bullet hitting that same car. So lie to me again, and I'm out of here tonight." Her fingers kept tapping.

She planted one elbow on the table and planted her chin on her hand. She waited. Tap-tap-tap-tap. Her eyes bored into mine.

I sucked in a deep breath. "I apologize. You are right. Those were bullets not rocks, and most likely meant for you." Her expression didn't change. She reached into her pocket and laid a small dark object about the size of a box of matches on the table and slid it over to me. I picked it up and examined it closely. *This must be the tracker June told me to look for.*

"I found this in the purse I bought at Macy's."

"Ah, mind if I look through the rest of your stuff. Might be another." *I'm on thin ice.*

She shook her head. "I double checked everything. I'm confident it was planted on me at Macy's. I even considered a personal body cavity search, but no, there aren't any more."

Why was there one in the first place?

Chapter 7

Ledger
"Why would someone want to track you?" I wasn't relieved that she was the target rather than me.

"Well, I had a run-in with someone I knew in Africa at Macy's. She was surprised that I was still alive. I think my broken leg and this shooting can be traced directly to her. Of course we have no direct proof, and even if we did, she has diplomatic immunity, so end of story."

How is it she knows someone with diplomatic immunity? I changed the subject, "I see. Well then…" I asked, hoping for an opinion from one woman on another, "…what do you think of Dr. Mixon?" I shifted in my chair. This whole conversation was foreign to me.

Rosalie tortured the mashed potatoes on her plate with her fork. "I think she worked hard to get to where she is." *Short and true.*

"That's all? Any opinions on her veracity? Her motivation in giving me information about Dr. Schwartz or the revised Gizmo manual?" *Yes, I was stirring the pot as fast as I could.*

Rosalie hesitated before she shared her opinion on anything, so I waited. "She is telling you as much as she can and being as truthful as she can. She is, or was, or both, mixed up in something not of her doing. You are just another intrusion, and maybe a threat, into her life."

I got to, "How am I—" when she cut me off sharply.

"No woman 'likes' to be forced out on a date, Skip, or Ledger, or whatever. You did that by going through her boss for that meeting." She pushed her plate back and struggled to stand, but she waved me away as I started to help her. Her face was angrier than I had ever seen it. "And, most importantly, she is *scared.* Scared of you. End of story. I'll be by the door at 7 a.m. sharp. Good night." She scooted away down the hall to her room. I heard her door slam shut.

I asked for it, and I got it. That was the Rosalie I'd forgotten. I'm glad she didn't lose that clarity in expressing her opinions. I knew I could count on her for that. All that she said begs the question of what could Dr. Mixon be scared of? *Why me, and who other than me?*

I didn't need to pack much. I'd left my island barely a week ago with my passport and a leather portfolio. This morning I am taking them and my new Gizmo manual for my return. I'll bring over a tailor from St. Thomas to alter the clothes hanging in my closet at Drake's Key.

Estafania had breakfast and coffee ready. The apartment was quiet and lacked energy. Rosalie was already at the table eating. She looked at me from under raised eyebrows as I sat down across from her. "Good morning, Skipper."

"Good morning, Rosalie." I glanced into her eyes. They told me nothing. "Coming with me to Drake's Key?" I expected her to say "no."

She picked up her coffee. "I'm not a quitter, at least not today."

This is definitely not how I expected things to go between us. My phone rang. It was early and I hadn't eaten yet. I needed food before I lifted off on a long flight. The ringtone was Vic's, so I rose and walked towards my office. "Yes, Vic."

"Boss, there's been a death here. You are coming today, aren't you?"

Uh oh. "Yes. We're scheduled to leave my airport at 8 a.m. What happened?"

"A break-in last night. Three people got into your office. As far as I can tell, they didn't take anything. They interrupted someone working late and killed them to make their getaway."

"Is there surveillance video?" *This was bad for me, bad for business.*

"Maybe." He sounded tentative. He never makes an accusation before he has proof.

"Have Peaches send me the video ASAP. I'll look at it on the plane."

"I can't do that. Peaches is dead." *That didn't sound right.*

"Repeat. I didn't quite catch that. *Who* is dead?"

"Peaches, Boss. She was strangled, but we caught them. I might be going fishing today. I'll be back before your plane bounces on the runway." Vic hung up. Fishing is Vic's way of telling me he is disposing of a body or two. *What story did he tell the police?* I tried to eat my breakfast, but I couldn't. Peaches was with me from the start of Drake's. She knows more about my business than anyone. Even me. I have no idea who can replace—

"What's with the thousand-yard stare?" Rosalie asked.

"It's…" *Where to start?* Take Rosalie or not? She's got that same look in her eyes as last night. "The truth?" *How do I even say this?*

She gave me her "what else would it be" look and

waited, as I weighed what I needed to say and do next. I never thought I would say something like this. I took a long drink of coffee. I figured I just had to put it out there. "My assistant Peaches was murdered. Strangled in my office. Still want to go?"

Her eyes popped for a moment. "We still have business to finish of our own. I need to know your world to understand who you are now. Do I have a death wish? No. Am I going with you? Yes." Rosalie stood and kneeled on her scooter with her broken leg. "It's now or never for us, Skip. My bags are by the door. I'll pee, get my purse and sweater, and I'll be by my bags in five. This island of yours should be a great change from New York drive-by battery and shootings."

****

After the plane took off, I turned to Skip. "I want to tell you a story, of sorts." He said nothing but kept his eyes on me. " 'I'm not a quitter.' That's what I told our daughter Allie last night before I knew about the second attempt upon my life. Now I'll have to come clean with her about her stepfather's death, since I raked you across the coals about telling the truth.

" 'I'm not a quitter.' That's the last thing I said to my husband before he died. We'd heard machine gun fire in the night. It was getting closer to the hospital. Some patients were taken out by their families.

" 'I will wait until the last woman leaves,' he said. 'Then I will join with you by the river. I have a canoe waiting to take us to the coast,' he told me." *As he held me close for the last time.*

" 'I'll wait five more minutes,' I said scared, but more afraid that I would never see him again. I mopped the feverish foreheads of the two remaining women when the doors burst open. The husband and son quickly picked up the mother and daughter, kissed Damon's cheek, and fled into the darkness.

" 'Now…,' Damon said putting his arm around me, '…now it is our time to go.' He led me to the car and pushed me into the back seat. 'Lay down. Cover yourself with the blanket. Quickly.' The gunfire moved closer by the minute.

"The roads were pocked from bombs—separatist rebel bombs we were told. I harbored doubts. The car hit a bump so hard I was lifted completely off the seat. I landed half-way onto the floor. It hurt when I breathed in. My ribs, I thought.

"We went a few more meters and hell erupted underneath our car. An explosion near the front on Damon's side ripped the door off. I was deafened and have little memory of being pulled out. My back was on fire from pain. Someone pulled Damon out and he laid by the side of the road his life bleeding into the dirt, and I couldn't stop it. I clung to him saying I wasn't a quitter, he shouldn't be either, but I couldn't hear his answer.

"Dark-skinned people, friends we knew for years, risked everything to help us. They led me to the safety of a jungle hiding place. They applied a bush poultice to my back to help with the pain. Later they took me to the river and made sure I was in the canoe Damon paid for." I stopped to wipe my eyes and blow my nose.

"I never heard where he was buried. I've never been back to help the Reverend Smith at his clinic. I nor Allie for that matter had a chance to say goodbye to him. He saved my life more than once that week. I've never told Allie the full story."

"I'm stunned. I don't know what to say."

"When you told me of the second attempt upon my life, I thought, 'Better killers than you city boys have tried, and I'm still here.' Now I'll have to come clean to Allie about the death of her stepdad, whom I suspect she loved even more than she loves me or you.

"I have never been so petrified in my life as I am now. If I tell her the truth, I may lose her. If I do, you better be worth it. So far you are only a sperm donor, but you better become her safety net and parent and whatever else she needs in this life—you hear me, Skipper Warren? You better *damned* well be worth it!"

I scooted to the other end of the plane so I could cry in private. I hate crying in front of other people, especially if I may never see them again. I went into Skip's bedroom on the plane, collapsed, and bawled myself to sleep.

****

While Rosalie slept, I took a call from Vasily Yakov Raskolnikov. "Vasily, what a surprise. How is the oil business in Azerbaijan these days?"

"Very good, Ledger." He spoke with that heavy Russian accent that could be charming—if he so wished or threatening if he needed it to be. "And you, you are well? No wife yet? How is this possible?"

"Not yet," I laughed for his benefit. "Too busy these days. I still owe you a visit to Baku."

He responded with, "I will forgive you if you let me come to Drake's for the Chairs."

"The Chairs? You want to watch the Chairs?"

"*Nyet*, Ledger, I want to play in the Chairs."

Whoa! "Play in the Chairs." *That was a surprise.* "Why, if you don't mind?"

"You know, I have a great amount of money, and

yet it does not please me. It is a source of much discontent and suspicion. I have been studying with my priest, and I have come to a decision. I am to become a monk and perhaps one day a priest."

Whoa again! I didn't see that coming. "What does all that require?"

"I am still discovering that myself, but I am sure owning and managing an oil empire as I study or minister to congregants are incompatible. Sadly. my wife passed away and I find I am not as interested in finding a new wife as I might have thought. I realize I have led my life too much in the temporal world and too little in the spiritual. Perhaps I am jaded, perhaps I am naïve, but I fear we have missed much in this life. Don't you?"

"Your words do resonate with me. What else have you been up to?" *I can't say I've had any spiritual side to my life, truth be told.*

"Growing a beard. Can you believe that? I mention it so you will recognize my fat face. I have not cut my decadent long hair though. That will be done by the priests."

"Will you be going into a monastery or seminary? I apologize; I don't know the correct term to use."

"*Da*, but I do not know where yet. Most likely in Russia. You remember my family immigrated to Azerbaijan from Russia, from Volgograd when I was only seven? So somewhere in that area of Russia perhaps."

"Vasily, I will put you in touch with my accountant, Beryl."

"Good. I expect to see you the last week of April. I think I take one last voyage on my yacht *Skvashina*. It means oilwell." He laughed heartily. "Those Soviets had no imagination. My first hotel was named The Coalminer. *Das svidania*, Ledger. See you in April."

Vasily is close to the last guy I would have expected to play in the Chairs. I need to make time to have a billionaire-on-billionaire talk with him. *This might be the slowest, or shortest, Chairs ever.*

****

Back on Drake's meant back to business. Rosalie installed herself in Peaches' office. When I remembered to check in on her she had already introduced herself to my IT manager as my assistant and had new passwords for all our systems before lunch. She was using Peaches' desk and computer.

"What are you doing?" I asked.

"I'm not going to sit around and watch you implode because your most important manager died."

"What?"

"Peaches. I didn't come here to twiddle my thumbs, or scooter around the Maze and the grounds—which I have already done by the way—and watch you flounder around like a chicken with its head cut off. That's not why I'm here. So if I can do even a small part of what Peaches did so you will have time for me and Allie, then *that's* what I'm doing."

"Oh, then thanks. What's next?" *Right now she reminds me more of my old Army sergeant than my late secretary.*

"Singh. Be here any minute. New contract it says on your calendar."

As if on cue my potential new general manager walked into the outer office. "Come in, Singh. I've got a contract waiting for your signature." Singh was a good three inches taller than me. *Not many guests will challenge you, Singh.*

As I followed Singh into my office Rosalie whispered, "Sit on the same side of the desk."

I sat on the same side of my desk as Singh, and I admit it *did* seem more personal. "Here is a copy for you to review. I don't expect a signature today." I handed him my basic department manager contract with a few additions.

"Yes, thank you sir. I do have a question or two."

"Let's start with the issues you want to discuss." Singh was always straightforward. He didn't play games. I liked that.

"Sir, I am to be married in the spring. I will require two weeks off to travel home. I will need accommodations for two adults when I return."

"What, no honeymoon? Better make that four weeks off."

Singh's face split with a grin. "Yessir, thank you, Boss." *Sincere but not obsequious.*

I had a sudden thought. "Max and Marie won't be returning. Will their suite suit you and your bride? I'll have it redecorated to her taste, of course."

Singh's grin widened. "Yes, I expect so. May I look at it today?"

"Check with Vic. I think all of their personal things have been removed. Does your bride currently have a job?" *I always liked to employ both spouses if I could.*

"Yes, Gyanleen is a preschool teacher. We both have university educations, so it is of special interest to us." *I liked her already.*

"That's important to me too. Now you've been here…what three years?"

"No sir, four. Four years in security, the first year in

the casino."

"Good. You must have a pretty good idea of Mr. Drake's responsibilities then." I detected a slight pause before he answered. He probably caught on to Dex's side hustles.

"I believe I have an idea of what you need in this position. But I am a quick study. I will read this tonight and come back tomorrow if that is suitable."

"That's fine. I've got another thought. I wear a tux at night, but you'll need a new wardrobe. I'll get you an advance. Can you have some sort of daytime uniforms made in India, and then something more elegant for the evenings. Both should reflect your heritage. You will be much more the face of Drake's than I am, Singh. You'll be the first contact for our guests if they need help. Do us up proud—silk, velvet, gold threads—classic, but please stand out in the crowd."

He intoned, "As if the sword isn't enough?" His smile revealed a row of perfect white teeth behind his thick black mustache and beard and the required turban.

Yes indeed. My new general manager will be an attraction himself. "I understand it's required by your religion. The guests don't have to know if it's ceremonial or not." We laughed at this comment. I suddenly started a mental count of the Drake's employees who regularly carry a blade. *Besides me there's Singh...*

****

I wrote down a few notes about my life after I left home. Somehow Rosalie and I had to address that for both of us. Oklahoma seemed so remote and truly a lifetime ago. It's been a week and Peaches' funeral was fast approaching so I tried to compose a few remarks for that too. It made me realize Peaches always had my back.

She knew me better than anyone else at Drake's but on a personal level. She could read me and know if I needed a drink or an antacid tablet, if I was getting enough fruit and veggies, and if I needed alone time. *How could I admit this to a room full of people I barely knew?*

Vic stopped by with Bad, my Ghurka security guard. "Got a quick minute? Bad has something you need to hear." My top two security guys didn't come to gossip. *This must be hot.*

Chapter 8

Boss

I waved Vic and Bad in. We all stood as Bad talked. He wore his khukuri knife on his back. I've never seen him without it now that I think of it. *Another blade*, I counted, *and Vic makes four, at least.* Bad handed me a photo of an Asian couple. "These people came with the cleaning crew. I saw them talking to a lot of our employees and showing them this picture." He passed me a photo of me, but before I transferred back with Dex, so now it's an original photo of Dex, if he's still alive. "They asked about the man in this picture. They wanted to talk to him. They wouldn't tell me what they wanted to talk about."

"Where are they now?" *I'm somehow relieved they're still alive.*

"Locked in the shark tank."

I laughed at that. Guests pay to be lowered in a glass pod into a pool of sharks, the embodiment of death and dismemberment. I suspect these two "guests" won't be equally amused. I checked my watch and grabbed the banana I planned to eat later. "Let's go."

We approached the pool when I saw Allie waiting. "What's she doing here?" It made me nervous to have her in the middle of the seamier side of security at Drake's.

"Helping," Bad said as he motioned for the pod to

be raised. The assumed assassins didn't look happy. The pod swung closer to the edge of the pool, but still over the water. Bad turned on the intercom into the pod. "This man is the owner of this island." Bad handed me the mic.

I held Dex's photo they showed around. "This man does not work here. He is no longer on this island. Repeat. He is no longer on this island." I lowered the mic as the man and woman in the pod talked between themselves. We listened but neither Bad nor I spoke Chinese.

Allie turned her back to the pod and switched the "Speak" button off on my mic. "Mr. Xin will not be happy if they return without killing the man in the picture. If he is not here, they must leave the island. They are devising a lie to convince you to let them go. Dad, don't make it easy or they won't believe you." *Her last sentence shocked me.*

I turned on the mic. "The police are on their way here to arrest you." I waved for the pod to be lowered again.

"No. No! We collect money this man owe for betting." They looked down as they spoke.

I stopped the pod. "I don't care what he owes you. That's your problem. I don't like you sneaking on this island. This is *my* property. You are trespassing."

"Okay. We go now, yes?" They looked pathetic until I realized that if I hadn't changed back with Dex, I'd most likely be dead by now.

I clicked the mic off and turned to Bad and Allie. "What do you think? Scared enough?"

Allie said, "A skosh more, please." She was dead serious, and I could see she was in her US Marshal mode.

I turned around and opened my mic. "You have one

hour to get off this island." I looked at my watch.

"How we get off?"

"I don't care. Swim. It's forty miles to the next island. If you are here in an hour, you will be swimming in *this* pool." I impulsively threw the banana into the water. The pool erupted into a frenzy of snapping razor sharp teeth slashing water onto the see-through pod.

I was impressed. *I'll have to remember that move.* I switched off the microphone and turned to Bad. "Take them to the cargo port and put them on the next ferry. Thanks, Bad. Let's go Allie." We turned our backs and walked away. I said, "Your mom is probably waiting for us. So Chinese, huh?" *She's one cool cookie, my daughter.*

"Yeah. It was that or Arabic, and I hate falafel. So Xin, huh. I hear the price on your head is five mil. The cheapskate."

****

I've been to funerals before, but this one was unlike any other. I realized how much I depended on Peaches. I recognized this was my first funeral for a person I cared about. She excelled at her job. She treated me like her own flesh and blood. How was I going to handle Drake's business and my own affairs without her?

There was a knock on my bedroom door. "Just a moment." As I finished my tie, I looked in the mirror. Who am I? *What will people say about me when the time comes?* I heard women's voices as I opened my door.

"Dad, are you ready? What's taking so long? Didn't the tailor alter a suit suitable for a funeral?"

I walked into my apartment living room saying, "He did. It's just that I don't' know what to say at the service. I was asked to say something, and I just don't know..."

Rosalie spoke up. "My dad used to say, 'say something personal, something the mourners can relate to.' It's not about you, Skip, it's about Peaches." She adjusted my tie. I'd forgotten for a moment Rosalie's dad was a preacher. He must have conducted dozens of funerals, perhaps for people he didn't know well. *What did I know about Peaches?*

We met Vic in the resort lobby for the ride to the church. "Just so you know, the governor is coming. Oh, I found this under the Gizmo after Dex disappeared." He reached into his pocket and pulled out his fist. As he opened his hand, out dropped a gold object that stopped on the end of a short chain. There, dangling from the chain was my grandfather's pocket watch I thought I lost when Dex and I transferred bodies. He handed me the ornate watch I used during the Chairs. "It must have dropped out of his pocket." I'd thought no one was as good at a deadpan face as Vic, but Rosalie was his equal.

Rosalie exclaimed, "That's your old watch, Skip. You were awfully proud of it when your grandad left it to you. I'm glad you have it back. May I see it?" She turned it over, running her fingers over the deep engraving on the back.

"I lost two things when Dex and I transferred back. That watch was one of them."

"What was the other?" she asked as she opened the case. It was still there: her high school yearbook photo, and it surprised her.

"That," I said. Here I was face to face with Rosalie as she was then, and Rosalie as she is now. *I need to figure out how to connect the two.*

It seemed Peaches Petty was well known in the Virgin Islands. The Reverend Otis greeted us as we arrived at the church. "Mr. Warren, the church is very grateful for your contribution to this service. Just look what your people have done here today already." He pointed to the large canopies set up with folding chairs for shade with water and juice dispensers.

"Many people will be here today, many more than we can fit into our small sanctuary. This was very thoughtful of you."

I felt I needed to say something, *but what?*

I heard Rosalie's voice. "Reverend, I am Rosalie Abatsong, a friend of Mr. Warren's. If I may, he is grateful for her long service and loyalty to him. Peaches was his assistant but also someone who watched out for him. I'm tempted to say she even adopted him in many ways."

The Reverend Otis chuckled. "I understand that. She put me on a diet last year after my heart attack." He patted his slim waistline with obvious pride. Again I tried to talk to no avail, but the Reverend continued. "The use of Drake's shuttle boats to ferry people from St. Thomas and St. Croix to Drake's Key is truly generous. Peaches had many friends and family across the islands." Then he pointed to the Drake's staff shuttle bus unloading people dressed in somber clothes, with an occasional splash of color. "And this...these buses make all the difference for the many people to be here."

The Reverend Otis leaned in closer. "Over the years she told me of the many generous things you have done for us. Life on this island is very different than it was under the previous owner. Let me thank you for that, sir. I remember you in my prayers every night. Now, I see Miss Petty's brother. I must speak to him. I'll will see you later at the buffet." He shook my hand vigorously.

I squirmed from the reverend's words. I didn't have the first inkling on how to conduct myself here. This was only the third time I'd been to this little church. I felt ill and my stomach churned. As I scanned the crowd, I spotted portable toilets set up under a shady group of palm trees and behind a discreet canvas screen. As I bolted towards them, I sent up my own prayer. *Vic, thanks. You thought of everything!*

****

We sat together in the tent after the service, a family but not a family. How should I introduce Rosalie and Allie? Would that make them neighbors or targets?

Allie finished a dish of passion fruit ice cream. "Dad, the buffet did Drake's proud."

"Yes, Skip, I'm stuffed. This was one of the most interesting funerals I've ever been to," Rosalie added as she sipped an island iced tea.

Allie started in on a cone of piña colada ice cream. "How's that, Mom?"

"Well for one, I've never seen a woman wearing a hat like that in a coffin. Peaches was dressed to meet her maker. If I were St. Peter, I'd let her in just for her outfit alone. She was a generous lady. I've never seen so many people at a funeral."

I looked around. "Many of the staff are here, but they live here and were friends with Peaches." I nodded to the occasional face that seemed familiar. I watched for faces I didn't know. Xin's men could hide easily in a crowd like this.

"Still," Rosalie said, "I went to a lot of funerals growing up. Did you know she was so well liked?" Rosalie mingled before and after and talked to many of the people here.

"Well, not in particular. We usually just discussed work." I only recognized a few faces from my staff at Drake's and not always by name.

"So you did know that—" She was cut off as the Governor stopped by our table.

I stood to shake his hand, but he passed me by. "Mrs. Abatsong, please don't get up." He turned to Allie. "You must be her daughter. I'm so pleased to meet you both. Peaches spoke warmly about you."

He turned to Rosalie as his aide spoke in his ear. "I must be going but I will put out the word, Rosalie. You will be hearing from us soon. Thank you again, Mr. Warren. The Petty family prays you continue your good work." He pivoted and shook another hand.

When I calculated he was out of earshot, I turned to Rosalie. "You met the Governor? What 'word' was he referring to? Why will he be calling *you* soon?" *I was losing control of my own little island on a regular basis.*

"As I was saying before the Governor arrived," Rosalie said, "you did know he is her brother, right? I asked his advice in finding you a new secretary slash assistant, that's all."

"Wait a minute. You didn't run that by me first, and no I didn't know he was her brother. It never came up. You know you used to do this in high school too, running my life behind my back…"

Allie executed a perfect eye roll. "Okay, you two. I am sick of hearing about when you were kids. No wonder you haven't made any progress into the here and now."

Her mom retorted, "What pray tell do you recommend, miss know-it-all?"

"I'm glad you asked. I have been thinking about

that, and I have an idea."

Rosalie looked at me, and I shrugged. She responded with, "Go for it, sweetie." *Our daughter was right, of course.* We hadn't made any headway in the few days since we came back to Drake's.

"Here it is. You can't cover every day, so take it one year at a time. Commit an hour a day. You each get half but hit what you think are the most important things. I'm staying for two weeks, so I'll facilitate the discussion. I'm part of the story too."

We two supposed grownups glared at each other but each of us said, "Yeah."

"Good. Dad, you get the first thirty minutes. Let's say an hour after we get back, we'll meet by the statue out your back door, the one of a woman and child sitting and reading a book. Mom, you'll have the last half hour after dinner. Now for heaven's sake, get up and talk to people. This *is* a funeral, you know."

****

Mom occupied Peaches' desk as Dad and I walked in. "Another few days and I'll have this place so I can find things," she said. "How's your afternoon going so far?"

"Swimmingly," I answered in a cheery voice. "I ran into Dad by the pool earlier."

"Well, Skip. It looks like you're up. Shall we go out, sit down in the shade, and get started? Or should we just make a run for it while we can?"

"Geez, guys, you act like you have balls and chains shackled to your ankles. I for one am glad to move forward, I'm not getting any younger, you know."

Dad and Mom sat down across from each other, and I sat by Dad. I started with, "It would have been so much easier for you two if your dads had reconciled and admitted you two were first cousins. You most likely wouldn't be sitting here now, but neither would I. That was a reminder that both of your stories are a part of my own personal history. Play fair, be nice. Most of all be true to yourselves and the memories you have." I passed around glasses of island iced tea and a plate of Mom's oatmeal cookies, her banana-coconut-macadamia nut recipe.

Dad chewed on a cookie. When he finished. he drank half a glass of tea and started with, "I reported to the Army recruitment center in Tulsa two weeks after my high school graduation. My parents wanted to take me, but the only one I wanted to see that day was you, Rosalie. But we didn't dare, did we?"

Mom shook her head and swallowed hard. She told me this part before. It always makes her cry, so I handed her a box of tissues.

"The Army put me and two dozen other recruits up in a motel. The next day I was sworn into the Army, put on a bus, and taken to Fort Leonard Wood in Missouri." Dad's eyes never left Mom's face as he covered the first week of basic training as a tear rolled down her face.

I imagined the young, idealistic man breaking from a confusing life he found too restrictive yet surrounding the girl he adored, the girl he planned to spend his life with. He didn't have to go, but it was the first step in their larger plan. She would catch up later.

"During the second week of basic training I got my 'battle buddy' who turned out to be my best friend for life. Earl. Hooah! We started basic training doing three-mile hikes with gear. At the end of ten weeks we could do ten miles easily.

"I was too tired for anything at the end of the day, but I wrote to you twice a week. At first you answered every letter. As time went by fewer letters came…" Dad finished ten weeks of basic training, and it sounded so harsh but necessary. Physical challenges, battle skills, first aid, drills rain or shine, night and day. Alone, in pairs, in teams, so many combinations and permutations, never knowing which one might save your life or cost you it, or that of a buddy.

"After basic I spent seven weeks in advanced individual training in Internment and Resettlement. My first assignment was at Guantanamo as a prison guard. That's where I was when I got your last letter, and the letter from your mom with your promise ring. She said there was an accident, and you died." He stopped and chugged the rest of his tea. His voice softened when he said, "So did I, Rosalie…at that moment Skipper Warren died. My father's letter was the cherry on the top. 'Don't come back,' it said, so I didn't."

Dad looked at me and whispered, "I'm sorry, Allie. I didn't…I didn't know—I didn't know anything."

I stood and took his hand. We walked out into the quiet side of the garden. I suspected Dad was used to holding in his emotions, maybe even denying them, or burying them so deep they might never be seen. I didn't dare let that happen again. If he couldn't learn that his authentic emotions could be safely acknowledged, this relationship I'd been hunting for my whole life died just as I found him.

Chapter 9

Boss

"Hi Boss, I never expected to see you here this summer," my summer manager Rex said.

"Funny how plans change so quick, isn't it? Just so you know, Vic left this morning for his two-month vacation."

I was not sure what *all* Vic did around here. I suspected it was more than I needed to know or wanted to know legally speaking. "Rex, how are the preparations going for the upcoming season? Got everything you need?" It looked like I would have to manage the updating and remodeling for the next season.

"Yes. Scott is here. He's conducting a soccer camp for anyone who wants to come. I might just go myself. My kids are in soccer camp in Pennsylvania right now. Randy is so busy with the track I've hardly spoken to him. You put a fire in his belly, for sure."

Rex was right. I was walking to clear my mind when I saw Randy two days ago with a surveying transit. "Surveying equipment—that was fast." I was pleased.

"Chet keeps this stuff in Engineering when we aren't using it. You do own the whole island, you know. We use this stuff quite a bit. I'm still a licensed surveyor, so I got to it after our contract meeting. I'm just playing with the location of the running tracks—"

The loud silky purr of a fine motorcycle engine split

our conversation as one sped past on the track. *Who was that?* "When did we get a motorcycle at Drake's?" I asked.

"We didn't, but we should. That's mine, but the girl's new. She showed up here two days ago and asked to try it out. She's licensed and pretty good. Got great reflexes and *great* legs. Do you know her?"

"If her name is Allie, I'm getting to know her better every day." I suddenly felt *protective* of her. That was new. I needed to get back, but I had a topic of conversation for dinner.

I saw Rex still waiting near my office. "There is one more thing, Boss. Who is that women who took over for Peaches? Is she married or anything?"

Was he hitting on Rosalie? *On my girl?* "You'll have to ask her that yourself." As I walked away, I again felt like I was losing control: probable assassins on my island, my employee hitting on my girl, and my daughter racing around on a 1,000-cc high-performance motorcycle. Most of all, I couldn't imagine what Rosalie might say tonight when it's her turn.

****

My afternoon was jammed. First, I returned a call Rosalie took earlier with Mr. Davi Miguel Blanco Moran. I did a five-minute search and learned Mr. Moran was a Brazilian cosmetics king, mid-fifties in age, and an industrious worker. He owned an empire in South American based on cupuaçu, a plant related to chocolate. *How does that work?*

Mr. Blanco Moran's phone rang. zzzt-click-click-click-*Damn.* I found myself hearing that old dial sound even with my digital phone. I realized it was soothing: zzzt-click-click-click-I wondered if there's an app to add that to my phone. Maybe I could commission one.

"Hello, Mr. Warren. This is Davi Moran, but please call me Davi."

"I go by Ledger. What can I do for you today?" Davi's English was excellent with what I suspected a woman might consider a sexy accent. *Especially a woman who liked foreign men.*

"I have two things I wish to discuss. First is the Chairs, and second is trees."

This sounded like business and pleasure. "Where shall we start?"

"The Chairs. I'd like to play the Chairs next...next May, is it?" He sounded tentative.

"Yes, the first week in May. You don't sound very sure of this, sir. Why are you thinking of this gamble?" *It's only June and I may have my first Player.*

"To be honest, I am tired of running an empire after decades. I want to help the economies of my fellow Brazilians. I have spun off businesses that my children own and manage, but I have enough assets outside of Brazil to play."

I've heard this story before. "Are you married?"

"Yes, a former Miss Brazil. Spectacular I must say. Also, not faithful. She is one of those women who make a career of shopping and surgery. I found out she bought a new boyfriend I am not supposed to know about, so I have called my lawyer. There is a prenup in place, but I have the stronger hand and evidence."

I've heard this before too. "Are you prepared for the worst outcome?" So many people never think it would happen to them, especially the men.

"Mr. Warren, some say Brazil is the plastic surgery capital of the world. I can become whatever I wish no matter if I win or lose, can't I?"

I saw what he meant. Our doc tells me the Brazilian butt lift is one of our most popular plastic surgery options. I often wondered how those women stay upright in the pool with all the new fat in those "Brazilian butts."

"Fine. I'll send you the forms for application. Now what's this about trees?"

****

Dinner was over. "Year one, Mom. Your turn," I said.

Mom sat across from Dad. "I was a 'good' girl. Everyone said so. Yet there I was seventeen and late. It only happened one time, that night of your senior prom in May and yet—" Dad's lips squeezed together as if he was afraid to speak.

"A quickie marriage was not in my future. I wouldn't let it be. I lived and breathed Skipper Warren. You were *my* life, but I was not about to snuff out *yours*."

Dad looked perplexed with his eyebrows knitted together.

"You were the smartest kid in the senior class. Everyone in town knew you were going places, that you would 'be somebody.' How could I destroy that and profess to love you? I borrowed some nursing text books from the school nurse. I pored over the section relating to pregnancy. There was no mistaking the symptoms.

"For weeks I lied to my mother. Not to her face, but still... She bought my sanitary pads when she bought groceries. I took my monthly box to the school nurse and gave them to her for 'the poor girls who couldn't afford them,' or those who have an emergency at school, as I did once."

Mom paused for a moment to regroup. This is weird

listening to how my life began.

"My mother found out by accident. That night at supper, Granny Lou, who adopted Daddy at birth, offered her opinion on the matter. She said, 'Second and later babies take nine months, but first babies come any time. You, Lewis, took five years and two months as I recall.' My dad did not laugh."

"I always liked your granny," Dad admitted.

"She liked you too, I think. Anyways, my mom said there were two options: go to a neighboring state for an abortion or give my baby up for adoption. 'We'll go to Texas tomorrow,' she said. " Mom reached over and took Dad's hand. "I think they were afraid of who the father was, and their answer was still 'not that boy.' My mom intercepted some of your letters and kept them from me. The day Rosalie was born she sent that letter to you that said I died. She let me know about it. She always claimed the last word."

Mom took a breather, ate another cookie, and drained my glass of tea. She was working up to something big, something 'ugly' as she said before we left home. I went and sat by Dad, putting my head on his shoulder, and entwined my arm around his. *I know what's coming next.*

"I refused to go to Texas long enough to turn eighteen. I overheard my mom on the phone speaking to a private adoption agency. She planned to snatch my baby—our baby—while I was still in the hospital and sign her away. When I heard that I got legal counsel. My lawyer came very early the day Allie was born. He helped me sign myself out of the hospital with my baby before my mom came."

I hugged Dad closer. "That lawyer was your father,

Skip." I felt Dad shake.

"*My* father—?" he whispered.

Mom stopped him. "Not yet, Skip. Let me finish before I lose my nerve. Your folks took us in. They gave Allie and me a home for years. We carried on a long discussion about your future, my future, and Allie's future. We all knew you would try to come home as soon as you could, that you would drop college and any idea of law school. I couldn't stand the idea of you working in any job you could find, and I knew you would. You, the brightest boy in town. I couldn't let that happen, so I asked your father to write his letter after my mom sent hers."

Dad stood, but I wouldn't let him leave. I clung to him with all my heart and willpower. "Not yet, Dad," I begged.

"Skip," Mom said. "I'm sorry. We tried to write the letter so there was a choice. I was wrong. I didn't see how you would think it said, 'don't come back.' I didn't see how we couldn't help but end up like the other kids we knew who went that route. I thought after you finished college I could find you again. I tried and tried. We all tried, but you vanished. I was convinced you were dead up until I saw you on the Marshal's plane. I'm so sorry."

Dad was still shaking as I put my arms completely around him and cried on his chest. *Now we can make progress.* I hugged both of them. *The worst was over.*

There was a tremendous explosion offshore and we turned away as we felt the blast. Panes of glass broke while the orange-yellow light annihilated the night. Dad instantly put his arms around us and turned his back to the window while moving us to the door. "Keep your heads down," he directed.

We waited for a second blast, but no other explosion occurred. We went over to the damaged window where we saw a huge yacht headed away from shore in flames. Black smoke dirtied the moonlit sky. We saw people jumping from the ship. Dad ran to find Bad. Mom scootered to the clinic to help Doc. I ran after Dad in case—I didn't know why; I just ran after Dad. As a Deputy Marshal my instinct was to think this was an attempt on Dad's life gone horrendously wrong.

****

As Boss I had no trouble commandeering a security jeep and drove to the cargo port. I found Bad and most of my summer security force at the port arranging a rescue effort. No one in port was injured, but we could already see a fuel spill on the incoming tide. I pulled on a spare pair of overalls and rubber boots and jumped on my tugboat *Big Buoy* with Bad.

"What happened," I asked. I noticed the night breeze pushing away from the shore; *that might keep some oil and debris at sea.*

Bad scanned the wreck searching for lifejackets, swimmers, bodies, wreckage, and the obligatory sharks. "When I searched the two assassins, I found a communication device but acted as if I hadn't." Bad pointed for the *Big Buoy's* captain to sail towards the upwind side of the wreck.

"As we waited on the dock for the St. Thomas police to arrive, a fast inflatable boat sped into the harbor, barely slowed down, and the two detainees jumped into it. It took off in the direction of that yacht offshore. None of our guards here have guns, so…"

"You can't see around the entrance; how did you

know which direction they were headed?"

Bad produced an awkward smile. "I planted a tracker on them, hoping it might flush out accomplices. That's the *Night Song* in flames. Recognize it?"

"Yes, I do and I'm thinking that's how Xin, Lau, and Velasco left Drake's." I suspect Xin didn't want any witnesses left associated with his assassination attempt on my life. If they took Dex on that ship, we'll never know what happened to him. We watched as our own inflatables sped around the distressed yacht. I heard a loud cracking sound. The ship split in two and sank in a pool of bubbling seawater and fuel. Flotsam and other debris was already rising to the surface. As the tide was coming in, our chances were better of finding survivors and bodies towards the beach. I directed most of the rescuers in that direction.

Bad already notified the US Coast Guard. They and our local environmental cleanup up crews would begin work at once to collect as much fuel and oil as possible before it rolled onto the shore, fowled our pristine beaches, and smothered wildlife.

I called Singh. "Contact Adair Inc. in San Juan. Get them here ASAP." Already my second tug *Little Buoy* was deploying floating booms to contain the spilled liquids. Another ship was bringing out sorbent sponges that soak up oil and fuel. The inflatables picked up two survivors. The island ambulance with lights flashing took them to Drake's clinic: they were our assassins from earlier in the day. Experience taught me the crews would work through the night and for days more. I didn't count on an environmental disaster in my own back yard. For the moment it would have to be my top priority, even more important than saving my own skin.

To top off my day, I received a personal text from Mr. Harry Hansan Huang. Mr. Lau died yesterday, or the day before, I lost track because they crossed the dateline. An autopsy was ordered, but who knows how long that will take, nor what they might find? Scrambled eggs, perhaps, for brains? *Is that a recognized "cause of death." If so, who will be blamed?*

Xin was still mad and now worried he might have whatever Lau died from, especially if he was exposed on Drake's Key. The bounty on me was raised to ten million. That would bring out serious hunters looking for my head on a stick. *Do I call, raise, or bluff?*

A month after the *Night Song* exploded, the majority of the heavy lifting in preventing a major environmental disaster was nearing completion. The two survivors were still in my clinic, their lives hanging by a thread. Security was easier to control on my home turf. I still had the remodeling to manage. *The month of June was going by too fast.*

Somehow Rosalie, Allie, and I managed to cover nine years in our lives—admittedly in pieces—over that month.

"Dad," Allie said at breakfast, "please pass the bacon. And how about bringing your brain here to our table as well as your body."

She's young and will burn off all that pork, eggs, and fruit by lunchtime, I mused with envy. As I pushed the platter towards her, I responded, "I guess my plate is full," I said as I tapped my head. "What's on your plate, today?"

"I've been talking to the woman who survived the blast. She's Chinese, and I don't think she expects to see her home again, so I sit and listen while she talks."

I looked to Rosalie who just scootered to the table. "She's right," Rosalie said. "I doubt she makes it to the end of the day. Pass what you didn't take over to me, please."

Allie passed the platter, finished cleaning her plate, and stood. "But first I'm off to the track to take my new bike for a spin. You didn't need to do that, Dad. But wow!" She leaned in and gave me a huge hug with a side of kisses on the cheek. Rosalie got the same.

"Year ten today. This is a biggie for you, Mom. See you guys for lunch," she said as she closed the door.

"A big year, for me too," I added. "Good time for a recap. As I understand it, you moved in with my parents, your mom got her teaching certificate, and then got a job—"

"Yes, but she also left my dad, filed for divorce, and left town. His congregation didn't like the scandal, so they didn't renew his contract."

"Your dad got the short end of the stick. I've heard of that before. He did nothing wrong, yet he gets the blame." *Some people think church is a showcase for saints, while others see it as a sanctuary for sinners.* "Then you finished high school, got your nursing degree, and your dad was a missionary, right?" I polished off the cornbread Rosalie made last night. I'd forgotten how good it was with strawberry jam.

"Pretty much. And you have some lingering PTSD from a massacre you and Earl came across, started taking college classes, graduated with a degree in criminal justice, and graduated from law school. You were a very busy boy, Skipper Warren." She pulled the last of the fruit salad towards her.

"PTSD? I never said—"

"I heard you…I saw you talking to Earl, remember? If you didn't already know that you do now. You seem to be handling it well, but counseling never hurts. Is year ten a biggie for you too?"

PTSD? Me? Well…that could explain my dreams, or should I say nightmares? I ducked my head as an answer. *How will I justify my job as a lawyer for a prominent family—a prominent crime family at that?*

Chapter 10

Allie

I rolled out my motorcycle Dad bought me—to make up for all the birthdays he missed, he said. I heard a low wolf whistle. I did not appreciate that kind of male attention. I loosened my chin strap and turned to chew off a chunk of the whistler's ear. "Just who do you think you are," I said as I lowered my helmet. A man stood behind the barricade and, since he was the only other person around, I lit into him. "What do you think—"

He whistled again, but this time I noticed he was not directing it to me but to my bike. "I think that's one killer bike," he answered. "Had it long?"

He was tall, tan, and handsome if you like that sort of thing. I felt my face flush and I turned away to hide it because that thing *was* the kind of thing I liked. I surmised he was a summer guest. I hoped he didn't think I was part of the fun and games.

"Do they have bikes to rent here now? I didn't hear about that before I came."

I straddled my bike, started the engine, and rode off the center stand as I yelled, "Ask Randy inside." I headed towards the rainforest stretch of the racetrack as I felt the purr of the superb engine tingling my body. That same satin purr filtered through my helmet, filling my ears with warm white noise. My leathers warmed up and caressed my body like a familiar hand.

"Honestly, kiddo," Mom liked to say. "You talk like that bike and you are in a very sexy relationship."

"Until the real thing comes along, why not?" We both laughed.

I savored the smell of the salt air blowing down my neck, the clear sky, the quick response of my bike as I leaned left and right. Then I spotted Bad at the edge of the forest. I looped around in a U-turn, hung my helmet on my bike handle, and hopped over the barricade. I waved as I walked towards him.

"Good morning, Bad. Is this your special place?" It looked like a tiny shrine behind him.

"Good morning, miss. Yes, my special place. I pray and offer food to the spirits."

I looked around. "What spirits are here?"

He looked over his shoulder and lowered his voice a few decibels. "Ghosts," he whispered. "Angry ghosts." His expression gave me no reason to doubt him.

I had no idea how to react to this statement much less respond. I moved to sit on a large, moss-covered rock. Bad waved for me to stop, and I did. He offered up what I understood to be a prayer and placed cooked rice and fruit in the shrine. After bowing, he turned to me and said, "You may sit. The rock spirit is appeased."

"I see you've cut some bamboo. I didn't know it grew on Drake's Island. What are you going to do with it?"

Bad said in his surprising British accent, "We don't let it grow here. It'd be too invasive. I brought it in from Florida." He reached behind his back and drew forth one wicked looking knife.

"Whoa! What's that?" I moved backwards on my rock, ready to beat it back to my bike.

"Oh, this little thing? It's called a khukuri. Functional, lethal, and mythic," he said in an offhanded manner. Then he deftly wielded his knife to strip a bamboo stalk of its leaves, cut it to lengths, and then into strips. "Today I am making an effective old-fashioned fish trap. I can't get the hang of the fly rod the Boss uses, but I do know how to catch fish." He worked efficiently and fast.

"Lethal, huh. You sure are making quick work of those stalks. See, I do know that bamboo is a grass and not a tree, and some kinds can be eaten. But how is your knife mythic?"

"Many people write that if a Ghurka pulls their khukuri, it must taste blood. If I do not inflict a cut on an adversary, I must cut myself to satisfy its spirit. As you see it is mostly used as a work tool."

"So, your knife has never tasted blood then." I was relieved.

He never looked up as he said, "I never said that, Ms. Warren."

Talk about dynamite in a small package. I fake checked my watch. "Enjoyed the chat, Bad, but I got a Chinese lady to sit with. She's not doing well."

"Ms. Warren, I know you speak Mandarin. Ask her if she has particular funeral practices in her family. She may rest better if she knows the correct practices will be followed. Although she came here to kill your father, she will be gratified to know her own death will not be forgotten. She may prefer cremation." He returned to his weaving as I walked back to my bike.

After showering, I went to the resort clinic. Mom was humming as she gave the only patient left a sponge bath. Considering the scooter she was perched upon she was doing an excellent job of it. When she was done, we sat, and she offered me mango juice.

"How is she today?"

Mom shook her head. "She is too badly burned to be moved. She was handcuffed to the bed, but the police took it off two weeks ago. Where would she go even if she could get up? We're just keeping her comfortable. Talk to her about her children."

Mom related to the side of this woman who left her own toddlers she will never see again in the hands of megalomaniac Xin, known for selling his own children. I saw her as the assassin who came here to kill *my* father. We agreed though that this dying woman's life was complicated. *But whose isn't?*

****

Dinner was quiet that night. I already knew a lot about Mom's year ten. I finally got a daddy like all the other kids. Well, not *quite* like all the other kids.

Mom started. "Even though I still don't speak to my mother, I have always had a warm relationship with my dad. When I moved in with your folks, Skip, he would send me money, and we would meet for lunch in the next town. After my mother left him, he went to Africa as a missionary. This much you already know.

"In year ten I moved to Dallas. Much more work for me there. That year Allie spent the summer with your folks at their lake cabin."

I jumped in. "It was great and sad. Momsie always yelled at me 'Allie, check the biscuits. Don't let them burn, sweetie,' and Popsie was like 'After the biscuits are finished, let's go fish off the dock.' "

"Why sad?" Dad asked. Mom and I were quiet. "Did something happen to my mother?"

Mom put her hand on Dad's arm. "She died later that year. Ovarian cancer. Nasty stuff I'm sorry."

"And no one told me?" he growled, the color rising in his face.

"We tried. As time went by you seemed invisible. That's when I started telling myself you were dead. Really dead."

Dad's face was stark and pale. He was not quite trembling, and I took his hand. He looked to Mom and admitted, "Yeah. I did a great job of disappearing, didn't I?" We sat in the quiet as he allowed stifled grief and regrets to wash over him. At last he released a long pent-up sigh that signaled us he was ready to move on. He kissed the back of my hand and squeezed it gently.

"Since Allie was with your folks, I took a leave of absence and went to help my Dad at his mission in Cameroon."

"Is that where you met Damon?"

"No, but I did meet his mother, Miriam. She was touring some of the bush clinics to acquaint herself with the HIV, family planning, prenatal, and neonatal services the Reverend Smith, as she called my dad, and the local doctor were providing. She seemed very concerned, very attentive, even friendly. She asked me, 'Miss Smith, the Reverend Smith tells me you are a nurse in Texas. Do you know my son Dr. Damon Abatsong?' "

"Honestly, I stifled a laugh, but I said, 'Mrs. Abatsong, Texas is much larger than Cameroon. It's impossible for me to know all the people there.'

"She didn't take kindly to that, but she added, 'He told me you live in Dallas. My son lives in Dallas. He works at Dallas Lying-In Hospital at—'

"I was so shocked I rudely cut her off. 'I know where

that is. I started a job across the street last year. It truly is a small world, isn't it?' Her smile seem chilly when she responded. 'Yes, indeed. He is a good boy, but he neglects to write to me. Would you be so kind to take a small gift I have for him? The mail is so unreliable here.' I felt that since I was rude, I had to agree.

"She showed up weeks later as I was preparing to return home. 'Roz-ah-lie, here is my son's information and gift. Please hand it to him personally. You are sweet to do this for me, *chérie.*' She did the French air kiss but only one cheek. She turned and left without looking back.

"We followed her to the door and watched her car drive away. Then, and only then, Dad said, 'You do know you should never accept a package from—'

" 'Yes, Dad. I do know. Let's have a peek, shall we?' In the kitchen I picked up a butcher knife and as I reached to slice open the wrapping paper, he put his hand on mine and said, 'Wait a minute. I've got a better idea. Come on.'

"We went to the surgery and cranked up his old x-ray machine. I loaded the film. Of course we had to step behind the lead shield during the x-ray, but after a quarter of an hour we had pictures from all sides."

Allie said, "I remember her a little. She didn't strike me as the homebody worried about her 'little boy.' "

"In her perverse way, she was. That's why Dad was suspicious. I developed the films—"

Dad's phone started vibrating and dancing around on the table, a rude, spoiled brat demanding attention. "Sorry," he apologized. He looked at the caller ID. It read Harry Hansan Huang. "I need to take this. Should I leave?"

Mom signaled with her hands for him to sit, I poured us more iced tea and cut each of us a piece of key lime pie, my own recipe.

"Hello, Mr. Huang. How are you this morning...I see...Yes, I have had visitors recently...Really...Do they know what it is...I see...I see...That could be a problem. Yes, sir. The same to you. I appreciate your call." Dad put down his phone, picked up his fork, and dug into his pie. "That was Mr. Huang. He may not make the Chairs after all. Seems there is a new strain of flu going around again, and Mr. Xin is in the hospital in intensive care."

We ate in silence. I swallowed my next to last delicious bite and couldn't restrain myself. "Flu, huh? Couldn't happen to a nicer guy. Is Xin blaming that on Drake's too?"

"No. Huang says until Xin's health situation is resolved, no one will take the 'contract' on me because they're afraid they won't get paid, that is if they live long enough. It seems word about the *Night Song* reached China." We sat in silence for a few moments, then Dad looked at Mom and asked, "What was in the package? A live snake, an elephant-foot trash can, an ivory tusk? What?"

His question broke the tension, and she said, "None of that. Miriam's local crafts."

I burst out laughing. "Miriam? A crafter? Who would have thought it?" I put the last delectable bite of pie into my mouth.

Mom chuckled and said, "Not too far off. Voodoo dolls, kola nuts, and candy cocaine."

Dinner was moving along beautifully until Mom mentioned voodoo and cocaine. That's when I choked on my pie. Mom pounded on my back until I stopped gagging. "Voodoo what?" I croaked out as I spit out my pie.

"Well, a vodun fetish according to my dad." Mom didn't seem too upset as she handed me a napkin.

Dad's eyebrows shot up. "How did he know what all that voodoo was about anyways?"

"I asked him that very thing. Is there any more pie, sweetie?"

I reached for Mom's plate. "Yes. The last time I checked there wasn't a heck of a lot of voodoo going on in Oklahoma."

"Not that I know of either," she added. "Dad told me he had to acquaint himself with his local African competition. He said there were parallels with the religion of voodoo and Christianity, particularly Catholicism."

Dad and I both chewed over this last comment but neither of us made a connection. "Okay, you two," she said, "think about this. One God, accessed through intermediaries such as spirits in voodoo and through saints by Catholics. Most people are asking for the simpler things and not the death or bad luck of an enemy. And the Reverend Smith said in the past slaves were forced to convert under pain of death, so they attended church and still secretly practiced their old religion."

"Mom, I just can't picture Miriam doing any of that."

"Any of what? Do you know anything about religions that believe in resident spirits? I certainly didn't, but my preacher dad does." Now that I thought about it, I *did* know someone who might be able to explain this idea to me: Bad, Drake's Ghurka security guard. *Our local intermediary with angry ghosts.*

"What did you do with the package?" Dad asked.

"We opened it, of course. The fetish was a wooden carved good luck charm for success and love. Nothing unexpected. Reverend Smith said the kola nuts were an offering to the spirit of the charm, but they couldn't be imported raw into the US."

This was a topic I was slightly interested in. The importation of agricultural products is carefully regulated. "What did you do with the nuts?"

"We cooked them in boiling water for twenty minutes, cooled them, and rewrapped them. Dad said they wouldn't be confiscated since they were cooked and not capable of germinating. The Reverend and I laughed. We figured we had outsmarted Miriam if she was intent on getting me arrested."

"And the candy?" I asked.

"We opened one and it was processed cocaine. That definitely would have gotten me arrested and in deep trouble. We substituted locally bought candy from the marketplace. Even if we had used the old wrappers there would have been a cocaine residue. Then we rewrapped the whole package in its original paper. Miriam went with me to the airport and through customs. Since Mr. Abatsong was a diplomat, their luggage got checked through uninspected. She bullied the poor clerk to treat my baggage as if it were hers. She removed her husband's name from the package, handed it back to me with only my name on it, and I stuffed it into my carryon and left."

"And the cocaine?" Dad and I asked simultaneously.

"We flushed it down the outhouse with a bucket of water. I had to pump the water by hand, and luckily no

103

one saw us use a whole bucket or we would have had some explaining and apologizing to do."

Dad and I laughed. "I'll never use the lake outhouse again without seeing that picture in my head," I squealed.

Mom went on. "After I returned to Dallas and got over jet lag, I called Dr. Abatsong. At first, I thought he would be reluctant to meet because he was a very prominent doctor, but I was wrong. 'Dr. Abatsong, you know my father, Reverend Smith in Cameroon at the New Day Mission and Hospital, I believe.' "

" 'I do. And you are?' His voice was warm satin with a slight nasal pronunciation."

"His daughter Rosalie."

" 'Rosalie the nurse?' he asked.

"How did he know that I wondered? 'Yes.' "

" 'Miss Rosalie, and how may I help you today?' He sounded friendly enough."

" 'I just got back from Cameroon and your mother asked me to bring you a package.' I heard something in a language I didn't quite understand. He didn't seem happy though.

"He said, 'My Mother Miriam Abatsong asked you to bring me a package? And you made it to Texas? When?' "

"I knew our suspicions had been well founded. 'I got home eight days ago from Cameroon. Well, I was wondering if—' "

"He stopped me. 'Stop right there. I have to meet you.'

"We met that night for dinner." Mom said, "I don't remember where. After introductions, I gave him the package."

" 'This is the package Miriam gave to you for me?'

He shook it and looked at it from every angle."

"Yes. I hand carried it in my carryon and I pointed to my satchel laying on the table."

" 'And you did not get stopped, searched, or detained? Not even once?' "

"'Uh, no. Why do you ask?' This was a game, I thought."

" 'Miss Rosalie, you are a mystery and an enchantress. You are the first person who has successfully delivered a package from my mother. How did you ever do it? I must know. I absolutely must know. You do know you should never accept a package from a stranger like that, don't you?' he scolded."

Chapter 11

Allie

"I do know not to carry a package for a stranger, Dr. Abatsong." Mom told Damon how she and the Reverend Smith opened the package and 'sanitized' it so it would make it through US Customs. "He laughed until he cried," she said.

"Now, Doctor, please explain that package to me," Mom asked.

Damon wiped tears from his eyes and told her, " 'It was a test. Miriam wanted to know how clever you were. She just mixed up a little voodoo package to get you in trouble.'

"She used voodoo on me?"

" 'In a manner of speaking, but she does know how. She was having a little cruel fun at your expense. The last person she gave a similar package to has spent seventeen months in an African jail charged with smuggling drugs. The person before that was stopped from entering the US because of the plant seeds,' he said.

"What about the wooden fetish? What was that for?"

" 'That truly was for me. It's a voodoo charm for love and success. Normally one needs to feed the fetish so they will facilitate wishes. Miriam uses kola nuts, which are plentiful at home, and candy. If you were caught and involved, she would deny anything was in the box but the charm and the candy that *you* obviously replaced with cocaine.' I chuckled at the irony. It worked. The charm worked, but not as intended. We were married before the year was out."

I chimed in with, "I got to be the flower girl at the wedding. Damon sent me to Space Camp the week of their honeymoon, so I didn't feel left out. It was super."

"How did your mother-in-law feel about you outsmarting her?"

"Skip, she's the woman I ran into at Macy's. I'd say not well, wouldn't you?"

It was Dad's turn at bat. I knew a little about him from my recent DNA research that found him. He didn't have a criminal record.

"I already talked about the Army. Afterwards, I went to college in New York and earned a degree in criminal justice which got me a job with a bank. Since I was older than the grads who didn't have military service, it gave me a leg up. I looked older, I was more mature, and I didn't sneak out early to happy hour after work."

I couldn't help but say, "I can't imagine you opening and closing checking accounts and cashing paychecks."

"And I didn't do any of that, Allie. I investigated financial crimes. My darling daughter, the FBI came recruiting me. I had done four years of public service in the Army. I wanted to give the private sector a shot."

"Drake's seems a long way from banking, Skip."

"Yes and no. I learned the ins and outs of the money trails, the crooks, the crimes, and who was who in that particular zoo. But I did save enough money in three years to quit and go to law school. That brings me closer to the topic of the night: year ten."

The waiter brought in dessert and coffee. Yum.

Banana fritters with custard sauce. I must steal this recipe. After he left, Dad started again.

"I wanted to stay in New York. I had former bank clients who hired me part-time when they needed a clandestine investigation. I needed the cash to pay my expenses. I applied to three law schools. All of them accepted me, so I picked the top ranked of the lot: Columbia."

"Dad. You went Ivy League? That's bragging rights."

"I didn't pick it for the shrubbery. I knew if I did well the doors and wallets of top companies would open to me. I graduated top of my class. I had impressive banking credentials, I knew how to conduct a forensic audit of a company's books, I was a veteran. It was a trifecta of qualifications. I also built up quite a network in the banking community. Of course the FBI hit me up again and I declined. Four top law firms interviewed me. I wanted a job where I could remain anonymous while making a killer salary."

"From what I hear those jobs are killers too. No personal life, no friends," I said.

"Exactly what I wanted. The family I had didn't want me, or so I thought. The girl I loved was dead, and I never wanted to feel that pain again. I didn't have any friends from high school, and who needed those hicks anyway. Sorry, but that's what I felt. Most of my Army buddies died with their boots on except for one, and he was in New York."

"Earl?" Mom asked.

"Yeah. Earl Chester DuBois. Still my best friend even though we seldom see each other. I accepted a very lucrative offer from a prestigious Manhattan firm located on Broadway. It didn't bother me that my main client, and at times my only client, was a crime family."

I was shocked. "How could you? You don't have a record, so how did that go?"

"Oh, I convinced myself that everyone has a constitutional right to representation. That's what I did to the letter of the law. I kept blinders on but stayed on the legal side of the street. I avoided Family dinners in case Family business came up."

"That is so disingenuous. Who are you fooling with that 'letter of the law' crap? Who—"

He cut me off. "No one, Allie, but myself. I needed to believe it was okay that I worked hard and earned this. My life was in the toilet if I didn't...and I was too chicken to kill myself."

Mom and I looked at each other with concern in our eyes. *Maybe my great idea wasn't so great after all.*

That night was the first night Dad took me for a drive around the track in his red 1990 Camaro IROC-Z convertible. The top was down, the moon was up, and we were in the middle of a conversation about what *I* did during year ten. *It was the best night of my life.*

****

"Skip, Have you seen these new uniforms Singh got from India? They are fabulous. I want one in each color," Rosalie gushed.

"Wow, you aren't kidding. No one will even notice the Boss walking around with Singh in the house. Good for me."

The summer progressed as normal as it could in a place like this. I hired a local company to manage the remodeling and had Singh supervise. The poor guy was so distracted from his upcoming nuptials that he almost had the wrong suite redecorated to his bride's specifications. She might not have appreciated the mirrored ceiling and stripper pole.

The Gizmo was boarded up during the remodeling; I was no further along on what came next for it. And August was about to be in my rearview mirror. I kept coming back to Dr. Mixon and I thought I knew why she looked familiar. My approach would be much different when I called her this time; I needed a favor from her.

"Skip, have you ever had traditional Indian dancers entertain here? Maybe near to the cricket match. Or even the field hockey match. Have you seen Allie out on the soccer field practicing? She's ruthless."

"No but pass that idea along to Max in New York." Rosalie was brimming with ideas on an hourly, nay, a minute-by-minute basis.

"So, how are you doing at finding a replacement for Peaches?" I had my fingers crossed.

"Oh, you don't want to know. Three of the female applicants heard a rumor that room and board in or near your apartment was included. Monthly bonuses and personal shopping sprees were mentioned. One old dear had great keyboarding skills but filed everything in the order she typed it. Her doctor told her that as her dementia progressed, she would lose even more skills such as reading, but her kids wanted her out of the house during the day.

"The last applicant was a young man with a police rap sheet who wanted to learn the casino business so he could upgrade his floating crap game and attract higher bets. He didn't know enough to lie about it."

None of this sounded promising. I certainly didn't want to be deflecting passes from my employees. I tried to remember how we found Peaches—ah! Dex found her. I bet he never knew what hit him. "There is a commercial business program at the high school. Call and see if they have any bright, earnest, honest candidates—you know what I mean. Sanitize those qualifications for me, will you?"

"Aye, aye, Captain. Bye the bye, you had a very important breathless call while you were out. A Mrs. Bunnie Snuggle. I wonder if Bunnie can type?" she smirked. "Check your inbox for her contact info."

I went to my office and called Bunnie. I heard her decrepit porn king keeper—I mean husband, had passed away since they were here last. What could she want?

"Hello, Bunnie. This is Ledger Warren. Let me offer my condolences on the death of your husband...You are very welcome. What can I do for you? Plastic surgery...oh, breast reduction in November. Yes...and the Chairs? Are you sure about that? It seems a bit rash on...Would Harold have...Yes, indeed, he is dead. Yes, I'll have the clinic call you to make the first appointment of the season." Bunnie seemed to have grown up since I talked to her last.

"Anything else I should know about before I head out to the gym?" I asked Rosalie.

"No, but it will be just us tonight, I'm afraid. Allie has a date."

"A date? My daughter has a date on my island?" I knew Rex might be sniffing around, or was that Rusty? "There doesn't seem to be anyone, at least that I know of."

"She said you already knew him."

"All the filthy rich guys are gone." Now I *was* confused. We'd been making progress in catching up, but we'd put off one special year for last and when Allie would be here from San Juan. I imagined revisiting Damon's death would be traumatic for mother and daughter. "Is that it for now?"

"I'll be out for a few hours after lunch. I'm helping Doc with the school immunizations and then later conducting a prenatal clinic. I've sent your calls to my phone. Just one more thing. I've gone through Peaches' desk and have an idea of where everything is as far as Drake's records and contracts. But I don't know where I should keep this." She had that I'm-up-to-something smirk on her face.

What kind of a joke was she pulling on me now?

She pulled out a small box about the size business cards came in from her desk drawer. It was covered in dark pink glitter. Some of the glitter fell onto her desk.

"What's this?" I picked the garish box up. It was very light.

"A serendipitous present. Merry Early Christmas." She grinned from ear to ear. "Turn it over, Skip." She beat a drum roll on her desk. "Da-da-da-dut—da-da!"

I did as she asked. On the bottom side was a neatly typed label that simply read "Mermaid Eggs – 2009. Not for human consumption." *Merry Christmas, indeed!*

****

Thanks to Rosalie I had the 'mermaid eggs,' the fuel for the Gizmo. I couldn't try loading a new egg into it until the remodeling was done. I sure didn't know how to test it to see if the mermaid egg was loaded correctly. I'll ask Chet to help with that.

Worst case scenario is we transfer a winner and loser from the Chairs and see how it goes, but that could be disastrous, probably unethical, even illegal, and the end of Drake's.

I pulled out a business card from my wallet and dialed. "Hello, Dr. Mixon. This is Ledger Warren. Do you have a minute to chat?"

"Hello, Mr. Warren. I need to thank you for your generous funding of my research. I had no idea you were interested in the topic. I see why you asked some of the questions you did. Now, what can *I* do for you?"

"Three things, I think. First, I've found the mermaid eggs. The instructions sound too simple. When I refuel the Gizmo, if all I can see is the meter resetting…well that's not very reassuring. Did the professor have any ideas about verification testing?"

I swear I heard her laugh all the way from Brooklyn when she said, "Did you try waving a dead chicken over it?"

"A dead what?"

She laughed again. "That's an old joke in the tech business. Honestly, I think if the lights and bell work before you push the green button, it should all work. Don't go all the way in the cycle, and if you do, someone must be in each booth. If you push the green button a second time in less than five seconds, it cancels the cycle. Otherwise, turn the damn thing off at the power switch. That's what I heard."

"I see," I said as I scribbled on a notepad. "So you are not sure that an actual transfer occurs without two people in the booths?"

"What would there be to transfer? I seem to remember one of the grad students saying that—and this is strictly hearsay—that the professor put his dog in one side and his cat in the other, ran the cycle, and waited to see which one rolled over on command."

This seemed too crazy to be true. "More whimsy, I suppose?"

"Maybe. With some people you never can tell. What else is on your mind?"

"Honestly, I need a favor for you to consider." I went ahead to tell her about Earl and asked if he would be a good data point in her study. I gave her his contact information in case she was interested. "There's one more thing about Earl. He and I were in Bosnia together...Thomas Mixon was your father, wasn't he?"

I heard a muffled "yes" over the phone. "Dr. Mixon, you father was the best NCO I ever served under. He was a complicated man, but he made Earl and me into seasoned and effective soldiers. I hope I'm not speaking out of school, but Sergeant Mixon coped with the stress with alcohol, and he wasn't alone. I'm not condoning what happened, but I understand what drove him to do what he did. I believe he took his own life afterwards because the sober reality shamed him more than he could bear. He loved you more than I can tell you.

"Life isn't fair, so treasure his love to shelter you when hard times come. Feel free to call me any time...You are entirely welcome. Bye now." I understood why she had been afraid of me, and why alcoholism was her research topic.

****

Rosalie and I were on our way to the pool in response to an invitation from our daughter. It was late August and things were settling in. The remodeling was well underway. The beaches were close to sparkling again. Best of all Rosalie was free of her leg boot and scooter.

"Do you know what this all about?" I asked. The sun

was sinking into a cobalt sea, and the air was cool and soft.

"Not a clue. Allie is a lady who knows how to keep her lips zipped. She can be very private, in my experience."

We turned a corner and there was Allie all tanned and toned. A man also very tanned and toned and dressed in summer slacks and an open-collared shirt sat next to her. They both stood as we reached the table.

"Mom, Dad, I'd like you to meet Alderich Muñoz. Alderich, these are my parents Rosalie and Ledger."

Alderich extended his hand to Rosalie and then to me shaking with a firm grip. "I'm very pleased to meet you both. Especially you, Mrs. Abatsong. Mr. Warren and I have already met, of course."

I was taken by surprise. I didn't remember Alderich. *When could I have met him?* We all sat down.

"I took the liberty of ordering island iced teas and nachos all around unless you'd like something stronger. *Cerveza*, perhaps?" Allie announced.

"Maybe later," I said.

"Me too," Rosalie added.

Allie looked towards her date. "Alderich and I met a few months ago on the track as I was enjoying my birthday motorcycle. Seems we both like to ride."

"I'm sorry to be rude," I began, "but I don't remember meeting you, Alderich. Could you refresh my mind?"

He smiled. 'Yes sir. My pleasure. We first met about five years ago when I came here with my own parents Ruth and Stanley Muñoz. Of course I've been here every year since with them."

His parents were two of my most dependable guests

and spent weeks here at a time. "Of course. The mustache is new, isn't it?" To be honest I was nervous around anyone I didn't already know. Now I was embarrassed but I sat back, relaxed, and kind of checked out. I heard voices but they didn't clearly register in my brain.

"What do you do, Alderich," Rosalie asked.

"I'm a biomedical engineer. I design and test prosthetics, especially leg prosthetics. I love all things mechanical. In fact I'm working while I'm here and Allie is helping me."

"Really? She told me she's been dancing, playing tennis, and snorkeling. That doesn't sound like work."

"Mrs. Abatsong, come by the basketball court in the morning around 8 a.m. and I promise you will get the picture. Right, Allie?"

"Yes, for sure. And don't forget field hockey practice before dinner. I want to be ready for the pros when they come…"

Chapter 12

Ledger
The next thing I knew Rosalie was shaking me. "Wake up, Skip. Allie and Alderich are gone. Come on. It's bedtime for us."

I scratched my head. "Did he say he was working here? The summer season is over. I don't remember that we have any guests staying in any of the rooms."

She gave me a light punch on my arm. "You dope. He's Allie's guest and staying in her room. I don't mean to nag but if you're going to be Allie's Dad, you're going to have to step it up."

****

Rosalie and I were courtside a little after 8 a.m., as Alderich suggested. There were two people on the court battling it out. I recognized my daughter's red hair, but I expected the other player to be Alderich.

"What's going on? That's not Alderich, is it? That man has a prosthetic leg. Is he helping Alderich with product testing?" I looked around but didn't see anyone else.

I heard Allie call, "Tie game. I need some water," as she came over to us. "Good morning, y'all. Want to join us two on two?"

"Thanks, but no thanks. Where's Alderich, sweetie," Rosalie asked.

From behind Allie we heard his voice. "I'm here.

She's giving me hell today."

I admit I wasn't too polished as I stared at his gadget leg. I wondered how many of my Army buddies were wearing gadgets like that.

"Is that a transtibial prosthesis, Alderich? It's a beaut," Rosalie said. "Is this what you design and test?"

"How did you know that, Mrs. Abatsong? I'm the one who's impressed."

"I've seen lots of amputations in Africa. Bad men with big machetes do a lot of savage harm, but Africa has never seen anything like your prosthetic. You are uniquely suited for your job. Good luck…Oh, I get what you meant. You test by subjecting it to real situations like dancing and sports. Cool. That's putting a new wrinkle to combining fun and work, isn't it, Skip?"

"I'd say so. Give my regards to your parents the next time you see them. Tell your mother I've added pork adobo to the lunch menu at her suggestion." I turned back to Rosalie. "We've got work to do. Ready?"

"Sure thing. Bye, see you guys later."

After we were out of earshot of Allie I said, "I just realized something about myself. I'm prejudiced against people who have lost a limb, and I don't know why."

"What? Do you think he is less of a person? Surely you don't think that."

"I don't know. I just had the idea that my daughter deserved a whole man, and I know that's crazy."

"Skipper Warren, a lot of women are attracted to what's between a man's ears and NOT what is sticking out of his shoes. Get over yourself!"

Seems like there were a lot of things I needed to "get over."

****

"Ledger, your New York manager is on line one. Something about a hostile takeover," Rosalie announced.

I picked up. "Suzanne, a hostile takeover of what and why?" My hackles were up. Hostile takeovers were nasty and expensive.

"Boss. It looks like we've got a bridezilla on our hands."

"A *what* did you say?" I was lost.

"A bridezilla. A bride who has outrageous demands from everyone concerning her wedding, And they don't mind using kamikaze tactics to get them."

"Got it. Now who is this bride? Anyone I know?" *How is a wedding connected to a takeover?*

"The bride is Kana Kawabata. Her father is the third richest man in Japan, but she ranks as the number one spoiled daughter."

"Her name rings a bell. Was she the young lady who insisted I book the Chippendales into Drake's for her twenty-first birthday? Who insisted her dad rent the whole of Drake's for the week? And who demanded Tom Cruise come in uniform and fly her around the island? It's all coming back to me."

"You hit the nail right on the head."

"What's the deal with the wedding?" I remembered the daughter was a royal pain.

"She wanted to book Drakes exclusively for a week in June, when we are mostly shut down, but wants the full casino, nightclub acts, everything." Suzanne took a deep breath. "And she is on our banned guest list. She wants that dropped. We said, 'no thank you' and she wasn't pleased. Another thing, she wanted a full up game of the Chairs with wedding guests as Players but rigged so she won all the bets."

"So why wasn't that the end of story?"

"Bridezillas get what they want. Daddy wants to buy Drake's to make it happen no matter the cost."

"But I am the sole owner."

"Yes, but he is trying to buy up a controlling interest in all your Japanese companies as leverage to hold the wedding where his darling child wants it. He already has stock in some of your companies. Maybe he can pressure some of his friends to sell him theirs too."

Suzanne was a very meticulous person. It's one reason I hired her. "Didn't you once tell me something about his name?" I heard a little giggle from her end of the line.

"His last name roughly translates to 'the bank or side of a river.' "

"Yeah. Sounds like he wants to sell me *down* the river today. Suzanne, start the contingency plan in motion. I'll be there tonight. See you later." I opened the door to Rosalie's office. "We need to get to New York today. Call Mike and tell her we're going in an hour. Call Estafania and June." I started to close the door, but Rosalie stopped me.

"We? Does that mean me too? Please, please. Ginger is in the hospital, and I want to visit her. I'll call the backup driver."

"Sure. Get packed or shop when we get there." I had a quick thought. "But please stay away from Macy's."
Who is Ginger and why does she care?

****

Rosalie, my self-appointed interim secretary-cum-assistant, took a call routed through my personal communications satellite to the plane as we flew to New

York. She had upgraded my network, so every plane, vehicle, ship, or railcar was connected in. I could carry on with business anywhere on the planet no matter where I hung my hat.

"Skipper," she said pointing to her headset. "It's Leona Bassett Butler for you."

"Who is she?" Her name wasn't familiar.

"Sole owner of LBB Pharmaceuticals. They make the phenomenal drug New Dawn that seems to be slowing down aging in the brain. She wants to talk to you, and no one else, and NOW!"

I put on my headset and searched for her on my computer's billionaire list. Okay, okay, not too shabby at all. "Miss Butler, this is Ledger Warren. How may I help you today?"

Although we'd never met, she called me by my first name. "Ledger, I *must* play in the next Chairs. Make room for me."

That was a first. "Miss Butler, I would be delighted but let's chat a bit first, to see if it might be possible. What's your hurry to play this coming year?"

"My husband died yesterday and…"

"I am sorry to hear that—"

She cut me off, "…and I must divest myself of my companies before I can collect my inheritance from his estate. So, greed, Ledger. I will never get my portfolio divested in the time before the deadline set in his will, and his fortune makes mine look like peanuts. All my current assets make up my bet in the Chairs."

"Who recommended me to you, or have you been a guest at Drake's before?"

"Nope, never been there, but my lead biotech researcher was in your last Chairs and told me about your game. Pretty spectacular, but exactly what I need."

"You do know that you are expected to compete as if you want to win, don't you? Spectators place private side bets…"

"Sure, sure, I'll give it my best. So, am I in or not?"

I knew an insincere answer when I heard it. "In, most likely. You'll be hearing from my accountant Beryl to start the process. Anything else I can help you with?"

"Absolutely. What's the wager limit at the craps table?"

"I'll have that information sent to you as well. Anything—?"

She hung up on me and I looked at Rosalie. "What did you think?" I wanted a fair game. "I can't afford to have people lose deliberately. Other guests will think the Chairs is rigged."

"The lady was honest, I think, determined, and how often do you get a Player who hopes to lose it all?"

"More often than you might think." She wasn't the first, she probably won't be the last. I wonder if her biotech whiz was Player Six, AKA Dr. Brain? I knew she'd be back in her game before long and it was only September. "That New Dawn sounds very promising." *Maybe I should be hoping I end up with her portfolio or at least invest in it.*

****

The day was already hot, so Alderich and I stopped our motorcycles in the shade of a turpentine tree. We took our helmets off and the breeze at once cooled our salty sweating red necks.

"Now that I've got you alone and away from your parents, how about a kiss, a real kiss?"

"Sure thing." I liked kissing and I really liked

kissing this guy. He was smart, athletic, and easy to talk to. *What's not to like.*

"You're a good kisser, Allie." He grabbed a water bottle from my bike. "Uhm, can I ask you about your dad?"

"Shoot. What do you want to know?" I twisted a dark curl hanging down in his face around my finger.

"First, he obviously didn't recognize me earlier. That's no biggie, but he seemed focused on my leg. Your mom acted like everyone has a prosthetic leg, but your dad was a little…weird."

"Mom's a nurse, so no worries about anything medical. I don't know about Dad. I'll ask him." I wanted Dad to like Alderich almost as much as I did.

"No, don't do that. It's okay." He put his arms around me and drew me close. He was taller than me but not so tall I needed to stand on my tippy toes. Just the Goldilocks height as my grandma used to say.

"You brought it up. I don't like to leave things dangling and unexplained. Now I have to know too." As I leaned in for another round of kissing, an old building caught my eye. After I got my five minutes quota of smooching in, I walked to that side of the track nearest the building.

I saw a greyish cone-shaped building that was flat on the top. I noticed a group of smaller stone buildings without roofs, and they all looked to be falling down and unoccupied. I wondered what part they played in Virgin Islands history. I pointed to them. "Do you have any idea what those were?"

"I'm not positive but I have an idea. Is there a historical museum or library here? They remind me of some buildings I've seen before."

"We'll probably need to go to St. Croix," I suggested. "I think there's a collection or something there, but I've never seen it."

"Let's clean up and have breakfast. Then we'll hop in the plane and head that way." *A boyfriend with wheels and wings. Way to go, Allie!*

****

June dropped Skip off at his NYC office and I rode to the hospital with him up front, as always. "What happened, June, that Ginger is in the hospital?" I hugged the bunch of peonies I had grabbed at the florist shop.

"She has more problems with her legs, and she fell. I ducked out to get us lunch and found her on the floor in the bathroom. She was having trouble breathing, her eyes wouldn't focus—I called 911 and they got there quick."

"Did they think this was related to her infusion therapy?"

"I don't think so. They warned us from the start that treatment would work for a few years but then it went downhill fast after that. That's what I'm afraid of, that we reached to top of the hill and it's a cliff in front of us now."

"That's tough. How long have you been together?"

"Since we were ten."

"Ten-years old?"

"Yeah. We met at the orphanage. Hit it off right away. Been together ever since."

"That's quite a story. How long ago was that?"

"Twenty-four years. Seems like just last week I beat up a bully who was beating on Ginger. That's how we met."

"Kids?" I asked tentatively.

"Nah. That was never in the cards for us."

I wanted to do more than I was for Ginger. "Could we get her something to eat? Hospital food is so bland."

We stopped and got a hot bowl of chicken and rice soup and a chocolate milkshake to go. I knew if she was as bad as I feared she might prefer the milkshake. I knew the last flavor we can taste near the end was sweet. I knew that June was in for a rough time. I knew Ginger was almost out of time period.

A small silver frame sat on Ginger's bedside table, the one I'd seen in their apartment. It was sweet. One slightly taller kid with dark hair and a somber expression with his arm wrapped around a carrot-topped boy's shoulders as he laughed and pointed to something off camera. Written above each was a name written in a childish scrawl: June and George. I put the vase of peonies on the table behind the photo. "Hello, Ginger," I said as I leaned in for a kiss on her forehead. It was warm.

She was running a slight fever. "Hi, Rosalie. Thank you for the cards. And peonies again, my favorites."

June sat by her bed and kissed her hand. "We brought you some soup and a milkshake. Let's try to get some of it down you, okay?" He spooned milkshake into her mouth alternating with a spoon of soup that he cooled by blowing on it. He touched it to his lips as a parent would to check the temperature before offering it to a sick child. June was a kind person. I stifled a sob as my heart went out to them.

"And afterwards would you like me to help you with your makeup and hair?" I asked. I could see she had lost weight. Given what I knew about muscular dystrophy, Ginger had lived longer than expected.

June fed more soup to Ginger. She was having trouble breathing and swallowing. I doubted she'd see

Christmas. When she had eaten all she could, he carried her into the bathroom. The toilet flushed and water splashed in the sink.

It's my turn to help them. June kept me from going into shock when the car hit me outside of Macy's. *What can I do to help?*

Chapter 13

Allie

"Alderich, that project on St. Croix did a great job of documenting the genealogy of many of the African slaves brought here. How did you think of that?"

"I was surprised that most of the current Black population here descended from slaves. I thought of it because I spent two weeks on St. Croix scuba diving, and I rented a former sugar mill to stay in. Allie, are you thinking what I'm thinking?"

"That someone here might have some voodoo knowledge to banish those evil spirits of Bad's?"

"I'm thinking we start with the Reverend Otis."

"We'll need to be diplomatic. Maybe I can start with…"

****

"…so you see, my grandfather Reverend Smith in Africa gave me the idea to talk to you."

"I didn't realize that voodoo or— what did you call it—vodun was practiced in Cameroon," said Reverend Otis.

"My stepfather's mother was originally from Benin, right next door, and it is recognized openly there."

The Reverend Otis asked, "But why are you asking if voodoo is practiced here?" He leaned in slightly but no longer smiling.

"Do you know that Drake's has a Ghurka security

employee?" *I bet he didn't see that coming.*

"A what?"

"A man from Nepal who is a British citizen and a former Ghurka soldier. They're legendary in military circles."

"Hmm. I did notice an Asian man at Miss Petty's funeral. Was that him?"

"Was he shorter than I am and wearing a large, curved knife on his back?"

"Yes. He did not come into the church. What about him?"

"A few weeks ago I ran into him in the forest by a small shrine he built. He said there were angry ghosts in the woods and he was trying to appease them. After I learned about the past slavery on the island, I wondered if there was a connection and if some of the people here might want to..." I didn't know what to say next.

"...might want to do the same or might want to assist him?" he said. He just looked past us and out across the rain forest.

"Reverend, I know history and life are full of pain. I've come to regard this island as my home, and the people here as my neighbors. I apologize if I'm out of line."

He tilted back his head and added, "Thank you for your concern, Ms. Warren." He walked us to our car. "If I should want to contact your Ghurka, whom should I ask for?"

I wrote down Bad's name and phone number on my business card. Alderich and I left in the car I borrowed from Dad, his 1960 MG Roadster in British Racing Green.

When we got to the garage, Randy reported that no

one was on the track, so we took the MG for a spin. Near Bad's shrine I pulled over and pointed out the altar.

Alderich said, "There are many who believe in ghosts and spirits in the Philippines. I didn't realize you were one too."

"I didn't until a few months ago when I found a ghost of my own, and you know him. I'm hungry. I'll tell you about it as we eat." *Voodoo. First Mom, now me. Be careful, Allie girl.*

****

A new season at Drake's Key was about to begin, and as the owner I had a looming problem. I didn't know if the Gizmo worked. I didn't have enough Players signed up for the Chairs and I needed eight minimum, to make it interesting, but I preferred more. I had twelve Players last year which made for quite a mix of contestants. Ever since season two, when I had a late dropout, I've needed at least eight.

My season two dropout was C.C. Corona, a self-made detergent millionaire who could buy whatever he wanted, except, as he put it, "A little peace and quiet." C.C. had five ex-wives, nine squabbling adult children, and a couple of ex-companions suing for palimony. When it came to women, he couldn't say no, until the next one came along.

Six months before the Chairs he was in a tragic industrial accident and ended up in a wheelchair. He still wanted to take part in the Chairs asking if he could have someone act as a proxy for him. I couldn't allow that. Every contestant would want a 'designated hitter' if I had. Because of C.C. every contract has fine print covering that situation.

C.C. showed up with three nurses and cried the

whole evening. As predicted, his expectant heirs battled over his estate, all being unable to break his will leaving it all to—surprise, surprise—his three nurses. I've always had a "spare contestant" in case such a situation arises again. I need four or five more Players to make a go of it this year.

Rosalie buzzed me. "A Mr. Leonard Flatz is on line two. Shall I put him through?"

Leonard? He's the smartest guy who ever worked for me. "Please."

"Hello, Mr. Warren. Do you have time to chat?" Humble as always.

"For you, of course. I see you're doing quite well for yourself, but that's no surprise."

This guy couldn't fail if he tried. "Thank you, sir…"

"Call me Ledger. It's about time, don't you think?"

"If you insist. I'm calling to ask if I may play in the Chairs this season. If I don't lose, legitimately of course, I want to come back until I do."

I was shocked. I asked Rosalie to hold my calls. "I have to say that I've never had anyone make a standing request like this. I'm going to need some convincing."

"I don't doubt that. I feel you know my business ability already."

I did and there was no doubt. He was one of five high level interns in my largest company. At the end of the trial period each gave a presentation on a knotty problem we had with our supply chain. Leonard went last.

He identified all the problems the other four had between themselves plus a critical one they all missed, including myself. He presented a plan that solved each problem followed by a groundbreaking implementation plan we put into place the next fiscal year. "That is an understatement," I said.

"Thank you. Let me ask you, are you familiar with a company named Afrodesiac?"

I racked my brain. What kind of a company would have a name like that? "I can't say that I am."

"I'm the founder of Afrodesiac. When you look it up, you will find as president a 'Julian Denzel.' That's me. Leonard Flatz wasn't sexy enough for a company that makes wispy lingerie and pheromone-enhanced fragrances like *Come to Me, Big Boy* perfume for the African American market."

My mouth hung open in shock. Leonard Flatz, the guy with a Department of Defense clearance higher than mine. Leonard Flatz, the guy who admitted under the influence of one ounce of champagne that he had never kissed a woman. Leonard Flatz, the five-foot one inch, fifty pounds overweight—I *must* have had the wrong guy in mind.

"Uh, well, that seems a long way from what you were doing for me…"

"Yes sir, it is, but it was an idea and dream I nurtured for many years. Along the way I lost some weight, had vison correction surgery, and changed my name. I'm still short but I find money does overcome that for many people. I've become very successful, but I don't trust the people I meet."

"I quite understand. Why do you want to gamble on losing all that?"

"I've given this a lot of thought. I have many people who depend on me for a living. I know I'll always have my brain and can do anything. What I want is to start over, just step away without hurting anyone else. Is that possible do you think?"

"Why don't you just sell your company? That sounds like an easy solution. If you lose that's exactly what you will do, step away. But if you end up in a different body…well then, that's a new set of problems."

"I see that. In fact, I am hoping that is the case. I know how to be a man, but I'd much, much rather be a woman. That's the secret that led to me forming Afrodesiac, sort of an entry into the feminine world. I actually wear all of the clothing…"

TMI! Waaay too much information. Then my brain rebooted. "Leonard, let me put you in touch with my administrator for the Chairs. She's a lovely person named Beryl. Anything else on your mind?"

"No, I thank you from the bottom of my heart."

"One more thing, uh, Julian. I'd be proud to have that brain of yours working for me in any role. Consider it an open offer…Yes, I do mean it. Bye for now." I shook my head as I hung up. *I'd hate to see that brain go through the Gizmo too many times. I'll have to discuss that with Leonard, or Julian, before long.*

I checked the calendar. September was history. *I don't dare get too comfy just because no one tried to kill me this month. That I know of.*

****

"But Mr. Warren, I'm sure you'll make an exception for me, won't you, and for my wife?"

"I'm sorry, Mr. Higginbotham, this competition is explicitly listed as having an additional fee. Your wife has the boat exclusively for the day. You are welcome to go along as a spectator." That was two days ago.

Today was the second day of the annual November Sailfish Tournament. A Virgin Islands-wide competition in which Drake's guests compete against the best fisherman in the world. I was at the dock to see the boats leave. "Good luck. See you at weigh-in."

This tournament was famous because Ted Williams, the baseball legend, loved fishing more than baseball. He came here every year to hunt sailfish. His old fishing guide told me something I've never forgotten. "Yes sir, ole Mr. Ted used to say something 'bout 'hitting is fifty percent in your head' and believe you me, he thought the same 'bout fishing."

"If he loved fishing so much, would he have liked the catch and release we have now?"

He scoffed and spit on the dock. "No, Boss, he would not. He wanted that picture a' him holding that big fish, or that fish hanging up at the dock for the picture man. After being bored for so long waiting, he wanted to be sure he git that damn picture."

My opinion was that Ted found he didn't like the trolling technique used for fishing for billfish any more than I did. "Here you go, Boss. All baited." I threw my line out behind the boat and put my pole in a holder in the gunwale.

"Now what?" I waited as the boat pulled my line. I waited for a nibble as I drank a beer, then another. I waited as I ate my lunch. I don't care for trolling either, but it is a hit with some of our guests.

In my opinion, what Ted preferred was the fishing we have on our main river on the island. There's a different kind of waiting. The fisherman controls the rod, the line, the movement. He stalks his fish, following it into the very water where his prey is master. He teases the fish from its underwater hiding places, tempting it with a juicy treat or a flashy mystery, casting his line again, and again until the fish strikes.

I've often imagined Ted in waders working his way up our Big Bass Gut flowing down from the mountain, flicking his rod back and forth, tempting a bass into taking his easy to catch snack on a hook delivered right in front of its nose. "Come on, come on. Tasty treat free for the taking. Come to poppa."

When the fish bites, the reel fun begins. The lightening whine of a line unwinding from the reel as the fish bolts. The grunt of the man as he raises the rod tip against the fish to gain slack in the line which he reels in quickly and repeats again, and again. At every step, the fisherman or the fish has control in this watery tug-of-war. Repetition is your physical and mental challenge even as the outcome is uncertain. I decided I needed to get my fishing gear and hit the Gut myself. A few hours later I got a call from my security manager. "What's up, Vic?"

"Better get over to the cargo port. There's been an accident on the *Bandit*. It's bad, Boss."

Juan picked me up. He made good time getting to the *Bandit,* a special deep sea fishing boat, one of two we kept for guests. The boat was customized with three chairs. If you're only watching the fishing, the *Bandit* had everything you could want at sea including a waiter and a private chef.

"How many times have you driven to the cargo port?" I noticed a dust cloud from our SUV in the passenger side mirror. Palm fronds flew through the air away from the road and into the brush.

"Ten times, Boss. Why?" The trees were a green-brown blur as we passed them.

"This is only the second time with me." I felt I was

flying as the wind from my open window whipped my collar against my neck.

"Sure, but Peaches told me to drive the road both ways at least five times so I don't get lost or waste your time, so I did." I couldn't help but smile at his comment. *But I didn't think I'll be smiling when I got to the Bandit. Vic only called me when something exceptional happened, or something we'd have to report to the police.*

This tournament is important to supporting the billfish stock, or so I was told. We practiced catch and release and had everything we needed on board including a tournament official to verify the catch.

"Mr. Warren, we've installed a hoist that can measure the weight without touching the fish," he told me. "A laser tape measure takes the length. A quick photo is snapped. You can photoshop the proud fisherman in later. We cut the hook as short as possible trying to minimize the injury. Then the fish is lowered into the water and the tail loop is opened allowing the catch to escape to be caught another day." *Or so the theory went.*

Juan pulled expertly into the parking spot. Vic waited with our local police. I saw the slightly bloody deck of the *Bandit*. I didn't see evidence of a catch, nor did I see Mrs. Evelyn Higginbotham.

'What's up?" I asked. Vic pulled me aside.

"Mrs. Higginbotham. She's gone."

"You are sure? Maybe Doc can—"

"No, Boss. I'm dead sure she's gone."

Vic was telling me one of my guests was injured in the fishing tournament. "What happened?" I didn't see any obvious boat damage, nor did I see Mrs.

Higginbotham.

"According to all the witnesses on board, the lady hooked a big sailfish. After half an hour she got tired and told the mate to take over. You know how that goes."

My own experience told me. "I thought that fish three years ago was reeling me in."

Vic tilted his head. "Right, so you remember that the tournament rules don't allow for any help, and the mate told her so."

"That's the procedure, yes." I looked around. I didn't see the mate anywhere.

"She told him again, and again he—" I saw Vic was sweating.

"I get the picture. Belligerent customer." My stomach was tightening.

"So then she hauled off and slapped him. He's the one at the doc's right now. Her fancy nails slashed his face, and he may lose an eye." *Ouch.*

I heaved a breath. "I'll talk to her."

Vic said, "You won't be talking to her, Boss. She *really* is dead." And now he *really* had my attention. "The second time she went for him he put up his arms to protect himself. She bounced off, stepped backwards, and fell overboard." I recoiled at this admission.

"Safety harness and life vest didn't catch her?" I raised my open hands in exasperation.

He shook his head. "She refused both of them. Captain made her sign a release though."

"End of story?" *Please let this be the end of this story.*

Vic shook his head. "No. She was thrashing around on the surface and got tangled in the line. The fish got to the end of the line, turned around, got up to speed, and speared her though the back. It was deliberate. The crew saw the fish put its blue sail up like they do when attacking."

I started to talk when Vic stopped me. *More?*

"I'll tell you when I'm through… The fish couldn't get Mrs. Higginbotham off its bill, so it started to spin. Result was both of them wrapped up in the line. By now, plenty of blood was in the water. The fish and the lady were spinning around. Both of them were making plenty of noise. That attracted the sharks."

Oh Lord! Just when I thought this nightmare was over.

Chapter 14

Boss

Vic said, "You know what a problem the fishermen had after the sharks got protected? Well, now we just set up a shark cafeteria, and they came running."

My stomach churned.

"Before the crew could latch onto the fish and Mrs. Higginbotham and haul them out of the water, there was a shark feeding frenzy. When they winched up what's left…well you'll see. That's why there isn't more blood in the boat. What's more, this accident is all on tape. You can watch it later. Come on in the icehouse."

I steeled myself. I'm used to seeing parts of fish. I'm not used to seeing parts of people. We walked into the cold air sending a chill down my spine. My eyes adjusted to the darker room. I smelled the pungent odor of fish. In a tub the size of a footlocker I saw the head of the fish, its bill pointed towards the ceiling.

I caught myself and choked. Impaled on that bill was less than half of a human, both deep in the embrace of the fishing line. If I didn't already know, I wouldn't have been able to name the gender of the body from what remained. I needed to heave. I involuntarily bent over the trough where fish were scaled and gutted, and barfed stomach acid. Vic handed me a wet paper towel.

After I cleaned myself up, I asked, "How about her

husband? Was he on board?"

Vic shook his head. He was a whiter shade of pale than I'd ever seen him.

"That's lucky. Don't let him see her until the police are done and we can…you know…untangle them." I had zero experience in dealing with a grieving spouse for an accident like this. I wasn't in any hurry to meet Mr. Maitland Horace Higginbotham, recent widower. I checked my slacks and shoes for blood, perversely happy that it wasn't mine. Juan drove me to Drake's, but at a funeral's speed.

****

After waving goodbye to his wife from the dock, Horace Higginbotham boarded his yacht and made a beeline for St. Thomas on personal business. I was unable to get in touch with him by any means. This morning, a week later, he presented himself at my office.

Rosalie called from her desk. "Mr. Warren," she said in a formal voice, "Mr. Maitland Higginbotham is here. He received a note that you wanted to meet. Is now convenient for you?"

Cripes. His wife was stabbed and killed by a sailfish and ripped apart and eaten by blood thirsty sharks. *What do I say to him?*

"Show him in." This was a first I never imagined in my wildest nightmares. I moved to my semicircle of chairs. I find it's better to deliver bad news in a casual setting rather than from across a desk, as if a death was an impersonal business transaction.

Mr. Higginbotham entered wearing a pleasant smile followed by Rosalie. She closed the door and sat down by him. I didn't ask her to come in, but I was glad she did.

He said, "This seems rather odd. Did I break a rule?" He was trembling.

"Not at all. But Mr. Higginbotham…I'm afraid I have some bad news."

He relaxed and leaned back in his chair. "Well then, let's have it, old boy." He straightened his pocket handkerchief.

In a slower pace I said, "I'm afraid there has been a terrible accident, sir."

"Here, at Drake's? I am sorry to hear that. If I—"

"Sir, the bad news is about your wife."

Higginbotham acknowledged Rosalie. "My wife? What's she done now? She can be rather vexing. I have insurance to cover anything she could have done. You do have my solicitor's name and number do you not?" He looked again to Rosalie and started humming under his breath. She shone her soft eyes on him and smiled.

"She's dead, sir. You wife was killed in a freak accident during the fishing tournament."

Mr. Higginbotham hummed and leaned towards Rosalie. He looked back at me, and then back to her. "My wife is dead?" His humming got louder and was now familiar. "My wife is dead?" Rosalie took his hand. "She's not only merely dead?" he asked.

She replied," She's really, most sincerely, dead," as she gently patted his hand.

What's going on here? This is nutso!

Higginbotham leaned back in his chair, let out a sigh, and stared at the ceiling as he hummed. Rosalie said to him. "Wait here, Horace. I'll get Dorothy for you."

"What is going…?" She shushed me, opened my door, and beckoned to someone in her office.

In walked the doc with a young lady in a blue and

white checked dress who went to Mr. Higginbotham and took his hand. "Horace, let's go to your room. The doctor has a nice treat to help you sleep."

He rose and said, "Did you hear? Did you hear the witch is dead?" He kept humming and smiled nervously as the two led him out of my office.

I looked at Rosalie. "What the *hell* was that!"

She shook her head at me. "For Pete's sake. Didn't you ever see *The Wizard of Oz?*"

That was the song. I recognized the tune he was humming. The munchkins sang that after the wicked witch was killed. "Well, yes, but what was *that* I just saw?"

"When we couldn't get in touch with him directly, I looked up his assistant. Evidently, he has several. According to Dorothy, the lady you just saw, his wife was bad news and driving him literally insane. His solicitor and son flew to St. Thomas where they met in secret away from her. The son will be here later today to make arrangements for his dad and his stepmother."

"Okay, but why the Oz stuff?"

"Pure escapism. He let himself go to a place he remembered from childhood."

"But the witch— both witches were killed in the end."

"Yes, but the cowardly lion wasn't and that's who he thinks he is. Horace was a powerful man but terrified of his wife."

"He's not the first man I've met in that situation."

She said, "Look on the bright side. You won't have to worry about him skipping around the Chairs in May."

"What?" A scene of Higginbotham doing that raced through my mind.

"The Chairs? Your high-stakes game where you literally rake in tons of money—"

I cut her off. "I *know* what the Chairs is. What about Higginbotham?"

"You forgot, didn't you? He signed up to play in the Chairs…right after the cricket match last May."

I slapped my forehead and said, "Geez. You're right. I completely forgot. How did *you* know about him and the Chairs?"

"The late, great Peaches Petty prepared detailed files. I'm up to speed as of today." She started to giggle. "If Vic was here, he might say the solution to the Higginbotham problem was a bit *deus ex machina.*"

"You two and your Latin phrases. I can't hope for a house to fall from the sky to solve a tough problem at Drake's."

"Why not? Have you seen the weather forecast?"

****

Scott spotted me as I walked through the Maze, the behind-the-scenes corridors of Drake's. "Boss, got a minute?"

Before I could answer, my sports manager said, "I got a terrific idea for the spring."

I stopped when he said 'terrific.' I didn't want to dampen his enthusiasm. "Sure, let's have it."

"I had lunch with Singh yesterday, and we hatched up a new idea."

"Let's talk in my office." We discussed the track upgrades and the new running tracks nearby as we walked. Allie and Rosalie were chatting in the outer office. Scott was in front of me, and I saw him eyeball both of them as we passed. They both waved at him.

I left the door open as we sat in armchairs. "Okay,

what's this big idea?"

"Boss, Singh was telling me about his cousin who is a famous hockey player from India."

"Wait. They play ice hockey in India? It's hot in India. Do they have indoor rinks?"

Scott seemed confused but suddenly snorted. "Gosh no. Field hockey is played on grass and it's the national sport—"

"Of India? Any place else?"

"Yes, sir. In more countries than cricket is and—"

I heard Allie's voice from the doorway, "—and field hockey is an Olympic sport but not cricket. Why not bring in women's teams for an exhibition and a training camp, just cover the rules and basics."

I interrupted this conversation that I was losing control of. "I suppose this sport needs a separate playing field?"

Both Scott and Allie seemed very animated about this topic. He said, "No, that's the beauty of it. The field will fit with room to spare inside the cricket field, er, pitch. All we'd do is lay down different lines. And we'd use the same bleachers under construction now. We will need some gear and a place to store it. Hmm, perhaps under the bleachers?"

Allie asked, "Who's this cousin that Singh is talking about?"

"I don't recall right off the bat, but he was famous for some hotshot technique. They made a movie about him."

"Was this technique drag flicking perchance?" She practically drooled.

"Maybe, that sounds right." Scott was as confused as I was by now.

Allie bounded over and took my hand, "Dad, Dad, we have to do this. If Singh's cousin is who I think he is you will have to beat guests off with a stick,' she said laughing.

"You're her father?" Scott turned pale as he edged away from her.

"Dad, I always wanted to learn how to be a drag-flicker and this is the best chance I'll ever have. You know, some flickers can propel a ball almost ninety miles an hour!" She looked as if Christmas was upon us, and I was wearing red and white.

I was flummoxed. "You play hockey? When and where did you play because I sure don't remember field hockey in Oklahoma?"

"College. I went to college in New England. Everyone plays field hockey in New England." She was squeezing my hand hard.

"Is this a fall sport or a spring sport?" I was starting to realize just how much of my daughter's life I had missed. My hand was turning white.

"Fall, silly. Spring is for lacrosse, but the pros play hockey in the spring."

She released me and I shook my hand to get the color back. *Lacrosse?* I saw that in *The Last of the Mohicans.* Those players were out for blood. I'm seeing my daughter in a whole new light. I took a moment to run through the season lineup so far.

"Well there seems to be a lull about mid-season. Scott, can you and Allie work up a proposal for me for…let's say February or March?"

He grinned at Allie. I grinned at him. *Good luck, Scott. You have no idea what you are getting into.*

As they walked out of my office, I heard him ask,

"Are you *really* his daughter?"

That night Allie and I took our almost customary drive round the track in my red convertible. She talked nonstop about Alderich, hockey rules, famous players, and her worst injury. *So this is what having a teenager would have been like.*

****

Drake's had two post offices. The main building was here at the resort and was open all year round. The other was in the middle of the island, not counting the rainforest and mountains. All signs on Drake's designate road distances from the auxiliary post office named Rome, little more than a tin-roofed shack with a drink machine and snacks for sale.

Given this, the resort was about a thirty-minute drive to the south over a somewhat curved and bumpy road from Rome. The biggest island village is About Hell, shortened to just Hell by the locals who called it that because that's about how hot the temperature gets in the middle of July, if you consider eighty degrees Fahrenheit hot, which they do. Hell was about a twenty-minute car ride from Rome if it wasn't raining. And to our kids, Santa lived about a three-hour flight from Rome by reindeer express, unless there was a tropical storm.

I explained this to Rosalie months ago when she saw Christmas shopping on Peaches' June calendar.

"Why does Peaches start in June?" she asked me.

I shrugged my shoulders and faked a SWAG answer. "We give each child under eighteen a personalized Christmas gift and stocking. We have, I don't know—maybe a hundred and, uh, ten kids. Peaches put the names and ages in her file. Look it up." I caught some side eye from that encounter.

When November came around, I asked her, "How's the Christmas shopping coming along?" She was waiting for that for months.

"I'm getting close to being done for Allie and Alderich. My dad is easy, yours not so much. And you? What do I give a Boss who literally has everything? Other than more mermaid eggs." I saw a slight smile twitch at the corners of her mouth.

I played her game. "Great, and the island kids?"

"The kids? Oh, do you mean the *two hundred and three* kids on the island? Those kids?"

I was slapped down by the sheer numbers. Honestly, I had no idea. In my meekest voice I answered, "Uh, yeah. Those kids."

"Wait and see," was all she said. I'm learning that Rosalie was a very patient person, and that she would wait forever to spring a "gotcha" on me.

****

I was occupied in my office more than usual. The Japanese Bridezilla problem was complicated. Her father was pressuring every Japanese stockholder in all my companies to sell him their stock. At the rate he was going he would soon be dropping down the list of the richest men in Japan. I was distracted and at a loss for ideas. I toyed with my salad at lunch until I heard, "Skipper, I'm going to start eating lunch with Singh."

"Why is that?

"At least he acts like I'm interesting. What are you stumped on over there?"

"The Bridezilla Takeover Problem. I'm spending all my time outbidding her father and there's no end in sight," I said as if this problem was a case solvable by a detective or money. "Are weddings always like this?"

"No, not all of them. I don't have a lot of experience in wedding planning. I only did a small one once. Everything went pretty smoothly."

"How many million did *that* cost?"

She shook her head and rolled her eyes. "If I remember correctly under fifteen-hundred dollars."

"That sounds like a two-dollar wedding license, a Vegas wedding mill, and a grocery store cake. What poor bride did you stick with that? I hope you planned it for free."

Rosalie picked up her plate and glass and stood up in a huff. "I *did* do it for free. I was the bride. You know you can be an idiot at times. I've got two words for you: Kei Kameika."

She left and I didn't see her until dinner. Even then I was confused. I didn't know how to spell much less look up her short two words, and Kawabata was now trying to get me kicked off the Japanese stock exchange.

Chapter 15

Rosalie

Turkey and dressing were foreign foods to Singh as was the American holiday of Christmas. Meal planning for holidays had been Dex's job and now it was Singh's to ensure a holiday feast that was suitable for all our guests and staff. He, of course, turned to his new wife Gyanleen for help, while Ledger turned to me.

"As you can see, Gyanleen, we will have about three hundred and fifty people at Drake's as guests and staff. About half of those eat meat, about a quarter request vegetarians meals, and the other quarter will eat both. I'm thinking we should plan for two thirds meat eaters, and the rest vegetarians."

"Are there some traditional dishes with this holiday meal? Anything that 'has' to be included?" she asked, taking notes.

"Yes indeed, but I'd like to try a variation to the main course. Instead of plain roast turkey, I'd like to serve turducken." My mouth was watering thinking about a slice on my plate smothered with gravy.

"I'm sorry, ma'am, but what is that...exactly? I've never heard of it before."

"A turducken. It's a southern dish." I pictured sweet potatoes and cranberry sauce as sides.

Gyanleen scratched her ear. "Is that an animal, a bird, what? What does this look like?"

I laughed a little thinking what a live turducken might look like. "It's not an actual bird. It's a chicken stuffed inside a duck that is then stuffed inside a turkey."

She looked horrified with wide open eyes and mouth. "While they are alive? That's horrible!" Her face was a chalky white.

"No! No, not alive. After they're killed, and the feathers and bones are removed."

She didn't look convinced. In fact, she looked a bit green around the edges.

"We can import them already stuffed, and the chef will only have to cook and serve them. How's that sound?"

Color seeped back into her face. "And for the vegetarians?" she said.

"Have you ever heard of a tofurkey, "I asked.

At that, Gyanleen bolted. That's the closest I've ever seen someone run screaming from a room. I decided to put the menu in the hands of our most excellent head chef. After all was said and done, everyone had survived Thanksgiving up until now without my help.

****

Skipper had two words for me at dinner.

"Kei Kameika," he mispronounced. "Who or what is that?"

"Kei Kameika is the number one male movie star in Japan." I parceled out my words as I was still a bit peeved.

"And…?" he said stirring his cold soup.

"And your Bridezilla's groom." He rolled his hand for me to continue. "And this union is an arranged marriage." More hand waving. "Put yourself in his shoes. Given what you know about the bride, would you look forward to spending five minutes with her, much less a lifetime?"

His eyes widened and he shook his head. "So what might the reluctant groom do about this marriage if he wasn't in favor of being Mr. Bridezilla?"

I could see we still weren't on the same page. "He'd pray to his ancestors that some obscenely rich movie-lover would buy his contract and move him to America for a blockbuster movie still under development." Skip scratched his cheek. *Was he deliberately being dense?*

"For Pete's sake. Buy his contract. Call Rhonda the Red Witch and write in a character he, and only he, can play in her movie. Get him out of Japan and get him a language coach because his English is nonexistent. You'd have leverage over the father as to Kei's career and put considerable distance between the bride and groom." The light came on in Skip's face as I finished with, "Pass the butter, please."

He pushed the butter dish towards me and abruptly excused himself from the table with his phone in his hand. I heard him exclaim as he strode from my sight, "Here's the deal, Rhonda…"

He never came back so I ate his dessert along with mine: a French chocolate silk pie with crushed toffee and toasted almonds sprinkled on the whipped cream. It was the best thing that happened to me all week.

****

I sat by the pool as the waiter put two island iced teas down on the cocktail table. Rosalie joined me and kicked off her shoes. We sat in silence across from each other letting the work of the day slide off. The breeze roiled the palm fronds and they clattered and shook, but the cool air felt great as it diverted down my neck and inside my shirt.

Rosalie spoke first. "The fishing tournament, and fishing season in general, is officially over. Our other guest came in third in the tournament."

"Good. Deep sea fishing is a lot harder than it looks. I'm glad Drake's placed in the top three…"

"That you can talk about? Yes, I expect so. I never thought of fishing being so… dangerous."

"Let's change the subject."

"Okay. Skip, I think your New York driver June is kind of lost since Ginger died. I think you should bring him here as a part of Drake's security team and take him as a bodyguard slash driver when we travel. How do you feel about that?"

I could tell she put a lot of thought into this. She's probably been thinking about it since she got back from Ginger's funeral. I knew she trusted June after the Miriam Abatsong nightmare at Macy's. "I think that's an excellent idea. Do you think he would ever leave the city for Drake's?"

"I know he would. I'll send you the contract I wrote up. Is next month too soon?"

I shook my head. Peaches would have done that too. I got a great replacement in Rosalie.

"Okay," she said. We haven't taken time to talk about your trip. What was that about?"

My financial situation has to come out eventually. "Rosalie, I think Allie probably told you that I have money…" She held her cup in both hands as she sipped her tea. "Well, she was being modest; I have a lot of money. I own 158 corporations and hundreds of associated companies."

She stared at the palm fonds whipping over our

heads. I was slightly annoyed at her nonchalant attitude. "I hire managers, top managers to run them, but I have to show up and run audits, talk strategy, hire and fire—are you listening to me?"

"Yes. Hire and fire. I heard you. Have you noticed the white caps rolling onto the beach? Isn't the bad weather usually over by now?"

I looked up and around. The weather did seem windy and no one else was out on the patio. The pool staff was covering the fire pits and chasing embers that blew away with wet towels. I stood to grab Rosalie's beach towel as the wind snatched it up. As I stepped towards her there was a sudden crash as the glass on the cocktail smashed under the bombardment of a four-pound coconut from above. Glass stuck to my slacks, but shards cut into her leg nearest the table.

"Come on," I said. "You're cut. The doc will still be in the clinic." I wrapped another towel around her leg and checked her shoes for glass before putting them on her feet. Glass was everywhere but my guys were sweeping it up as we left.

While I waited, I heard Doc talking to Rosalie as he carefully probed her leg. "I shouldn't be too much longer, young lady. Has this happened before? I see a couple of old scars here…" The glass pieces clinked as they dropped into a metal kidney pan.

"Yes, but that's mostly from plain old shrapnel."

Shrapnel? Where could she ever have been when she was hurt by shrapnel? Yes, I missed my daughter's life but I missed her mother's too. I was slowly becoming determined not to miss the rest. "Let me take you to your room," I said pushing a wheelchair, but she stopped me.

"I can make. See you tomorrow." She left with only

the tiniest limp. Her scooter and walking cast were gone, but that little limp? I was pained to think it could be permanent.

Doc said after she left, "I thought we kept all the coconuts removed from around the pool. After that pool cleaner got brained—"

"We did, but don't mention that incident to her. We replaced all the tables with teak without glass."

****

Rosalie was resting, so I ate dinner alone. It was quiet, peaceful, and lonely until my cellphone rang. Neither my phone nor I recognized the caller's name, so I let it roll over to voicemail.

In the end I was glad to have some time to myself. Then I dressed in my evening tux and strolled through the casino, restaurants, and bars to do my meet and greet. I realized many of the returning guests were calling me "Dex" but were puzzled when we had a conversation.

I ran into my new general manager. He was truly resplendent in his new duds. "Just what I wanted, Singh." Admiring his lush beard gave me an idea. I made a note to visit the barber the next morning.

"Thank you, Boss. My wife has the eye for clothes. She is the real power behind the throne."

Peaches surely kept things efficient and running like a champ. Rosalie was turning out to be the same and then some. She was integrating into my power network outside of this island. I made a mental note to ask her in the morning at our daily start up meeting about this misidentification problem, see if she has any ideas.

So where did that table come from and was this a simple accident, or not?

****

My attempted beard was driving me nuts. I was constantly scratching my chin and cheeks. Drake's barber assured me the itching would quit after a few weeks. I could already see the beard was making a significant difference in my appearance, especially the gray that I was convincing myself was "distinguished." No one had ordered a drink from me in two weeks. *Maybe I should fake a Jersey accent too.*

Tropical storm Quigley was late in coming. We asked guests who were here to fly out or sail to safer areas of the Caribbean over Christmas until the storm passed. I expected them back for New Year's Eve. I had apartments in Jamaica for them if they wanted, an island that only sees a tropical storm about every ten years. We've been lucky since we opened Drake's and Jamaica has been a safe haven for many of our guests. We opened the underground storms shelters in the caves and all resident staff of Drake's moved in. The staff quarters are more akin to dormitories.

"I'm sorry, ladies…" I said to Rosalie and Allie, "… but you will share a private room off my office. I guess you can flip a coin for bunks."

To conserve energy and water, we had a shared toilet with all stalls, no urinals. The showers were shared but with individual shower stalls. We had one kitchen and picnic tables.

I showed Rosalie and Allie around. "The dining hall is this side of the kitchen. All meals are buffet and no special orders." A drink bar held ice, tea, coffee, juice, and milk. The shelter wasn't built for more than a few days occupation, but we had plenty of food and water and two auxiliary generators.

The rest of the island had the same supplies and a

few selective steel and concrete shelters with generators open to all residents. In Oklahoma we had tornado shelters, so this wasn't anything new to me.

Allie quipped, "Dad, Quigley has us down under." She fit right in with her movie references. "This is kind of like being at home, isn't it?"

I was mentally calculating what we'd have to do to get ready for the big New Year's party. "How's that?" I answered.

"Well, you have to wait for someone to come out of the bathroom before you can go in. Less privacy but you probably won't be caught in your birthday suit, unless you want to."

My underground suite consisted of a small office for two, three in a squeeze, with a couch and small conference table, and two sleeping rooms. Allie, Rosalie, and I were relaxing after our chili mac, coleslaw, and cherry cobbler dinner at a picnic table we shared with the Singhs.

"Allie, did you get through to your office?"

"Yes. I got lucky when that position in Puerto Rico opened up. Now I can see you guys every weekend or so."

"Where did Alderich take his plane?" He flew out yesterday afternoon and Allie chose to stay behind with us. Alderich left since we didn't have any place to keep his plane safe during the storm. My own planes flew to Panama and were already safely tied down in my private hangar.

"Jamaica. The storm isn't on-track to cross Jamaica at all. That's where his folks went in their plane, so he's with them."

I felt for once that we were a bit trapped in the small

space, hemmed in by the raging storm outside. I'd never had this kind of company before while sitting out a storm.

"Mom, you're pretty quiet. What's going on?"

I suspected Rosalie wanted to spill the beans about Damon's death that she did not spill earlier when we did "year twenty" of our catching up. I knew she was petrified of how Allie would react.

The Singhs walked away and left. Most of the other people already left for their rooms or to help with chores. The space became quiet except for the white noise of the roiling sea.

Rosalie looked to her left and collected her courage. "Allie, I need to tell you something…something ugly, and I know you will be upset."

"Okay. We don't keep secrets from each other. Dad, do you know what this is about?"

Thankfully, I did not, so I shook my head and kept my lips zipped.

"It has never been a secret that Damon's mother Miriam was disappointed when he showed up in Cameroon with a white American wife with a daughter. She was also unhappy that some women came to the clinic to have abortions, a service offered as a part of family planning." Rosalie rubbed one hand over the other.

Allie nodded mechanically, signaling Rosalie to continue.

"I went with Damon that last year to help in the clinic, as I had for a number of years. After two weeks, we went to Yaoundé to visit his parents, who were home for a visit on a UN break." She turned to me and said, "Skip, Yaoundé is the capitol. My father-in-law was a diplomat." She hesitated a moment before she plunged into the deep end. "We shared our exciting news at dinner. Damon took my hand and said, 'Rosalie and I are expecting a child…' "

Allie's eyes popped and she sucked in her breath at the announcement of a baby. I suspected this was news to her. *It was a bombshell to me.*

I had never considered Rosalie might have had another child with her husband. This realization shocked me, but I made an immediate and tactical decision; I kept my mouth shut.

"Mom! A baby? Why didn't you tell…"

Rosalie signaled Allie to stop. "Just wait, please. Damon's dad clapped his hands and grinned. Then there was a loud crash. Miriam was bringing a bowl of food to the table but on hearing our news, she hurled it against the wall.

"She stood over him and shook her finger in Damon's face. 'How dare you! How dare you, Damon Abatsong! You come here and kill African babies in the womb year after year. And now you dare, you dare to tell us you are bringing a mulatto baby into the world with a white woman who already has a bastard child.' "

"She turned to me. 'You are a witch. My package should have gotten you into trouble. Instead you used my *own* magic and beguiled my son into marriage, and now this.' "

"Damon pulled me up from my chair, 'Come. We must leave now.'

"Miriam dashed to our room. She was a woman on fire as she thrust her hand with two pills towards him. 'You will not leave here until you abort this witch's baby.'

157

"Damon was as horrified as I was. 'Absolutely not!' he yelled.

"She screamed back, 'It should be easy for you. If you don't, I will.' She had been a midwife and done abortions herself, but many of her patients died. She knew Damon kept the pills in his medical bag.

" 'Damon, if she gets a hold of me, she will kill me,' I whispered.

" 'Most assuredly,' he whispered back. He looked around for an escape route not already blocked by armed men—one of the necessities of being a diplomat—so I snatched the pills from her open hand and swallowed them both."

Allie grabbed my hand as Rosalie continued. I was as shocked as Allie was.

Chapter 16

Ledger

Rosalie said, " 'Damon, we can try again.' That's what I said to him. I could not let him make that decision for me, nor let his mother gain control of him. We went to our room and barely came out until two days later, after the medication had run its course. We headed to the bush clinic."

Allie had tears rolling down her cheeks.

"Skip, could I have a glass of water, please?" Rosalie said.

I poured out a glass for each of us. I never heard such a horrific story from anyone I knew. I knew now just how strong a woman Rosalie was.

"We weren't out of the woods yet," she said. She repeated the ordeal she told me about on the plane ride from Miami to New York, about escaping from the clinic, the local English-speaking separatists on a rampage, the car explosion that killed Damon and caused the burns on her back.

Allie knelt in front of her mom and put her head in Rosalie's lap as they both wept. "How did Damon not stop her or you, Mom? Why?"

"There were guards. Damon knew I would only be allowed to leave that house after aborting our baby, or if I was dead. His mother had grandiose plans for him to follow in his father's footsteps as a mover and a shaker in their country, but not with me by his side. Damon told me that's not what he wanted. His calling was in medicine and with us." She put her hand on our daughter's hair and stroked it gently.

After Allie cried herself out, she went to watch the storm by the mouth of the cave. Quigley howled, whipping the water to foam, but we were safe. I went out and sat by her.

"Your mom told me some of that story before but not about the pregnancy."

"Why would he not protect her?" she mumbled. I never heard her so sad as I did then. It hurt to see her like this.

"He did. She forgot to mention that he made her lay down in the back and cover up, while he sat up front by the driver. She would have been killed if she had been sitting there."

"Yeah. What's your point?" She stared at the weather through dull eyes.

I took her hand in mine. "Your mom always sits up front. Even in New York. My driver, June, told me she insisted on that. The bomb was for the person in the front passenger seat, for her. Damon protected her up to the last moment of his life. And she ran into Miriam in Macy's in New York this May. Ten minutes later she was hit by the car. That's how her leg was broken.

"Imagine if you set out to kill your daughter-in-law and instead kill your 'golden child,' your only son." *In New York we'd call that murder in the second degree.* "She must have been very angry that Mom was still alive." Allie burst into tears again and cried on my shoulder "until the well ran dry," as my granny used to say. Now I knew why Rosalie had shrapnel in her leg, and why she knew people with diplomatic immunity. I knew why she told me I'd better be enough if she ever lost Allie. *I knew how I'd feel if I lost either of them.*

****

New Year's Eve

"I'm going in," Randy said. The new VP of Drake's racing division was at the resort for its famous Christmas/New Year's celebrations. The Boss was known to be particularly generous on this occasion where his guests and his managers rubbed shoulders.

"Better think about that a minute," warned Scott.

Rex, the summer manager of Drake's asked, "What do you know that we don't know?"

"I know that woman Allie is the Boss's daughter..."

Randy reared back. "I did *not* catch that when I met her at the track last summer."

"Besides," Rex added, "Allie has a boyfriend I hear."

Scott went on, "...and Allie calls Rosalie whom you guys are eyeballing—for good reason, I might add—Allie calls Rosalie 'Mom.' "

"Mom?" Rex and Randy repeated.

"Are you sure about that?" Randy asked.

"Yes. One hundred percent. But here's the thing. The Boss's last name is Warren, Rosalie's is Abatsong, and Allie's is either Smith or Warren, so I don't think the Boss and Rosalie are married, or not anymore."

"So, why does Rosalie work for the Boss? If you know so much, where does she live?"

"I don't know the answer to your first question, but according to housekeeping Rosalie lives in the Boss's private apartment."

Randy said, "Then I guess I just ducked a bullet."

"I don't know about that either," Scott said glancing over at Rosalie again. "Housekeeping says they have separate bedrooms and bathrooms and there doesn't seem to be *any* evidence of hanky panky. And Allie has a bedroom in there near her mom."

"Okay. It's just a dance. I'm going in," Randy remarked as he headed towards Rosalie who was dressed like a queen in a red sequined off-the-shoulder dress with enough of a swishy skirt to twirl and spin.

Across the dance floor the Boss spotted Allie as she came in alone. He waved her over. "Happy New Year's, Allie. Made any New Year's resolutions?" he asked as he gave her a special hug and she kissed his cheek.

"Yes, and my first one is to finally have a daddy daughter dance. Shall we?"

"Absolutely." He took her hand and led her onto the dance floor. "I like to dance but I get very few chances."

"Why? I'd think a handsome single man like yourself would be fresh meat for the ladies."

He laughed. "I always suspect they have ulterior motives if they ask me to dance. I never ask a single woman who is here with a guest. If I dance with a single or married woman for that matter, I feel I need to dance with all of them to make it clear that *I* have no ulterior motives."

"That's kind of sad. What about when you aren't at Drake's?"

"That's always business trips and meals. I'm lucky to get thirty minutes in at the hotel gym or a massage. Where's Alderich? I thought he would be here."

"Me too, but he had family business in Mexico City. He'll be here tomorrow. He has a lesson scheduled with your chess master day after tomorrow."

"He's meeting with Kasparov. I didn't know Alderich played chess."

"He said he was second in the Philippines' national ranking before his accident."

"Well, well, well. I'll have to think about that if he asks me to play. I don't suffer abject humiliation easily." Father and daughter laughed as another couple bumped into them.

"Oops, excuse me," Randy said before turning to see who it was. His eyes widened and his forehead started to glisten. "Sorry, Boss," he added as he turned away.

Rosalie's face appeared over Randy's shoulder. "Good evening, Mrs. Abatsong," Boss said with a wink. "Enjoying yourself?"

She smiled back with, "Most definitely, Mr. Warren. Lovely party."

Randy immediately led Rosalie in a direction away from the Boss. "Sorry, I was having such a good time I didn't see them."

"So was I, Randy, so forget it."

The dance ended and Randy walked Rosalie back to the punch bowl where Scott and Rex were chatting. Rex handed her a small cup which she quickly finished off.

"Okay, who's my next victim?" she asked with a grin.

Scott stepped up. "I am, ma'am, if you please."

As he took her hand and led her away she looked back at Rex. "Don't go away. You're next."

Rex turned to Randy. "That took guts, man. How'd it go?"

Randy laughed. "Great. She's funny and easy to talk to. It was fun until I crashed into the Boss. Then I was more scared than when I hit the wall at Bristol in my last season in NASCAR."

"Ouch. Look at Scott showing off. Of course he would be a good dancer. He used to dance on Broadway. Don't tell him I said that thing about Broadway. I wasn't supposed to tell anyone."

Scott and Rosalie ended up at the punch bowl again and Rex was ready. She pointed at Rex and away they went.

Scott admitted, "I had trouble keeping up with her. Did you learn anything else about her?"

"She's a nurse."

"I think I feel a fever coming on." The men chuckled. Scott followed with, "There's Boss's chief pilot Mike. I've never seen her in a dress before. Wow!" He handed his cup to Randy. "I'm going in."

****

The party wound down and Ledger went out to the patio, loosened his tie, and removed his tux jacket. He found Rosalie almost asleep on a lounge chair.

"Come on, Cinderella. It's after midnight and I'm turning into a pumpkin."

She struggled up and took his hand. In the other hand she held her shoes. "Take me home magic pumpkin. I've got a lot of shoes to try on tomorrow."

They walked unspeaking through the quiet halls to their apartment. Once inside she said, "We did our past. How about a New Year's kiss? For luck. For what comes next." She dropped her shoes, and he dropped his jacket.

She was unsteady on her feet, so he held her in his arms as she put hers around his neck. Their kiss was soft and slow and leading towards a second kiss when she passed out cold.

"Poor kid, She never could hold her liquor." For the

second time in the last year he gently undressed Rosalie, put on her pajamas, and tucked her in bed. "You'll be sorry tomorrow. The flamingo pajamas are an improvement over the flannel nightgown, by the way. Happy New Year." He placed a second kiss gently on her cheek and closed the door as he left.

****

New Year's Day

Drake's private planes landed at the cargo field, and Rosalie said I was not to come and spy. They held all of the islanders' Christmas presents that she sent off when we evacuated for the storm, except for a few things we stored in an unused cave.

"No peeking, Skipper. It's a surprise for the kids, a surprise for the adults, and a surprise for you. And I swore all my helper elves to secrecy too. Now shoo."

When I got up on New Year's Day, Rosalie and Allie were gone. I found a warm streusel coffee cake like my mom used to make, a hot pot of coffee, and a fresh mango smoothie in my apartment kitchen. You sure know how to slow me down, Rosalie, I thought as I hunted down a fork and knife. In a half-hearted attempt to walk off my coffee cake, I wandered into Drake's sports bar where the pregame show to the various bowl games was in progress as well as the Rose Bowl Parade on competing TVs.

"Looks pretty quiet," I remarked to the bartender.

"Yes sir," she said. "Our usual suspects are here slowly sipping their eighty-proof holiday breakfast chased by a nourishing cup of house made eggnog."

One year I told a former guest that our eggnog was designed to provide about twenty percent of a person's food energy for the day. When I checked in with him in the afternoon, I suggested he get some lunch at the buffet next door.

"I already had six of these," he said lifting his eggnog cup. "I'm good for the day including dessert."

That experience prompted me to change my feeding strategy. I waved to the bartender for a cup of chowder. "I bet you forgot your soup course. Try this. I eat it every day," I lied. "See if you can guess which liquor we use to 'sweeten' the pot." I stopped telling the eggnog story to guests after I started offering cups of lobster chowder and chunky gazpacho, basically a salad through the blender, in an effort to get some genuine food into those stomachs.

Next, I tried the Lizard of Oz Lounge. There sat a young couple whose wealthy families hated each other. Fortunately, the parents were also very anti-alcohol and that made this lounge the perfect spot for their offspring to meet and greet if you could call it that.

I ran into Vic in the Maze. "Boss, a lot of guests are sleeping last night off. A few didn't come back after the storm at Christmas. We're running short-staffed so local employees can be in About Hell helping Rosalie. I'm to deliver you there at three, so Juan will pick you up out front at two-thirty."

That left me a few hours, so I headed to the gym hoping to sweat out my hangover.

Juan picked me up on the dot. "Happy New Year's, Boss."

"Same to you, Juan. Do you have any idea what's happening today?"

"Yes, but Miss Rosalie swore me to secrecy. Did you make any resolutions?"

I thought about resolutions as Juan drove. When

Rosalie and Allie appeared in my life eight months ago and we started this ongoing experiment in getting to know each other, I decided to cut them some slack. After all I was the guy with all the money, the guy with offices and apartments in half a dozen countries. The guy with a fleet of airplanes at his disposal. I had to know more about the world than they did. Time has been proving to me that I was miserably wrong.

"Yes. Juan. I am going to cut myself from slack and listen to other people more. I'm a terrible listener."

"Today would be a good day to start, sir. A lot of people will want to talk to you." We bounced a few times over rough spots in the road. I made a mental note to have those fixed as soon as possible.

Now Juan's comment made me nervous. I hadn't considered the security risk to myself and Rosalie this event could pose. I checked my pocket. *Whew!* It had become a habit to pocket the taser Peaches gave me last year. *Thank you, Peaches.*

I thought we were lost when we pulled into Hell. I didn't remember a soccer field nor a baseball field, not even a park to be honest. "When did this happen?" *And did I pay for this and not know it?*

"You're joking, aren't you sir. Your daughter and Scott worked hard with the community to get this put up in time for today." Juan stopped in front of what appeared to be a repurposed cargo shipping container. Allie was on the opposite side of my car waving at me. I returned her wave when suddenly my door opened.

I turned to see who opened it and heard, "Welcome to New Years in Hell, Boss." It was June dressed in khaki shorts and a Drake's polo shirt.

"June! You made it." I got out and said, "Same to

you. Rosalie kept you a secret but I'm happy you are here." I shook his hand. I had never done that before. *Why not?*

"Me, too. I appreciate all you did for Ginger and me." He leaned in. "I'm acting as your private bodyguard along with my new friends Tiny and Bobby." *Friends?* Did he already know people on Drake's?

I looked behind June and there stood Peaches' two cousins Tiny and Bobby. She had impressed them into service last season as my bodyguards. It looked like Rosalie did the same. I waved at the men, "Hi, guys. Good to see you again." Bobby smiled and waved back while Tiny looked up from his plate of food and nodded. I looked around. People were everywhere. An unfamiliar woman approached me. I knew she was going to talk to me when she looked straight at me. I was glad Tiny and Bobby were so near. There were so many people here I did not recognize. *And that's a shame, Bossman.*

Chapter 17

Ledger

"Good day to ya, Boss." The approaching woman waved at me and grinned.

I knew that voice from my office. "Same to you, Sylvia."

She was a local woman who managed my accounting office at Drake's. "I'm going to be your guide today. If you look over there to the right, you'll notice one shop for the kids where they can get fitted for a new pair of shoes. They can choose from three styles. Next to it is the shop for the teens. And the two smaller shops at the far right are for the adults. That idea to get orthopedically sound shoes for everyone will save you money in the long run. So many of us who live here have all kinds of foot problems from bad shoes. Look, I found some comfortable sandals and my feet better already."

"Can we walk over there, Sylvia. I'd like to take a look."

"Sure thing, Boss. And thanks for the ham. It was delicious."

Allie came up beside me. "Dad, did you notice how the shipping containers are painted?"

"Yes. They're amazing. Who did that?"

"We got the high school art classes involved. This park was a community effort." She leaned in. "Of course Drake's bought all the supplies. These containers were ones abandoned in the cargo port." As we approached the repurposed shipping containers I spotted Rosalie in the kid's shop.

She waved us over. "Happy New Year." She leaned in close to my ear. "You own three shoe companies, if anyone asks."

"Okay." As I watched her measuring a child's foot it took me back to my own childhood. "Where did you get those. I didn't know they still used them. They don't look the ones we used to use."

"The one you remember is called a Brannock Device and we have them for the adults, but these are made for babies and kids. Every shop here has three or more. We, I mean you, bought so many shoes the company threw these in for free. We want to make sure they get shoes that fit."

I suddenly remembered what she said to me last night as we walked to the apartment. I slapped my forehead. "I see what you meant, about trying on so many shoes today. I thought you were talking about you."

As Sylvia guided me by the adult stores I noticed a barrel of old flip flops. "What's that for?" She pointed at the man just exiting the men's shop. He walked out of the shop and tossed his old shoes in the barrel. Then he saw me watching him.

"Mr. Warren, you don't know me, but I work in the desalination plant. These are the most comfortable shoes I have ever had…"

"Chauncey, isn't it?" I remembered his name because it seemed out of place at the moment.

His mouth fell open. "Yes, sir. Thank you, Boss. My feet thank you, and if my kids and wife's shoes fit like this, the whole family thanks you. And thanks for the ham. It wouldn't be Christmas without it." Then he lunged at me. He moved so fast I couldn't reach my taser nor my knife. He threw his arms around me and hugged me as if there was no tomorrow, turned, and left.

While my ribs still felt his hug, my heart suddenly understood that seemingly little things in life mattered the most. *Why didn't June stop him?*

****

People arrived on the island school buses or drove their cars. Families laid a blanket on the ground on the soccer and baseball fields. The lines at the food tables were replenished as fast as new dishes were set out. I got in line with Tiny and June.

"What's good, Tiny?" I asked.

"If you like gumbo start with the callaloo, Boss, right there in those bowls. It's traditional for today. Here, eat a Johnnycake with it. Uh, and thanks for the ham." He handed me a warm round yellow object wrapped in a paper napkin.

June added in, "Don't miss the fruit cake. It doesn't taste like any I ever had before."

At four o'clock the steel drums started playing Santa songs and the kids' ears pricked up. At four-fifteen sleigh bells started jingling through the sound system, first faintly, then louder. A cheer roared through the crowd as Santa made his entrance in a red sleigh pulled by six Virgin Island donkeys, because everyone knows reindeer live where it's cold, and donkeys live here in the islands, I was told.

I asked Rosalie who was playing Santa this year. "I've spotted all the men I thought you might 'volunteer' to be Santa."

"Oh, you'll recognize him, I promise," but I saw that "gotcha" look on her face. Now I was curious.

Walking behind Santa were a dozen elves who looked a lot like the island school teachers, and they knew every child on sight and by name. Following them was a very large wagon with colored lights blinking from front to back. I saw the elf driving had a gadget leg. and it made me laugh.

Santa moved from the sleigh and sat in an overstuffed red chair on a stage where all could see him as he waved and clapped. The kids stood up and cheered. The elves began taking Christmas stockings marked with each and every child's name and delivering them to that child which was guaranteed to lead to shrieking and joy.

The musicians played holiday music as people waited and some folks stood to dance and sing along. Within twenty-five minutes every child below the age of seventeen had received their stocking. The wagon left and another wagon took its place. There were nineteen children scheduled to receive bicycles this year. They knew who they were, and they ran up to the wagon giggling.

"Carole. Merry Christmas, lovey."

"Me, me. It's blue and pink, just what I asked for."

"Gerald. Merry Christmas, child."

"That's my name! Flames, yeah!"

To their delight, each bike had the new owner's name painted on the rear fender, so distribution went quickly as the light faded and the trees lit up with yellow, red, blue, and green lights in addition to the night lights for the athletic fields. The band stopped playing.

Santa beamed as much as the kids did. Then Rosalie led a young woman timidly up a ramp to Santa. He waved her over to him. "Merry Christmas, young lady. What did you ask for this year?" Then he looked at the small child in the buggy she pushed, a Christmas stocking tucked in by his side.

Rosalie leaned in and whispered in Santa's ear. Santa's eyes turned to the boy with a shaven head who was smaller than his eight-years. The boy could not speak but his shining adoring eyes never left Santa's face. Santa rose and stepped to the buggy. He gently lifted the child in his arms and smiled his biggest smile. Then Santa began singing, "Show the world and all its people, all the wonders love can bring…"

A hush fell over the park and the people. All eyes were on Santa, but his eyes never left the child in his arms as he sang and sang until he reached the end, "… Say it loud, make it clear, today." Santa held the child close and whispered in his ear as his mother burst into tears.

Santa gently laid the child in the buggy. The child's beatific smile never left his face as his mother wheeled him away. Rosalie led Santa, his head bowed, off the stage to the candy cane colored tent for him and his helpers to rest and change. I waited outside the tent for Rosalie. The band started playing again as the people picked up their things and headed towards the buses and their cars.

Rosalie's eyes were red, and she was wiping her nose as she appeared from the tent. She took my arm as she said, "Happy New Years, Skip. Let's go home."

As we followed June to the car I asked, "Santa was a surprise. Was that Richie—?"

"Yes," she said quickly.

"How did you ever get him?"

"I asked nicely, but I never expected this to happen. I didn't plan that song."

"I didn't think it was planned. It's the little unexpected things in life we appreciate the most, I've learned. I wish I could have time to thank him."

"You will. He's having dinner with us tonight. Just don't ask for his autograph."

I still don't know why so many people thanked me for ham. *Is that some kind of code?*

****

In the car Skipper asked, "What about the grownups? I didn't see any presents for them?"

"Good grief. How many people do you think we could—" and then I stopped. At least he was engaged in the welfare of his residents.

"The residents got generous gift cards two months before Christmas and hams a month ago. The mailboat ought to be busy for weeks. Might even need to use a plane a time or two or even the shuttle boat."

"I see. That was smart thinking. I bet they ate the ham during the storm. How did you think of that?"

"I asked around about traditional foods in the Virgin Islands for this holiday season. Ham was at the top of the list, so that's what the families got, good old bone-in cooked hams with all the trimmings. Plus every employee got a bonus in their September check."

He scratched his head. "Why the September check?"

"You never have shopped for kids toys, have you?"

"Does Allie's motorcycle count?"

"No. Sylvia reminded me that Peaches always insisted on it. It gives the folks time to shop before all the stores are empty. Plus, you put in better Internet service at the high school and the school's computers were available to families in the evenings after work to shop online starting in October."

I changed the subject. "June, how did you like the food at the party?"

He said, "Never had anything like it before, but I really like shrimp and that soup was delicious. What did they call it?"

Before I could open my mouth Skip said. "Callaloo. Did you try the johnny cakes? They reminded me of hush puppies or cornbread."

"Yes, those were different, but I don't know what hush puppies are, so I can't say about them. My sweet tooth dug those rum cakes. I never liked fruitcake, but I could learn to love those rum cakes."

I jumped back in with, "I sent a couple to friends in the States. Guys, you have inspired me to make my favorite comfort food dinner tomorrow. You are invited June. Dried lima beans cooked with a ham bone and hushpuppies with onion like my grandma made." I sat back planning my meal.

Skip cleared his throat. "I know we said no Christmas presents, but I wanted you to have this." He handed me an envelope.

"What is this?"

"The last letter I wrote to you. I got the one from Dad telling me you were dead, so I never mailed it." I took it but I knew I had to be alone to read it.

"I cheated too." I pulled an envelope from my purse with Skip's name on it. "Merry Christmas," I said as I passed it to him.

"So…what is this then?" He didn't open it.

"A notarized copy of Allie's birth certificate." He didn't say anything as he slipped the envelope into his jacket pocket, but he squeezed my hand and held it the rest of the way home. June dropped us off at the back door to the apartment.

As we walked into our apartment Skip said, "That was a great day today, even magical. You did a great job and thank you for the ham. See you at eight for dinner."

Why the thanks for ham? Should I tell him Richie Moran is in my phone favorites now?

****

It was the middle of January and business was starting to pick up. Rosalie reminded me at breakfast that Yvette, my casino manager, had an appointment with me. The subject was unknown, but she was on time.

"This is unexpected," I noted. "Is there a problem in the Casino?" She was dressed as only French women do; elegant, simple, classic.

"*Non, chérie.* There is a man I met during the summer, oh, I mean we met in Monaco at the Monaco Summer Music Festival. Boss, I am grateful you have an apartment in Monaco. It is *très* chic and so close by the casinos.

"It was a wonderful idea to take my Drake's gowns there and frequent the casinos at night to create attention for us. I get to vacation with my son and *maman* in the day, and work at night."

"It benefits us both, doesn't it?" Yvette got a free vacation in a gorgeous place and extra salary on top of that. She was a close colleague to the managers of all the casinos since that's where she started in this business. "Tell me about this man."

"He wants to play in the Chairs. He does not speak English well and is afraid he might lose because he would not understand the words. I explain to him he only needs to hear the music. When it starts, he walks around the beautiful chairs. When the music stops, he sits down fast. I show him a video from last year on my phone."

"Who is this man? What does he do?"

"His family has a famous French perfume brand you would recognize, *PourQuoi*. He is Monsieur Alain Gaston Fleury."

It was my turn to be excited. This brand included much, much more than perfume and they all do very well in Drake's shops. He would be an attraction in addition to a Player.

"And why does he want in the Chairs?"

Yvette answered with her classic incurious shrug. "I do not know, *chérie*. That is between you and him. Here is his number. An English-speaking translator will answer." She rose from her chair. "Do you think Monsieur Dex will return to Drake's? When I see you, it reminds me of him."

Dex return to Drake's. I was shocked that she asked me this, especially since he tried to poison her along with me. *I'll never understand women.* "No, not as an employee," I answered. She left without a word. *She must be lonely. Yvette and Dex? An intelligent, sophisticated French woman and a dangerous rounder from New Jersey. Strange bedfellows indeed.*

****

Scott and Allie ginned up a proposal quickly for both a field hockey camp and an exhibition game with women's teams. I was invited to check out the pitch AKA the playing field.

"Okay, Dad. Scott had an idea, so we've chalked up the field on top of the old cricket pitch. Normally there are eleven players per side." She pointed out that it fit neatly inside last year's cricket field.

"He also set it up so we can play Hockey5s. That's played on half the field with teams of five each. Kinda like three-by-three basketball. This way two games can go on at the same time."

"Where are you storing the equipment?"

"Since we were already building some permanent bleachers, Scott built an enclosed storage space underneath them."

"That's smart and a good use of space. When does everything start?"

"March. We have the camps first. Mornings is for guests, including me by the way, and afternoons for our school kids who want to try it. We've booked a couple of retired professionals for the camps, and I'm helping with the kids."

"Where will—?"

"In the lower guest rooms, which aren't used much this time of year. That way our pros are closer to the field but still can make it to the guest meal venues."

"And for the exhibition game?"

"I had to tweak the dates for that, Dad. It's mid-March to coincide with Spring Break. We got two women's college teams. We're allowed to pay them now, so that's an incentive for them to come. I worked part-time in college to supplement my scholarships. Please don't be mad." She looked up at me through lowered lashes.

"And where—?"

"In the empty staff rooms. They'll be out before the last week of the season so the extra staff you bring in can use them."

"How did you know about the extra staff?"

"Mom told me. You got a twofer here; Mom and me. We've been a team all my life."

She was right. I got two for the price of one. I considered what Allie and Scott did in a short amount of time, and that she wasn't here full time. "I'm not mad, Allie. You two had a late start on this and you just came up with a win-win deal. Let's celebrate this at dinner tonight. Scott, care to join us?"

Women running around wielding sticks that could split a coconut in half. Or my skull? Let the games begin!

Chapter 18

Ledger

As I passed her desk, Rosalie said, "You had a call from an old friend, I'm told. Here's his number." On the note pad Rosalie wrote "Bernardo Maurizio Fabian Ormanni" and a number that seemed almost familiar.

In my office I checked numbers that called me recently and there it was, the number I didn't pick up on at dinner a few nights ago. Bennie the Jet. The name gave me reason to pause and ponder if I should pass or should I play?

On one hand Bennie was a shadow from my earlier life as a mob lawyer. I was always careful to avoid the people and places I associated with mobsters when I was in New York. On the other hand I knew I owed him a favor. He was the reason I was "allowed" to retire from the mob life rather than take up residence in a Jersey landfill or the East river.

My retirement started with a win for my side in the courtroom. Wise guys have very long memories and longer networks like Nikko the Knife...

I felt the spray on my neck when Nikko passed me leaving court. He spat in my face and snarled, "You and your family are dead meat hung up for slaughter and skinned alive. Sweet dreams, counselor."

I didn't have a family then, but I did now, and I still owed Benny a favor. *Maybe one call is all I need* I hoped as I pressed "Dial."

He answered, "Ledger. You are a hard man to find. You'll have to teach me how to disappear like that."

"Bennie, you sound well. To what do I owe the pleasure of your call?" He sounded the same, his voice like oil on water, mellowing down and smoothing out the highs and the lows.

"Your name came up recently from an associate whose name I can't divulge. He told me about that nice little side hustle you've got called the Chairs…"

"And?" I only intended to listen. If this was an attempt to take over my resort or grab the Gizmo I might have to take certain presumptive precautions.

"…and I want to play in it this year."

You could have knocked me over with a feather. True, I needed another player, but did I dare invite organized crime into my most lucrative business? *Did I have a choice?* "That's a surprise. That seems out of character." I did some mental math. "Are you retiring?"

"Yes. And with John's blessing." John, our code name for our mob boss, must be getting soft in his old age.

I laid it out fast. "I need ten million up front and a minimum of twenty mil of legitimate assets as a bet. Do you have a money laundering front that hasn't been busted by the Feds yet that can pass that kind of cash over, without me worrying I'll have to surrender it later?" Maybe a little abrupt but this is strictly an old debt I was closing out.

"Easily. I paid attention when you got out and saw I wanted to do that one day too. I started around the time you left. I set up overseas trusts that I know you don't touch that I can live on comfortably if I win or lose."

"But the bet is clean? Anything besides the cash?" I didn't want to take a bath on this deal.

"I have a couple of businesses here, but I can't imagine I won't have to 'divest' myself of them to another associate. I do have some clean overseas assets though that are free and clear." I chuckled. He made all that mob activity sound so legit. *I wonder if the Feds have a wiretap on him. Or on me.*

"Are your wife and kids okay with this deal?" I remembered his wife had an opinion on everything.

"No, not by a longshot. I may have to give her those local businesses in the divorce. The kids aren't taking sides yet, but they are not in the mob life. They are legit and I want them to stay that way. Capiche?"

"Capiche," I said acknowledging what I perceived was his biggest worry. "What's your plan afterwards?" *Why did I even ask that?* "You going to take up dancing?" I was trying to deflect a prolonged conversation.

He laughed, "Maybe. You guys named me after that Jet's gang member in *West Side Story,* but I still enjoy a little soft shoe now and then. Beats sweating at a gym, and I don't have to leave home. Send me the paperwork. We'll have a drink for old times' sake."

"Sure thing, Bennie. Later." I hung up and called Beryl to explain the situation.

There it was, my eight Players assuming Huang pulls through. I don't remember any 'old times' worth celebrating with Bennie, and certainly not Nikko the Knife.

I'll gladly lift a shot and take Bennie's cash and smile while doing I, but I won't turn my back on him.

****

I drove my golf cart to the field hockey pitch. Rosalie sat beside me, in the front of course. This was March and the second week of camp. Allie took vacation time to take part.

"The grass looks good, doesn't it? And the pitch is neatly chalked. Very professional."

"Yes, Skip. The benches and bleachers look brand spanking new. Those bleacher seats look so comfortable I could sit in them all day."

The coaches Allie hired were dressed in dark navy shorts with tucked in cream-colored polo shirts. As I got closer I saw a logo on both of them that I didn't recognize. In fact, all the guests learning to play field hockey had on a similar polo shirt that was either navy, cream, or light blue. Allie came over to us when they took a break.

"Hi, guys. Wanna pick up a stick and join in?"

I answered, "The gym and weight bag is plenty for me. Allie, what is that logo on the clothing? I don't recognize it."

"I'd be in trouble if you did. That's a logo Scott and I designed and registered for Drake's field hockey. We gave every participant a free shirt and patch, and they are currently on sale in the Drake's licensed apparel shop. Guests can have a name embroidered on for free."

"Drake's has a licensed apparel shop?" *Since when?*

"As of March first. You and Mom get a free polo, of course. Just go in and ask for it. Tell them I said it was okay. Make sure you get the gold lettering. That means you guys are upper management." She chugged a bottle of a sport drink with the same logo on it. "I gotta go. Watch this. Dad. I'm getting pretty good at drag flicking. Of course my goal is to be *killer* at drag flicking, but I'll put in the time to perfect it."

Rosalie and I looked at each other with our mouths open. I felt old. "Tell them *she* said it was okay? When did *she* become a businesswoman?" Rosalie snorted.

"That's a revenue stream I didn't see coming," I stammered. We watched Allie line up to what looked like a golf ball on steroids to her right, squat down slightly and step forward with her left foot while dragging the ball along with her stick, and then POW! With a strong flick of the stick the ball was airborne and propelled forward until it smacked into a net fifteen yards away. She repeated the motions, and I noticed she hit the same spot every single time. "Our daughter is some athlete. Did you see that coordination? And the power she puts behind that ball. I wish I had that eye when I'm skeet shooting."

Rosalie looked at me with a question in her eyes. "You know what we have to do now, don't you?"

Yes, I did know. "Come on old lady, I'll help you into your seat," I joked. I turned the cart around and we made it in record time to the new shop. I chatted with the two employees, dressed in the same polos with blue lettering, an island couple who both played and enjoyed sports.

"I suppose you two are cousins of my late secretary, Peaches." I was joking, kinda.

"No, Boss. I am her aunt Venus, and my husband is her uncle Arnold. He was a golf pro in Florida for a number of years." She added, "I worked as a junior college women's sports coach for tennis, basketball, and swimming."

Arnold said, " Peaches made us promise to keep an eye on you if anything ever happened to her." We chatted for a few minutes while Rosalie browsed and picked out her "free" shirt. *Lovely people.*

Rosalie and I went back in the afternoon to watch the local kids at the field hockey camp. "What are those kids wearing?" Rosalie pointed to a group lining up for a scrimmage.

I raised my field glasses. "They have on tee shirts with an enlarged logo on the front." The tees came in the navy and the light blue. Each kid had a reusable water bottle—yes, with the logo. I had no idea where we could go with this merchandising, but Scott and Allie obviously did. They told me later that afternoon they were planning an online shop with apparel for each exhibition sport and each activity such as scuba or snorkeling, golf, the track, the casino, and a generic Drake's Key navy polo with a light blue collar, or light blue with a navy collar.

I said, "I might like one of each to wear around the premises in the afternoons or to play golf," which delighted Allie to no end. "Of course, someone might think I was a waiter."

"Not with your name in gold, Dad."

My favorite was the tee with a picture of the Chairs that read "There's more to do at Drake's than just sit around."

Rosalie admitted, "I like the shirts with the Drake's Dandies parrots."

I also leaned towards the water sports shirt with the Drake's Dancer nudibranch and coral. "I know it's just a slug, but I like this." *Who did the artwork?*

The best part was their idea to use the proceeds from shirts to support the sports park near About Hell. That was a great feeling. Allie did me proud. In hindsight,

Rosalie probably deserves a lot more of the credit, but I had the place and the financing. *I'm starting to know what it feels like to be a part of a real family.*

****

Alderich suggested a seminar or two on prosthetics for senior citizens. My left knee was acting up, so I agreed at once on the condition this was no sales pitch.

Alderich wore a spiffy striped vacation shirt and pressed khaki shorts. His gadget leg even looked polished up. His leather tennis shoes looked like they were straight from the box. I have to admit the kid cleansed up pretty nice.

Alderich helped a lady with a cane to a front seat and then started his show. "Thank you all for coming today. I am Alderich Muñoz and like you, I am a guest here. However, I am not quite like you in all respects." Alderich tapped his artificial leg with his cane so all could hear the clank, clank it made. I'm impressed. He's quite the showman. "Five years ago I was in an accident. When I came to in the hospital a week late, I was missing the lower part of this leg below my knee." He tapped it again.

"Now you don't need to have a traumatic accident to need a new knee." A picture of a state-of-the-art knee replacement appeared on a screen. "I have one in the leg that wasn't injured."

Ah, the old bait and switch.

"The causes leading to knee replacement are limited…" Alderich continued another fifteen minutes. Not a single person left.

Rosalie leaned against the back wall, her phone in hand.

I joined her. "What do you think?" I whispered.

"I'm thinking I need to get to my orthopedist soon."

"No," I said. "Make an appointment with my ortho doc coming in two weeks."

She looked at me. "Really?"

"Why not? It's an employee benefit."

"Employee benefit, huh. " Her phone vibrated, and she left to answer it.

When I left, Alderich had a crowd asking questions and taking names.

*****

"Rosalie, I think we should spin off the apparel as a new…" I noticed a young lady sitting behind Rosalie. "Who is this? Have we met before?"

She stood up and came towards me. I braced myself with my left hand on my taser.

She offered me her hand as she said, "Hello, Boss. I am Phibe, Miss Rosalie's intern."

I side-eyed Rosalie and saw she was smiling, so I relaxed. "Phibe, pleased to make your acquaintance. Do you have time to come into my office and talk?"

"Yes, sir," she said and walked straight into my inner sanctum.

We sat in front of my desk with the door open, a habit I was increasingly adopting. "Mrs. Abatsong has already asked you some questions or you wouldn't be her intern. What do think I should know about you?"

Rosalie brought in a tray with iced island tea, two glasses with ice, and the ubiquitous cookies. She poured as I reached for a cookie.

Phibe took a sip and said, "My name is spelled P-H-I-B-E. I am named for my four-times great grandmother who arrived here as a slave. I hope I make her proud. I am a quick student, Mr. Warren. I just graduated from the Commercial Program at the high school. I am skilled in computer software and applications. My third cousin, Miss Peaches Petty, told me a great deal about you. It was her admiration and fondness for you that prompted me to apply for this position. It is the best opportunity on the island for me."

I swallowed hard, not wanting to look the fool in front of this remarkable young lady. "And what do you hope to accomplish here, Miss Phibe?"

"I have two goals, Mr. Warren. First, you have a much better Internet service than I do at home. I hope you allow me to take college classes on-line after hours towards a degree in Business Administration specializing in digital marketing.

"Secondly, I hope to make an impact here. I know I can get experience from the inside on the operation of a global corporation."

Wow. "Phibe, Drake's Resort is a small business centered just here on this island, you should know."

"But you are an international tycoon whose holdings span the globe. I did my research."

I was speechless so I stood up. "Thank you, Phibe. Welcome aboard. Please keep your research to yourself if you don't mind." Phibe took another cookie and refilled her tea as she left.

Rosalie sent Phibe on an errand through the Maze and then stuck her head into my office. "Well, what do you think?"

I chuckled at Phibe calling me a tycoon. "Are you sure your degree isn't in human resources. She's a gem. You might be training a competitor for one of my companies one day."

"Or one heck of a manager," she said.

****

Singh's cousin Rishi arrived a week before the field hockey exhibition scheduled for the second week of March. As Allie predicted, we were booked up.

The cricket match last year turned into the season's biggest party, I was determined to do a better job of planning for both it and the field hockey exhibitions.

Singh set up daily talks for guests with his cousin who spoke on a different aspect of field hockey each day, followed by a large dose of personal experiences. Afterwards he wasn't shy about pressing the flesh and signing autographs. Drake's provided a photographer for professional selfies. Gyanleen acted as his translator.

I called on Gyanleen for help last October. I suspect this was around the time she and Rosalie discussed traditional Thanksgiving foods, so she was apprehensive. "Gyanleen, you are the expert in this area."

"Let me understand, Boss. You want me to help your chef to plan for two weeks of Indian dishes for next March?"

"Yes, and to help my entertainment manager Max in New York to find proper East Indian entertainment for half of the days. I suggest you go meet with Max in person and look for an Indian chef to bring in for a couple of weeks."

"Go to New York, just like that? Without a chaperone?"

She had a somewhat naive look. I knew she wasn't teaching at our primary school, so I was hoping to hire her to plan and run most of the field hockey week's activities, along with Allie and Scott. If that worked out, I wanted to put her on the payroll to help Scott and Max plan other special activities.

Where would I find a chaperone? And in New York?

Chapter 19

Ledger

This chaperone thing was new to me. I found Singh and asked him to educate me.

Singh chuckled. "Boss, Gyanleen is a married woman, so a chaperone is not needed. I suspect she had never traveled by herself. I know she has not been to the United States, so I will guess she is nervous or scared to be on her own in a foreign country. And in New York— a nightmare I've heard. Do you have any contacts in New York?"

I'd say one or two. "I see. Perhaps I can find someone to help her getting around the city. I do have an office there."

"I did know that you travel there often, but I was not aware of the office. Boss, there is a large community of Southeast Asians in New York in what is called by the odd name of Queens. Are you familiar with it?"

I chuckled. I had been spending more time in Queens than ever before. "Yes, I have heard of it."

"I have a cousin who is very close to our branch of the family who lives there. I will check, but I believe he has an unmarried sister who would be a suitable chaperone for my Gyanleen. I have never heard of any scandal about her, other than she is unmarried. Would that be a problem?"

"Not as far as I'm concerned. I was thinking to fly

191

Gyanleen to Miami to catch a flight to New York. You could go with her to Miami and see she gets onto her plane."

"A commercial flight to New York or...?" He seemed to be waiting. *Maybe for another choice?*

"Or we can have my New York pilot fly down to Miami to pick her up."

"That is sounding like a plan." His white teeth gleamed when he smiled.

"Good. Work with Rosalie and our pilot Mike here to iron out the details. Oh, don't let Mrs. Abatsong talk you into letting her be the chaperone. She seems to attract trouble when she's there and my credit cards take a hit." *That was a lie. I didn't want to take a chance on Rosalie being hurt again—or worse, killed. Nor Gyanleen either*

Singh agreed and sighed. "I am too worried about these things. I married a shopper."

"Well, let's channel that talent in a productive way." We two men shook on the bargain. I didn't mention the kind of trouble Rosalie had the last time she was in the Big Apple.

Gyanleen's trip went off without a hitch and now in March, our field hockey classes, exhibition, and Indian-themed entertainment and food were hits. Gyanleen hired a top-notch Indian chef. She worked with Singh's cousin, whom Gyanleen referred to as "auntie" and Max to book topnotch Indian dancers. Gyanleen even led a class for guests on the basics of Indian dance where I saw Rosalie giving it a try.

Two life-sized wooden Asian elephants showed up in early March, one in the lobby and one at the entrance to the casino. Since then various architectural features showed up overnight yet installed seamlessly as if they have always been there. I especially liked the pointed arch over the main lobby entrance that was reminiscent of the Taj Mahal, and the faux pierced marble screens with living jasmine climbing up them in our main restaurant and casino. Few people noticed me, and that was a good thing. My beard made excellent camouflage. However, I've noticed that the biggest attraction was my general manager; Singh—tall, dark, handsome, mysterious with his ever-present sword, and glorious in his new working clothes.

Was the sword functional as well as ceremonial? Add another weapon to my blade count.

****

Although field hockey was unknown here in the Virgin Islands, the student classes were full. Alderich completed an on-line class to learn the rules and officiate. Now he helped with the classes and exhibition games. He said he was writing a paper for publication in a sports journal. He's got more energy than I do.

"I'm calling it my longitudinal study on the reliability of my gadget leg and knee implant for athletically inclined recipients, and for those who run and stand as part of their job," he told me. " Did I mention I know two football refs and three basketball refs with implants?" Smart guy, Alderich, combining work and play.

Today was the exhibition game of the local girls' team followed by the college teams' game. Our East Indian celebrity hockey player stood at midfield for the coin toss. Rosalie and I sat with Singh in lawn chairs off to the side of the bleachers.

Singh said, "Boss, our girls are wearing white shirts

for the home team and dark blue for the visitors. They were randomly assigned to teams by Gyanleen and my cousin." He leaned in and whispered, "Between us they tried to make the teams as evenly matched as possible."

Good idea for beginners. I asked, "Where's Allie? She's not going to miss this for…"

Rosalie pointed across the field to the visitors bench. I strained to see where she was pointing when I spotted my daughter. *Yes!* She was a referee along with Alderich. Gyanleen coached the home team and Bad coached the visitors.

She poked me. "Try to show some impartiality. You are sponsoring both teams and all of them live here." She passed me a hand fan. "If you notice, the rules are printed on one side and the layout of the field on the other." She wore a Drake's visor and offered me one in a darker color.

Scott's voice blared out from the new speakers. "Ladies and gentlemen, parents and guests, boys and girls—let's get this game rolling!" There was a clattering of struck hockey sticks, and a cheer rose from the stands. "Our celebrity hockey player will toss the coin. The visitors' captain will make the call…and it looks like the *visitors* will put the ball into play."

"What happens next," I asked Singh.

He pointed to the middle of the field. One girl from the visitor's team was at centerfield. Her team and the defending team were spread out in a formation. "She has to pass the ball back to one of her girls at the rear of the field. That girl can then move the ball forward towards to their goal. And there she goes!" He jumped up and waved as the girls rushed by.

This game moved much faster than cricket. Each

player had gloves, knee socks covering shin guards, and a new carbon fiber stick. I was gratified to see each girl had on protective headgear, and I hoped that included mouthguards. My guest dentists spend too much time on our island kids teeth to have a tooth needlessly knocked out.

"I'd hate to get clobbered by one of those sticks," I reflected.

"If it makes you feel better, anyone who did that would be charged with a foul. Sticks can't be raised above the waist," Rosalie said. She shot up and yelled, "Are you blind ref? She was behind the line!"

I made my way to the refreshment tents at the south end of the field where I ran into Vic.

"Not quite like cricket, is it?" I commented.

"No, Boss. Those women can be brutal with those sticks."

"Are they that dangerous?"

Vic smiled with a slight smirk. "*Noli timere.*"

"Be not afraid? That's easy for you to say. My daughter practices in my apartment hallway. I've had the walls replastered four times already."

"What I said applies to parenthood too. Have you tried these crab and shrimp samosas? They are really something."

As we sampled the food, Gyanleen came by heading for the medical tent while holding her left hand. It was swollen and she was in obvious pain.

"I wonder what happened?" I said.

Vic replied, "Most likely a player whacked her finger with a stick that was illegally played above the waist. She'll lose that nail in a day or two."

****

I was late for the start of the college women's game. I saw Gyanleen, with a bandage on her hand, and Alderich were the referees. *What happened to Allie? Was she injured?* I sat by Rosalie. "What happened?"

"So far the home team scored two goals—"

"No, I mean where's Allie? Did she get hurt. I don't see her."

"That's because you aren't looking in the right direction. She's number six on the home team and she scored one of the two goals."

"Home team?"

"Yes, she's subbing for a girl with the flu. So far. she's keeping up but this is not your grandma's hockey game."

A pack of players moved past us so fast I couldn't tell them apart. It was a sea of ponytails and braids bouncing in the breeze. "Which one is Allie?"

Rosalie pointed. "Redhead, no ponytail."

This game made the earlier game look like it was played in slow motion. This game was high speed golf on steroids. This game required close attention from both players and fans. Even so, both sides were full of Drake's guests cheering and having a great time.

I hunted down Scott. "Great game, Scott. Did you say men played this game too?"

"Yes, sir. Wanna try for men and women next years?"

I gave him the thumbs up and went back to cheer on my daughter. This was my first time as a dad rooting for his kid and I was stoked!

****

Alderich and I waited outside Drake's main gate. As the last remnant of the sun melted into the edge of the ocean, we saw car lights blinking, beckoning us to another world. I didn't have the slightest idea who was in that old Chevy sedan. The rear door opened. "I am Phibe," said the woman sitting in the back. I recognized her. She beckoned me to sit.

"Mr. Alderich, sit with Alphonse." We did as we were told and the Chevy quietly merged into the dark. My pulse drummed in my head as we rode without headlights along invisible roads.

"Did you bring the things you were asked to get?"

I handed her a shopping bag with a half a dozen black candles, two bottles of Cruzan Black Cherry rum, and a bunch of purple flowers.

"May I give you some background on what happens next?" She picked up a small notepad covered in cursive writing and mysterious symbols.

"Yes, please." This was a first for me.

"First. You are only observers. Realize we are starting a process tonight that may take months. We can't atone for hundreds of years in one night. This is the first step, and I thank you for it."

That made sense. A simple "sorry" just won't cut it for such a big chunk of history, but I could do something for *this* island's past.

"Second. Do you know how magic is defined?" Phibe asked.

I didn't expect that. "I don't think so."

"It is simple. For magic to happen we need certain words, a desired action or result, and an object that unites those two things. Of course timing is important, as is location. This is a very large island. Expect this relief to require multiple ceremonies in multiple places. Let me explain the drums first…"

Alderich was all ears, and I could see I'd have a lot to tell Mom and Dad when they got back for the next season.

****

The island shuttle boat was an hour overdue. Juan drove me to the port to wait for Rosalie and Allie. *Why didn't I insist on them flying?* I was in a bind. We'd promised the truth with no secrets, Rosalie and me. A week ago I'd given my word to a man from our past, and now she would think I lied to her. I saw my ladies wave as they came down the gangplank.

"Dad, you spoiled us. My best mother-daughter trip ever!" Allie gushed as she hugged my neck. I even got a hug from Rosalie. They gabbed all the way back to Drake's, but I was preoccupied with what waited for us there.

"Why are we getting out at the clinic?"

"Rosalie, he made me promise not to tell you…"

"Who made you…?"

I saw Reverent Smith step out of the clinic door. Rosalie's eyes followed mine and she tore out of the Range Rover. Allie bailed out too. By the time I got out the two crying women had smothered the exhausted man. We moved into the clinic reception area.

"Dad, why didn't you tell us you were coming? Is anything wrong? Are you okay?" Rosalie demanded.

"Now, now, I'm fine, just tired. I didn't sleep well on Ledger's plane, but I'm fine."

Both women shot looks at me at the mention of my plane. Now they knew I was in on it, whatever "it" was.

"Why did you come here?"

I wondered that myself. I could see I had some explaining to do later.

Singh arranged for iced tea and sandwiches. I took a lobster salad to nibble on and kept quiet. The keeping quiet part had been working out for me since these two lovely ladies showed up in my life.

Reverend Smith explained, "Have you been following the news from Cameroon? The separatists are on the warpath and all foreigners were expelled. It was barbaric. People were slaughtered left and right…" He shook his head from side to side in what looked despair.

"But you are all right, yes? What changed in the country?"

"The main thing was the Abatsongs were accused of corruption and trying to overthrow the national government. Mostly it was about Miriam, but her husband was caught up in the outrage that followed. Anyone remotely associated with them was hunted down and butchered on the spot. I'm sorry but your father-in-law was one of those unfortunate men.

"Miriam is in jail awaiting a public trial. I'm afraid it won't end well for her. I knew I was on the list because of you and Damon. I called Ledger and asked for his help. I wouldn't be here but for the grace of God and Ledger Warren."

Rosalie took her Dad's hand and pressed it to her cheek. "At least you are safe now."

His fingers ruffled her curly hair. "Don't be mad at Ledger. I swore him to secrecy before I told him anything else. There were spies everywhere, my dear, even in my hospital. I couldn't risk anyone else."

Rosalie let out a sob and a weak smile found its way to her lips. "Come on, Dad. Let's get you settled in a room so you can rest. You have to be worn out. And then we'll have some sandwiches brought—"

Her dad said, "Wait, I'm not done. I brought someone with me. He's not well but I could not leave him to be slaughtered." The Reverend's eyes and shoulders drooped. He took Rosalie's hands in his.

"Who is that? Do I know him? Poor thing." Her eyes searched her father's face.

"He's resting in the examination room just in there…It's Damon."

Allie and Rosalie shrieked. I thought Rosalie's legs were failing her as she sank, but the Reverend held her up. "Come on now, but he may not know you." He led the women into the next room.

I choked on my lobster. I didn't know this part. *How could Damon be alive? Did I just help in the destruction of my own long-delayed family?* Tears stung my eyes, and I left to stand in a corner. The last time I cried was the day I received the letter telling me Rosalie was dead. Now I fumbled for my handkerchief.

I realized bitterly that life was messier than I could ever understand and in this moment it was completely out of my control.

Chapter 20

Rosalie

Allie and I stood in front of Damon's room as my Dad told us Damon's situation. "Be prepared, my dears. Damon was severely injured in the car bombing five years ago. He suffers from advanced blast lung, he is almost totally deaf, he is blind in one eye, he has some brain damage from a concussion from the blast, and he lost his left foot and several fingers from his left hand. He has a serious infection. He is sedated at the moment.

"Rosalie it was much too dangerous for you, for him, for me, for all of us if you knew he was…well…alive." He let this news sink in. "Let's go in."

The room was dimly lit. I did not recognize the gaunt man in the bed. His head was shaven, and a white beard hid his face. He looked a hundred years old. "Dad, this doesn't look like…" *I couldn't bring myself to say my own husband's name.*

"That's the idea. I shaved his head and let his beard grow as a disguise. When people came to the hospital, I said he was from another mission and dying from cancer. I said he had leprosy to explain his missing foot and fingers. That alone kept away many people who looked for him."

Allie bent over and kissed Damon's cheek. "Hi, Dad. I've missed you so much." She laid her head on his shoulder and sobbed.

Hearing her call Damon "Dad" invited a flood of tears from my eyes. I took his good hand in mine and laid my face in it. "Damon, love. I'm here. I'm here." The rest of my unacknowledged grief poured out with all my old fears. I saw Damon was dying. Too many signs I'd seen too many times told me so. Now I would have proof that he was gone from this life; Allie and I could say a final goodbye.

The doc asked us to leave so he could check on his declining patient. We stepped out to the waiting room. Skip was still there, looking pale, like he'd seen a ghost. I knew that Allie and I had. I looked around our little group. *What a mess. What a mess.*

****

Allie stayed with her grandpa while we waited. I washed my face in the rest room and focused. I managed to calm my mind. I saw Skip standing outside in the shade of the porch. I took a glass of tea and went to stand by him. I took his hand in mine.

"I didn't know about Damon, I swear. Your dad just said he needed to get out fast and he was bringing a patient."

"I know. How can I ever thank you? He was right, you know. There were spies everywhere. Hiding him was dangerous, but moving a man as well-known as Damon Abatsong would have been suicide for both of them. Dad did a great job in hiding and caring for him. It doesn't surprise me he wouldn't abandon Damon. They cared for each other from the start."

Skip took my tea and downed most of it. "What does this mean for us, Rosalie? You, me, Allie?"

I saw I was now in the same situation as Skip was.

People we loved, people we believed dead suddenly showing up in the here and now. "It's not the same with Damon." I turned to look into Skip's watery eyes. "He's dying, Skip. I'd be very surprised if he lives through the week, but I will be at his bedside as much as I can. So will Allie and Dad. Damon was some of the best parts of our lives. We'll be sure he doesn't die alone, or in pain, or forgotten. I'd like to inter him here on the island. Will Reverend Otis allow us to bury him in the church graveyard?"

"I'm sure he will. If not, we'll sic Reverend Smith on him." We both snot-chuckled at that idea. His wise crack blew the steam out of this situation and we both relaxed a notch.

I let out a big sigh of relief and it lifted a weight off my shoulders. I would have closure on my husband's death. I could allow myself to move on with the rest of my life. Somehow, I would convince my own father to retire here where I knew he was safe and loved. *This was a big, big day for me…I hope I never have another one like it.*

Damon never regained consciousness and died three days later. We buried him on March thirty-first in Reverend Otis' graveyard. Dad gave a short eulogy. I picked out the headstone:

Beloved Husband and Father
Damon Lord Abatsong
b. 1968 -d. 2020
Far from home,
Closer to God.

****

"Rude, crude, and socially unacceptable," that's how people see me. This is my second visit. I'll be 'parking' my superyacht *Stranger Danger* at the cargo port so I can use my vehicles. I plan to relax in comfort in my custom-made bed with my new yacht girl Bobbie Jean.

My name is Rudolph Karl Granger, but my customers and business associates call me Rudy or "Boss Hogg." I'm the undisputed pork producer in the Midwest. No one knows more about pork production than I do.

"Bobbie Jean, honey, have them bring my breakfast out to the deck…a bowl a' chili, a loose meat sandwich, and a double slice a' strawberry rhubarb pie…yes, I want a soda, no make that three. Root beer. Come on out here, sugar."

I've come to Drake's for a little danger and little fun, but mostly I've come to make a killing for April Fool's Day. I doubt Drake's Boss will laugh if he finds out.

###

"Sit with me, Alderich. They don't mind. Honestly, I take this Rainforest Tour every time I'm here for more than the weekend. I love it."

"These custom buses are really something. Why do you sit in the back?"

"Better view. I might want to look back at something and most people sit closer to the front. I spotted a movie star on the bus the first time I came. Lola something."

The guide announced. "Please find your reserved seat on our open-air bus. We have custom-made double-wide seats for each guest, but you may sit two to a seat if you like. Seat belts are optional.

"Welcome aboard, Mr. Granger, your seat is right over here. I apologize for the stairs but we want everyone to sit high enough to see our magnificent treasures. I ask that you not reach out of the bus. We do have some venomous reptiles in our ecosystem—"

"You got anything that'll kill a man dead?" Mr. Granger asked.

"Sir, I did hear a rumor about someone dying from snake poison, but I'd rather not try to prove it was true. In fact, our entertainment director published a technical paper on poisonous species unique to this island. So that part, I *do* take seriously.

Alderich leaned in close. "Is that true, about the poisoning I mean?"

"...to continue, do not reach out of the bus. Please do not touch or make a move towards any type of wildlife..."

Mr. Granger spoke up. "You don't mean the birds, do ya? They cain't hurt me, right?"

"Sir, the whole island is private, so technically the owner owns all the flora and fauna. You would be disturbing private property if you tried to touch them. Besides, wild parrots can do considerable damage to your hands, face, and ears, so you should take that part seriously. Do not touch or take any of the plants or flowers. That can bring a federal fine or jail sentence. You should take that part *very* seriously. Any more questions?"

Mr. Granger waved his hand. "Are we gonna hafta ride back to the hotel in this bus? Why didn't ya just bring us by boat? I can see the water from here." He pointed to the obvious undulating waves of the turquoise sea, sunlight glinting from the surface.

"Sir, there are sheer cliffs along that side of the island. You came the shortest distance possible. In fact you came the only way to get here." The guide turned back to the other guests. "Now let's move into the rainforest and look at some one hundred and fifty-foot-tall tree ferns. Not a tree, these ferns can live for centuries. Over to the left you see…"

Alderich nudged me. "Get many like him?"

I nudged him back. "Boss Hogg? You'd be surprised." Alderich didn't smile at my comment.

"Did you say Boss Hogg? That rings a bell, but I can't quite put my finger on it. Maybe it'll come to me later. How about a kiss? That's the real reason we sat in the back, isn't it." He kissed me like he meant it. I returned the favor. "Did I mention my folks are arriving in three days and staying for three weeks?" Alderich dropped casually.

So it's "meet the family time," is it? This should be fun.

****

Mom, Dad, this is Miss Rosalie Smith Warren, but everyone calls her Allie," Alderich said. "Allie these are my parents Ruth and Stanley Muñoz."

I reached out to shake hands with them, "I am so pleased to meet you both. Let's sit down. I imagine you are exhausted from your trip." We sat at a shady table with a harbor view.

Alderich ordered iced tea all around as our waiter passed out lunch menus. "I'll bring your drinks and then take your orders. Please note we have some new selections this year."

I said, "Mrs. Muñoz, one of the new selections was at your suggestion."

She looked down the menu and said, "I see. I must thank Ledger. Have you met him this summer, *ijo*?"

Alderich and I both burst out laughing. "Yes. Allie is his daughter."

She looked surprised and turned to her husband. "Stanley, did you know Ledger had a daughter?" Alderich's father shook his head and buried it in the menu.

I said, "Neither did he until last May, Mrs. Muñoz. Have you decided on what you want for lunch?"

A loud guest from across the pool was berating our same waiter. "I said I want three—one, two, three Southern fried pork chops. Cain't you hear right?" Mr. Rudy Granger was at it again. Alderich's parents had their heads together and were pointing in Boss Hogg's direction.

"Would you prefer to eat inside," I offered. They both grimaced. We stood and went inside and found a quieter table but still with a great view.

Alderich's dad asked, " Will that man be here for long?"

"I think he's just here for a few days. Why do you ask?" I asked.

"He and I are in the same business, so I've run into him at conferences. As Rudy Granger says repeatedly in his sessions, he has a master's degree in agriculture in meat production from some university in Texas. He is eminently qualified when he talks about his expertise and his personal experience. I have been able to reduce the waste products in my own production and increased employment because of him.

"However, that man you see over there, that Boss Hogg he is pretending to be—how do you say in English, a man from the country?"

Alderich looked at me and answered, "A hick?"

I added, "Or a redneck."

Mr. Muñoz continued, "Yes, redneck. I've heard that before. He plays that role when it is convenient for him. He acts rude, he acts like he doesn't understand. Do you understand?"

We both signaled "yes." *He liked to play dumb. He thought no one caught on to his act.*

Then Mrs. Muñoz added, "And we don't like his hobby. That is the main thing."

Alderich smiled condescendingly and asked, "What's his hobby, mama?"

She sneered, "He's an orchid thief."

That got my attention and Alderich's too. "An orchid thief?" I repeated.

"And Philippine cockatoos."

Alderich asked, "How do you know that?"

His dad replied, "Because our government has a warrant out for him for stealing endangered species and illegal trafficking of wildlife."

Alderich and I looked at each other. "Allie, do you remember Boss Hogg's questions from the tour?"

"Indeed I do."

"In hindsight, what do they sound like to you?"

"Like he's got a plan to do some illegal shopping in our rainforest. He asked everything but what time does the sun set? I need to see Dad pronto." I stood up to leave. "I apologize but I need to see a man about some parrots." I turned to Alderich, "And the best part is the USA has an extradition treaty with the Philippines." I leaned over for a quick kiss and left.

Was I too late to catch a thief and an international trafficker?

****

I rushed into Mom's office. "I need to see Dad ASAP!"

"He's busy with Bevey and Russell..." Dad's top forest rangers were already here.

I stepped into Dad's office. "Is this about some missing parrots or orchids?" I asked as I bent over, out of breath.

The three men looked askance at me, and Bevey said, "What do you know about it?"

"I have reason to suspect one of our guests is here to pilfer orchids, parrots, and who knows what else from the rainforest." I repeated Mr. Granger's questions from the tour days ago, and the conversation I had with the Muñoz family. "Please tell me you have cameras in the rainforest."

Bevey said, "Not everywhere..." and my heart sank.

"So it's true. He's wreaking havoc in Drake's Key rainforest, but we can't prove it."

Then Bevey added, "...they are mostly in the most accessible areas, like the tour route."

Dad asked, "Was Mr. Granger still in the restaurant when you left?"

"Yes. Playing the redneck to the hilt."

Dad called the harbormaster. "Is *Stranger Danger* still in our harbor...where was it headed?...Did it file a float plan?...That must be a first. Read it to me...Thank you."

Dad turned to us. "Bevey, call Fish and Wildlife Service in St. Thomas. Copy those camera videos and send them too. They'll need them for proof to get a search warrant. Ask for both search and seizure warrants. Tell them I'd appreciate it if they arrested Boss Hogg here before he gets back on his ship.

"I'll call the Coast Guard. His yacht left a few hours ago for Tortola to stock up on Pussers rum. Boss Hogg's orders. It's returning here around seven to pick up Mr. Granger. Then it's leaving for New Orleans, but that could be a lie. The *Big Buoy* will be loitering in the harbor and move in to block any escape route for the yacht once it's docked.

"We got this guy dead to rights. Allie, get your stuff. I wouldn't want you to miss this round of fun and games," Bevey said. "Tortola is in the British Virgin Islands. Mr. Granger may know his pork, but he doesn't know beans about geography."

****

I had time to see Alderich before our work at the marina. Our crime force would rendezvous at the harbormaster's office at 5 p.m. sharp with the object of hogtying Boss Hogg and recovering Drake's pilfered flora and fauna. I couldn't tell Alderich what was going on, but he had some ideas. But more importantly he had some disturbing news for me. His parents didn't approve of me nor of our relationship.

"I'm sorry I had to dash out…"

Alderich stopped me. "That's not it. They're devout Catholics and want me to marry a Catholic,"

"Marry? Who's talking marriage? We've only known each other for, what, a year?"

"I love you, you know that, Allie."

"I feel the same way about you, but have either of my parents brought this up? No, they have not. Have they ever acted out towards you? Have they ever acted like they didn't want you around me? No—"

"Well, sort of. No, your folks have never made any cracks about me being Filipino, but your Dad still calls my prosthetic leg my 'gadget' leg and that makes me feel like he thinks I'm less than a man." He was not smiling his beatific smile. *That part about the gadget leg was true.*

I realized I was being distracted, and I needed to be on my A-game. "Alderich, I can't do this right now. I'm working tonight and it may take hours. Don't wait for me for dinner. In fact, it may go on all night. I just don't know what will happen." I stood and rushed out so he wouldn't see the tears running down my blazing cheeks.

Chapter 21

Allie

I'd done an hour of yoga and meditation. My mind was clearer and more centered on my job looming in front of me. I took a hot shower followed by a long, cold soak. I worked to steady my nerves. This could go easy, or it could go to hell in a hand basket in a flash.

We had four different law enforcement entities coming together to arrest one Mr. Rudolph Granger and his crew, to search his ship, and to seize anything we might find related the commission of several federal, territorial, and international crimes. I was the lead for my office since I was on the ground already. I collected my badge, .38 Special, handcuffs, flashlight, and pepper spray. What else did I need? *Don't screw this up, Allie. Oh, yeah, that too.*

****

My Filipino parents updated me on my cousins in Mexico City while we waited for our beef samosas and pork belly sisig and drinks. I couldn't help but worry about Allie. She doesn't tell me much about… "Uh, sorry. What was the question?"

My mother sighed. "I said they asked if you were meeting us there next year. They missed you."

I can't even think about next year. My girl is somewhere out there trying to arrest an international criminal, while I'm here trying to show my parents what a good boy I am. I got up and went back to my room where I changed into gym shorts. I headed for the speed bag and slipped on my gloves. BapBapBapBap. I pounded for a good five minutes. I stopped and wiped sweat from my eyes and spotted the Boss on the body bag. "It looks like we had the same idea," I said.

He acknowledged me and kept up his assault on the 140-pound bag, working his core until his abs glistened. He picked up his water bottle and came over. "Is it working for you?"

"Not really," I admitted.

"Me neither."

"How about a little one-on-one on the court?" I had something to prove.

He smiled slightly, "I accept the challenge. Go easy on me."

Ha! Come on gadget leg. Show time.

The Boss gave me as good as he got. He had a better jump shot, but I had the better layup. We both needed more practice on dribbling. After the ten-minute buzzer rang, we sat and mopped sweat as we drank sports drinks.

"Allie plays like you do," I said.

"How's that?"

"Take no prisoners."

He laughed. "I suspect that's true in field hockey too."

"Plus she can fake me out ninety percent of the time." I laughed at that myself. We were both breathing hard.

"Where is your family from in the Philippines?"

"Cebu."

"In the middle then."

"How do you know that? Have you been checking up on me?" I laughed.

"On you? Not any more than any other guest. It's just that I visit the PI at least once a year to check on my businesses."

"Oh. Any sightseeing?" We had many beautiful and historic sites.

"Once. I went over to Leyte."

"Why there if I may ask?"

"My grandfather died there on 25 October 1944," Boss said.

"I'm sorry, sir. Did you go to the Landing Memorial?"

"Grandad did his duty to God and to country. I never met him, but I sure as never cared about MacArthur, so no, I did not go to the memorial." He was still scratching his beard.

"Mr. Warren, have you been exfoliating?"

"Have I been what?" He gave me a suspicious look.

"Exfoliating. It keeps you from getting ingrown hairs in your face. I'll show you how in the locker room. Now, old man, let me show you what my gadget leg can do." We went at it for another ten minutes, checked our phones for any messages from Allie, and went for a beer.

****

I didn't have my body armor, but I wore my windbreaker with "US Marshal" on the back. We assembled at the Harbor Master's Office as planned. Fish and Wildlife Service had the warrants, so I stayed out of their way. FWS figured Granger was pretty smug about his activities. Sending his yacht to Tortola while he leisurely ate an early dinner told us he wasn't on to us, or he was giving us the finger. Either way, there was always the chance of real danger. What we believed Granger had already stolen from the rainforest was worth millions and he wouldn't give that up easily.

Big Buoy was loitering in the harbor. A couple of our guys in shorts and tees had moseyed over near the pier parking where they posed for selfies. At 6:17 p.m. the *Stranger Danger* was directed to a spot by the pier directly in front of the Harbor Master's Office. I and the local police waited in a white panel truck labelled "USVI Tropicals, Gift Baskets, and Tees." Vic and Bad were out of sight.

The harbormaster contacted Hogg's boat. "*Stranger Danger*, request the captain check in on shore. There is a hold up on your fuel request." After securing lines, the captain, who looked smart in a fresh white uniform, presented himself. I followed him in.

Hank Ivy from FWS confronted the captain with the search warrant. "How's it going to be, Captain? Will your crew put up any fight?"

"If they do it isn't by my order. I just drive the ship from point A to point B."

"Want to make our job easier?"

He shrugged and then looked Hank in the eye. "Just so you know. There aren't any passengers in the guest rooms, just an attendant, on deck two so you don't need to knock."

"Captain, does *Stranger Danger* have a support vessel?"

I didn't think of that. Every big superyacht had a support ship.

The captain's face color matched his uniform. He said, "Yes…" and gave us "…*Granger's Ranger*."

Hank stared the captain down.

"It's anchored off the leeward side of Viequies."

Hank purred. "Puerto Rico, nice, and less than fifty miles away. Come with me. Let's go everyone. We're taking a personal tour led by the captain."

As anxious as I was to get on board, I waited with Vic and Bad and our local police for Mr. Granger who was in route from the resort. The rest of the team except Sal of FWS went on board. *I hope it's Granger who's in the limo and not his alter ego Hogg.*

****

I walked along the edge of the parking lot mindlessly counting the three-foot-tall yellow bollards planted in concrete four-feet apart. They were perfect examples of the KISS principle of "keep it simple stupid." In this case it was simple steel rebar-reinforced concrete pillars that kept cars from rolling out of the parking lot, over the pier, and into the water. Everyone knew what their purpose was at once. *Why isn't life as simple and obvious?*

Just as it was starting to get dark, his limo stopped in front of a bollard ten feet away from me, its headlights lighting up the reflective strips encircling the top. Mr. Granger exited the limo and walked between the bollards towards the *Stranger Danger.*

Sal stopped him. "Mr. Granger. I'm from US Fish and Wildlife. Sir, we are executing a search warrant on your yacht. We have evidence you have illegally harvested specimens of protected endangered species from Drake's Key."

"The hell you are. Get away from my boat," he yelled. Looking over at me. "Girlie, I know you work at the resort. Get on your phone and call your Boss. Tell him to get his ass down here now!"

I held pepper spray hidden in my left hand. "No sir, I do not work at Drake's—"

Boss Hogg came at me pointing his bulbous finger. He jabbed that finger into my shoulder, "I said now!" as he repeated the jabbing. I saw Vic move towards me.

As I backed away, I lifted my pepper spray and unloaded it into Hogg's purple face. I hit a bollard that made me both twist and fall backwards. The combined motion propelled me onto the hood of the car parked by the bollard. My wrist hit the edge of the hood, but not in a good way.

When I got up Boss Hogg was on his knees with Bad's badass khukuri knife across his overlapping chins. His eyes were squeezed shut. He was coughing up a lung. Tears streamed down his heavy jowls and cheeks. I started to say, "Don't rub your eyes. It just makes it worse," but thought better of it. I waved Vic and Sal over to where Hogg couldn't hear me. "I think my wrist is broken, but I want to get on the ship. Can we cuff him, and all go on the *Stranger Danger*?"

Sal said sure and Vic went to find a makeshift sling for me. Sal cuffed Hogg and laughed, "Boss Hogg, you stepped in the slop today. Assault and battery on a Deputy US Marshal."

"What Marshal?" he coughed.

I leaned in, "Girlie, Mr. Granger. Deputy Marshal girlie, to you." After first aid by Vic, including taping an icebag on my wrist, we all went aboard Hogg's superyacht.

Hank had all the crew and other employees assembled in the grand salon next to the master suite. The woman who sat down next to Granger was the only other passenger. The other task force members combed the ship starting on the second deck.

I noticed two potted fuchsia and dark purple Drake's Candy orchids on the side tables.

Hogg's girlfriend saw me looking at the orchids. "Beautiful, ain't they? Boss Hogg said they was just weeds growing on a tree. I never seen nothing like that, so he brought me some."

"Bobbie Jean, shut your trap," Hogg growled.

"The lady was talking to me," I said. I turned to her. "Got any more?"

"Sure thing, honey. Right by my bed, Wanna see 'em?"

I inclined my head and followed her into the master suite where she closed the door. The room was awash with so many plants I wondered what was left on the island.

Bobbie Jean said, "I was wondering how I was going to get you alone. When I heard it was Fish and Wildlife, I knew it had to be these. Deck two is jam packed full."

"Anything else?" I asked.

"Parrots, jeez they are noisy and messy. I refused to have any of them in here. Check the galley. The ship stopped by your aquaculture pens and I hear lobster is on the menu later tonight. I noticed they were all tagged. The reason I'm undercover is this ship has four marine diesel engines to power it. Only thing is, they have twelve in wooden cases as 'replacements.' I suspect some of the replacements are illegal arms headed to Mexican drug lords. Good to see you again, Allie. Sorry about the arm."

We hugged quickly as I said, "Professional hazard. I'll live. I'm in PR now. Visit when you get a chance."

We walked back into the salon.

Bobbie Jean, "She told me they's real pretty but they's flowers. What kinda flowers don't grow in dirt, sugar?" Hogg glared at his companion who leaned back and shut up.

****

I was admitted to the hospital in St. Croix. I texted Dad and Alderich and called Mom. "I'm scheduled for surgery in three hours. It could have been worse. I think your leg was worse."

Mom flew over at once. She opined, "If it's a clean break it should heal easily. It's not trivial and you'll be in a brace for a few weeks after a cast. Do you get any time off for recuperation? Maybe at Drake's?"

"I have to be here a few days, but I'll ask. How's Dad and Alderich taking the news?"

"I haven't seen either of them since you came crashing into the office yesterday. I'll hunt them down when I get back." She leaned over and kissed my cheek. "I'll be back soon. Text if you need me to bring you anything. Love you."

"Love you too." Since I couldn't eat anything before surgery, I laid my head back to catch a nap as I replayed the thrilling night we had on the *Stranger Danger,* now appearing as scenes of action and satisfaction as I slipped under my fuzzy warm blanket of sleep.

****

Alderich was jumpy. "Ledger, did you get Allie's text?"

"I just saw it. I can't find Rosalie, and my plane is gone. I don't know what that cartoon means though." Ledger sweated. His eyes were slightly bloodshot.

"Cartoon? You mean the emoji?" Ledger shrugged.

"It's called an emoji. That one means 'fingers crossed,' as in 'good luck,' or 'here's hoping.' Now, is Phibe in the office?"

"Who?"

"Phibe. The intern. She might know." The two men hurried to the Boss's office. Phibe sat serenely in Rosalie's chair. She jumped up as the men walked in.

"Phibe, do you—"

"I'm so sorry," the girl stammered. "Don't tell Mrs. Abatsong, please." She was shaking.

Alderich asked, "Do you know where she is—Mrs. Abatsong?"

"She left in Mr. Warren's plane for St. Croix about twenty minutes ago."

The two men left and walked out to the sidewalk. "My speedboat will take an hour to get there. You are coming, aren't you?" Ledger asked.

"No, you're coming with me. My plane is fueled up and ready to go."

"Lead the way," the Boss snapped, now in full "Allie's Dad" mode. Twenty minutes later they were airborne.

Alderich mumbled, almost to himself, "A sprained ankle, giardia, and now this…"

"What did you say?"

"Why did you let her go on this police action? You know what kind of a man Granger is. Who let's their daughter do that?" Alderich asked Ledger in an accusing tone.

"Wait a minute. I didn't let her *do* anything. Do you honestly think I would want her hurt? If that's the case, where's my parachute?"

Alderich glared at Ledger, took in a deep breath, and

said, "I wasn't accusing you of anything. Hold on." He called the St. Croix airport to announce his estimated arrival time.

"Ledger, you got a car in St. Croix at the airport?"

"Yeah, maybe. No, I bet Rosalie took it to the hospital."

"Can you call the driver and have him come pick us up, or do we need a cab waiting?"

"The reception out here isn't always great." He speed-dialed his driver and asked him to meet us at the airport. He settled back. "When did Allie get giardia?" he asked.

Alderich paused. "When we were testing a new hiking foot. We were blazing a trail through the forest towards the mountain. I don't know if you have ever done that, but it gets really hot and humid in there, and there's no breeze.

"That's further out in the boondocks than I go. I do fish the Gut and it's the same way."

"Well...the stream just looked so inviting..." Alderich smirked and looked out his side window. It was quiet in the cockpit. "Do you know the word 'boondocks' comes from Tagalog? It mean 'mountain' in the Philippines."

"Does it now? I'll have to tuck that away for the next trivia contest. Could you tell if the stream was catching any sewage or runoff? If giardia is on the island, I need to fix it before everyone has it. I don't need an epidemic on the island."

"No, but I think I could take your rangers back to the spot if they need to check it out."

"That would be appreciated. Doc treated you both?" Alderich nodded. "And the ankle?"

"This feels like the third degree, Ledger, but it was basketball."

Now it was Ledger's turn to react, so he changed the subject. "How are you handling being here with your parents and Allie at the same time? Have they met her?"

"Yes, they have…and…and they don't approve of her." Alderich frowned as he said this.

Ledgers' hackles rose on the back of his neck. "Why, may I ask?"

"They want me to marry a Catholic."

"I didn't know you two were so serious."

"Neither did we. My mom is always trying to play matchmaker. She has a whole litany of 'must,' can't,' and 'never' associated with my future life. May I ask you a personal question?" Ledger nodded. "Are you and Rosalie divorced or still married?"

Ledger looked out of his passenger side window. "That's a very personal question."

"Yes, I know but I have to figure out a way to get my parents to come around to her."

"We were never married. I found out Rosalie was alive, and I was a dad last May."

"So if Allie talks about her dad in the past tense, that man wasn't you?"

"Probably not. I know she was very close to him, and for that I am thankful."

Alderich pointed out the windshield and picked up the mic. "Ten minutes to landing. Be sure your tray tables are upright, and your seatbelt is buckled," he joked but neither of them laughed.

Chapter 22

Allie

Ledger, Alderich, and Rosalie crossed paths at the entrance to J.F. Luis Hospital. She was standing there looking for Ledger's car when it pulled up in front of her and the men stepped out. They all went in for a cup of coffee.

"For god's sake, don't go and wake her up. Her surgery is in ...," she looked at her wristwatch, "...ninety minutes and she needs the rest.

"How bad is it?" Alderich asked.

"I saw the X-rays and it's not complicated. It's broken but easily fixed."

"What happened?" Ledger asked.

She repeated what Allie told her about Boss Hogg jabbing Allie's shoulder, and her tripping over the bollard and landing on the car hood.

"So Granger AKA Boss Hogg didn't actually break the wrist himself?"

"Apparently not. But he's being charged with assaulting a Deputy US Marshal while engaged in her official duties right off the bat. That could be real prison time and a large chunk of change." She glanced at Ledger and added, "Well for most of us."

"That's *all* he's being charged with?" Ledger asked through clenched teeth.

"Oh, no, no, no! I'm not sure they're even through

adding the charges all up. The stuff he took is endangered *and* protected. He transported it all across international borders, so international trafficking occurred as well. Federal laws, international laws, why he even poached some of your lobsters from the aquaculture farm on Drake's. It's complicated and Allie was under the influence of a painkiller when she was telling me all this."

Alderich said, "I hope you guys stop her the next time."

"Whoa, Alderich. What did you just say?" Rosalie barked.

"I mean, you had to have known it was dangerous and what was going to happen. Why didn't you—"

Rosalie's face lit up. "Listen here, mister. I raised a smart, decent, brave woman. I raised her to be as independent as I could because lord knows the men on this planet are the source of most of the trouble. I don't tell my daughter *what* to do. I give her *my* opinion *when* she asks for it. She is an adult. I trust *her* decisions, and this is her *job*. Her job! Got that?"

Ledger put his hand on her arm, "Rosalie, he didn't—"

She jerked her arm away. "Don't 'Rosalie' me. If you two don't change your tune before she wakes up, don't even show your faces in Allie's room. She doesn't need your attitude or your condescension and neither do I." She turned and stomped out of the room.

"I'm taking the car." she yelled over her shoulder. "You two are grounded!"

****

Allie's bed rolled back into her room late in the afternoon. Even the nurses were impressed. Someone bought out every florist on the island. Her private room was transformed into a jungle of green leaves, yellow tinged palm fronds, and orchids of every color. In the corner was a large "Get Well" poster on an easel. Alderich and Ledger sat by her bed waiting as she started licking her lips and making small, short noises.

"Alderich…," she said, "…you're here."

"How did you know?" he asked as he kissed her ear.

"My nose still works," she purred. She inhaled deeply. "Why don't you just—"

Alderich cut her off. "Uh, babe. Open your eyes. You have company."

Allie partially raised her heavy lids. "Daddy," she said. "…you came." She held out her uninjured hand and slowly said, "Take me for a ride in the convertible."

Ledger chuckled and moved a chair close to the bed. He took her hand. "My pleasure, sweetheart. Look! It's a beautiful night. There's not a cloud in the sky, and the moon has already set. Here we go, turning left onto the track. There's a million stars out tonight just for you. Ooh! Did you see that shooting star? Make a wish…"

She closed her eyes and leaned her head on Alderich who sat on her bed savoring her trust and the perfume of her soft red curls.

****

Hank Ivy from Fish and Wildlife Service came by two days later. "Allie, just checking in on you, girl." He handed me a chocolate shake and I almost kissed him for it.

"Thanks. Hospital food is as boring as the paint in the halls. This is great." I sucked as hard as I could, but nothing came up the straw.

He pulled out a long handled plastic spoon in

cellophane. "Just in case. I can never get up enough suction either." He sat beside my bed, unwrapped the spoon, and handed it to me.

"Speaking of which you should have heard the sucking sound Boss Hogg made when we explained that by sending his boat loaded with his stolen flora and fauna to Tortola it left US territory and entered British territory—it was beautiful."

"And the service boat in Puerto Rico? You got it too?"

"Even longer than the yacht. We confiscated it, the helicopter, and the minisub. Found a tag from a Drake's lobster in the sub, so it was used for poaching, and we can prove it. The video they took is icing on the cake. There were orchids and parrots on both boats. If only the parrots could talk, we'd have taken a victim statement."

We both cracked up.

"How about Bobbie Jean?"

"She was arrested—"

"But she's—"

"—undercover, I know. We arrested her in front of Hogg, so we didn't blow it for her. She's already back in the states, and she was right about the weapons. All in all, this April is one huge win for law and order. Hogg will be in the federal hog pen for life."

I was spooning the shake into my mouth and trying to avoid a brain freeze when Alderich came in with burgers. *Now that's a big win in my book.*

****

Before I knew it, the end of Drake's season was here. Vasily Raskolnikov signed up to stay for two weeks at Drake's, the last week of April and the first week of May: Chairs week. He was due to arrive just about dark.

His yacht *Oilwell* sent a message requesting a pier-side berth for the first week.

"Boss, The *Oilwell* showed up right on time, sailed into Drake's harbor, and backed into the berth. After tying up and checking in, nothing happened," my harbor master reported as Rosalie and I awaited the arrival of our daughter at Drake's resort airport.

Unusual but not unheard of. "Clarify what you mean by 'nothing happened,' " I asked.

"Just that, Boss. No one has been off the ship since it docked. No one has been seen out on deck moving about or sitting. Only the required in-port lights are on."

"Any room service orders go out?"

"Not that we saw."

"No visitors from shore or another ship?"

He shook his head.

"Okay. Let me know if anything changes."

"Aye, aye, Boss."

Moments later, Allie stepped off my private plane. "Dad, I love your Friday night commuter transportation. I can be here faster that I can drive to my apartment." She hugged me and planted a warm kiss on my hairy cheek. I loved it. Her mom got the same.

I picked up her overnight suitcase and her hockey equipment bag that she seemed to carry more than a purse. "Come on out of the heat. We waited dinner for you."

"I could definitely eat." As we walked down the hall towards our apartment Allie stopped and said, "I want to show you how my dribbling has improved, and you won't believe my drag flicking move. It's lethal."

I took a call from the front desk as she rummaged through her equipment bag. She got out a stick and dropped several balls onto the carpet.

"Boss, Mr. Raskolnikov called to ask if you would meet with him. He says you have never met so could you meet him at your office to talk."

Never met, huh. I pushed the panic button in my pocket to call Vic and Bad, the two best security guys I've ever had. "Sure. Is he on the way here?"

"Yes. Two minutes tops."

That's not time enough to get my Glock. "Stay here, both of you."

Rosalie said, "I'll take Allie's suitcase to her room. Be right back."

Shit! No time to argue with her. I need to make my stand now. "Stay here, Allie. Please, baby." I moved forward down the wide hall keeping myself between Allie to intercept the ersatz Vasily Raskolnikov.

They must have run here because in a matter of seconds two burly men in ill-fitting Eastern European suits approached me. I was only expecting "Raskolnikov." Since I had met him in Baku at a conference several years ago, I knew what he looked like. He had sprouted a new beard but kept his long hair according to our last conversation. The man approaching me was clean-shaven and bald and definitely not Vasily. He stopped eight feet away. "Mr. Warren? I am Raskolnikov. Happy to meet you."

I held up my hand for the men to stay put. "Sir, you are not Vasily Raskolnikov."

"*Nyet?* But you are Boss, yes? You are the man I come to do business with."

"Where is Vasily?" My knife was in my hand but still in my pocket.

He shrugged his shoulder in a disinterested manner.

"That is not important."

"To me, it is. If you want to leave here, you will answer me. Where is Vasily Raskolnikov?"

"Alive. Now we do business. I come for ten million."

Bounty hunters. What was their connection to Vasily? "Ten million. For what?" *Xin was in this somehow, or his contract on my life was.*

"Your head. Xin pay us to take it or you pay us not to take. Easier you pay us now. We do not care."

"That's pretty bold. Does Xin know you're here?" I was stalling for time. *Where is Vic and Bad?* "Is Xin even alive. I heard he was sick."

"If Xin die, then you pay us now to leave. Or we take your head for free since we take trouble to come."

"So another bounty hunter can still show up? I don't think so."

"Okay," he shrugged, "We collect from Xin." He made a quick step forward now brandishing a knife.

As the bounty hunter moved towards me, I heard, "Dad, drop to the floor." I hit the deck.

Wham! I looked up to see my attacker on his knees in front of me. His hands covered his broken and profusely bleeding nose dripping down the front of his shirt. A bloody field hockey ball rolled down his paunch of a stomach and dropped onto the floor.

"Down!" Allie ordered again.

I hugged the floor even closer.

Wham! A second hockey ball hit him square in the right eye with a cracking sound, and he fell over, his hands covering his bleeding face.

The second man abandoned his partner and turned. He ran down the hall in the opposite direction dropping a sack and machete along the way. I heard a whooshing sound from behind me. The second man lurched forward hitting his face on the stone wall at the end of the short hall and fell to the floor. Neither man moved, but the first man was moaning and swearing.

I got up and went to check on the second assassin. He had a weird round thing with a handle sticking out of his back. "What the hell…?"

Rosalie came up beside me. "It's my hunga munga. It's an African throwing knife, a wedding present. Hard to miss with three blades." She went to the man and checked for a pulse. Then she put her foot on the man's back and proceeded to rock her knife back and forth until it came loose and pulled out.

I stood there with my mouth hanging open and my eyes agog.

Rosalie shrugged. "What? You said I could bring it."

I could *not* process what just happened. Allie? Rosalie?

Vic ran up, took a quick look around, and handcuffed the first man. Then he said, "Mr. Raskolnikov is safe. These guys and three others boarded the *Oilwell* at sea. They took over the ship with the help of two of the crew. Is everyone here okay?"

Regaining my senses I replied, "I think so. Where's Bad?"

"On the *Oilwell*. His khukuri tasted blood tonight. I'll clean this mess up, Boss." Vic leaned into Rosalie and said softly, "Nice job. Practice *does* make perfect."

"Uhm, Dad, I have an idea."

I needed an idea about then. "I'm listening." I removed my hand from my pocket.

"Let's assume that these men were here to assault you, or more likely kill you, during an act of extortion. That's what I heard anyway."

"Okay. Then what does that get us?"

"As far as I can see they had already committed an act of piracy and kidnapping on the high seas, much more serious crimes than extortion and assault."

"Possibly, so I'll grant you that." I didn't know what my law-abiding daughter was getting to. *Was she abetting a crime, or would she have to arrest me for one?*

"Mister second banana over there was killed in an act of self-defense. He most surely would have your head in his bag if Mom and I hadn't acted. I felt, and I suspect Mom did too, I felt that these guys wouldn't leave any witnesses in any case. Nothing to adjudicate there, right?"

"Just 'attend' to the body." I looked at Vic. "And the top banana with the broken nose?"

"At sea, a captain judges mutiny and piracy. Perhaps the real captain Raskolnikov, or his ship's captain, would assume that role."

I considered what happened, what the outcome might have been if my ladies hadn't stepped in, and what might have happened if they just stood by. I couldn't help but put my hand on my throat as I ran through Allie's argument.

"Sounds good to me. Vic, take thug number one to the *Oilwell* and explain the situation to our guest Vasily Raskolnikov. Help him in any way he requires."

Allie added, "Vic, fingerprints, photos of tats, DNA samples, please."

The corners of Vic's mouth turned up a notch.

"I said fingerprints, not actual fingers, Vic!"

I stood in true awe of my ladies. There was only one thing left to do. "Rosalie, Allie, let's wash up and go to dinner. I hear there's Baked Alaska for dessert."

****

The *Oilwell* sailed out of our harbor as we got to dessert. We didn't hear a thing from it except for the normal coming and going chatter. As I sat watching the harbor the next morning and sipping my first coffee of the day I saw my own personal boat leave. Vic was at the helm. *Going fishing?*

The *Oilwell* returned after four more days as if nothing had happened, The best I could do was hit reset and go on with the few days left in this season.

Chapter 23

The Scorecard

This was it, the first week of May. The end of the season and the Chairs. Five more days and I could relax if I don't count the cricket match. I had an interviewer again this year for a 'proposed' book about Drake's, and I have given him the following list and notes on each Player.

Player One: Mr. Bernardo Maurizio Fabian Ormanni, a retiring New York business owner. He has known me for many years, but other than this not much seems to be available in the public record. He is sixty-three years old. Likes to dance, read, and bet on horse races. Two adult children. Speaks English and Italian. Police record unknown. Fingerprints on file for licensing to practice law in New York. No known social security number. (Odd since it would be needed for licensing.) No driver's license. Appears to have several passports under different names. In divorce proceedings. Has one New York Supreme Court Judge, one New York Senator, and three rare book authorities on speed dial. Estimated net worth thirty-nine million.

Player Two: Senhor Davi Miguel Blanco Moran, a Brazilian cosmetics king, and avowed tree hugger. Funds a personal initiative to preserve the rainforest through sustainable methods. Partnered with me in an experiment to grow cupuaçu, a Brazilian tree, on Drake's as a new economic opportunity for my residents. I ran the idea past my own arborist and forester to be sure they wouldn't endanger our native rainforest. I've allocated two test areas of ten acres each and so far, the trees seem to be adapting but we are still trying to introduce a local insect to the trees for pollination. In divorce proceedings. Four adult children. Speaks Portuguese, Spanish, and English. No police record. No fingerprints on file. He is either fifty-nine or sixty-one years old, and records vary. Has David Beckham on speed dial. Estimated net worth 402 million.

Player Three: Ms. Bunnie Snuggle, the current owner of a men's magazine empire, and a recent widow. Age thirty-nine. Her late husband exploited her from the time she dropped out of school at fourteen. She is well known to a certain type of magazine reader. Note attached photographs. Originally from Arkansas, where she started an initiative to provide better education to all elementary school students three years ago. The Snuggles were frequent visitors to Drake's. Speaks English. Hobbies are cross-stitching, crocheting, and knitting. No children. No known police record. No fingerprints on file. No driver's license. Has the Secretary of Education on speed dial. Estimated net worth 613 million.

Player Four: Ms. Leona Bassett Butler, the sole owner of an extensive pharmaceutical empire. Age forty-six. Also a recent widow anxious to claim her husband's portfolio, but she must divest of her own assets to claim his within a year. Admits to being motivated by greed. Started as a nutritionist. Is a licensed pharmacist in the US. No children. Three stepchildren who are estranged. Speaks English. No hobbies outside of gambling.

Investigated three years ago by the IRS for questionable accounting practices. Outcome pending. Released affidavits from investigation redacted. Fingerprints on file. Has several high-priced lawyers on retainer and on speed dial. Estimated net worth 1.7 billion.

Player Five: Mr. Leonard Flatz, currently known as Julian Denzel. Age thirty-one. An absolutely brilliant guy. Can do anything in a company. Founder of Afrodesiac, a line of products aimed at the African American market but expanding into Africa next year. He aspires to be a female through the Chairs. (Is frightened of gender reassignment surgery.) Makes YouTube videos on applying makeup and fashion. Speaks English, Spanish, Swahili. No police record. No driver's license. Hold several federal-level security clearances. Fingerprints on file in several locations. Never married. No children. Estimated net worth 516 million.

Player Six: Monsieur Alain Gaston Fleury, owner of a world-famous line of fragrances and designer retail goods. Named sexiest man in France six years running. He speaks French and Italian but doesn't speak English comfortably. Collects African art and weapons and seduces women. Ballroom dances at professional level. Water skis competitively but does not know how to swim. Follows Monaco football and financially supports the sport in Monaco, where he lives for most of the year. Frequently seen with actresses, models, and celebrities. Divorced. No children. No police record. No fingerprints on file. Has president of France on speed dial along with three French fashion houses. Estimated net worth 478 million.

Player Seven: Mr. Vasily Yakov Raskolnikov. Oil

tycoon from Southwestern Asia. He is in training to become a Russian Orthodox monk after the Chairs. Former freestyle wrestling champion in Azerbaijan. Former hobby of racing camels as owner and jockey. Avid chess player. Travels by yacht when possible. (Owns two large yachts.) Speaks Russian, Ukrainian, Arabic, English, Azerbaijani, and Turkish. No known organized crime connections or police record. No fingerprints on file. Widower. No children. Has Russian and Azerbaijani presidents on speed dial. Estimated net worth three billion.

Player Eight: Mr. Harry Huang, recovered nicely from yet another seasonal strain of flu. Widower. Estranged from son. He is a Canadian-born investment banker and author of several bestselling self-help books on investing. Part-owner of a Canadian professional hockey team. Likes and plays basketball and ice hockey. Was a circus clown in China for five years. Speaks English, Mandarin, Cantonese, Japanese. Hobbies are nature photographer and close-up magic. Distant cousin of earlier Drake's guest Lau (recently deceased.) No police record. No fingerprints on record. Has Jackie Chan on speed dial. Estimated net worth is a minimum of 750 million to 2 billion.

Not a bad mix, after all. No matter how the Chairs play out, I'm the big winner as usual. *Why don't I feel as satisfied as I usually do?*

****

"What shall I call you?" I asked.

"I think Alan would be fine, Boss," the interviewer told me.

These interviews were becoming a yearly feature at Drake's. The Chairs was in four days, so this interviewer must be busy. "You got my notes, I think. And the story hasn't changed since last year?" *In case any guests asked me what was going on, I needed to have my story straight.*

"I am collecting stories about Drake's Key for a future book, no names to be published."

"So no information with Players' names or outcomes from winners or losers in the Chairs. Good. Alan, may I ask a personal question? Your facial…" I tried not to look at the scars.

"The scars? Real or not? Safer for you not to know."

"And those hearing aids?"

"What hearing aids?"

"Okay. Let me introduce you to my new General Manager, Mr. Singh. I've already briefed him on your function here. Got your eye on anyone in particular, Marshal?"

"Again, better you don't know, better you don't call me Marshal. Just carry on as usual."

****

The day I was dreading was here: the cricket match. Last year's match turned into a full-blown spectacle. All we were missing were floats and zoo animals. This year I limited it to three hours. How much chaos could happen in that time frame, I thought arrogantly.

Our teams this year were new to the regional league. The Nighthawks, called the Hawks by fans, and the Oystercatchers, called the Crackers by their fans, referring to their practice of cracking whelk shells to eat the resident sea slugs.

The stands were already full, the food concessions up and running, and the noise at a respectable level. Tiny, Bobby, and June were deployed around me and a

Chinese clown was juggling for Rosalie and Allie. I got a call from Vic just as Scott called the coin toss. Juan was already waiting for me and June at the field parking lot.

"Vic, I'm on my way. What's the problem?"

"It's the elephants."

"What elephants? The wooden ones in the resort?"

"No, sir. Real live elephants."

"How many and whose are they?" *I spoke too soon about circus animals.*

"Two. The Indian owner of the Nighthawks owns them. They've been cleared by USDA for entry, and they've been unloaded from a private superyacht. They even got a truck to transport them and it's on its way to the cricket match now."

"They're bringing them here! If they are legally here, what's the problem? I'm almost there. Wait until I arrive."

"Bring some boots or a change of footwear, Boss." He hung up.

As Juan stopped by the dock, I noticed one of my small Bobcat front loaders at work. Vic waved me over to it. I didn't have any boots in the vehicle and before I could ask Juan to fetch me a pair from the harbormaster, I was up to my ankles in the problem.

"Crap," I said. The area around the elephants was just that: pounds and pounds of...elephant poop.

Vic pursed his lips trying to not laugh. "So according to the elephant trainers these babies produce about 200 pounds a day of this stuff."

"What do they do with it?"

"They shovel it overboard at sea."

"This stuff could have live seeds that can overtake our protected plants. Have the Bobcats shovel it back onto the yacht where the elephants came from. Didn't they need a permit for that too? And call the resort, get that Bobcat ready to shovel at the cricket match."

"A permit for dung? Maybe. I know Barbados requires one but that's not US territory."

"Call Fish and Wildlife in St. Thomas. They might know." I looked down at my ruined shoes. "Anything else?"

"Yeah. The owner of the Oystercatchers is British, and that's his yacht over there at pier three unloading." I jumped from a loud animal roar. Then Vic said, "What about the lions?"

My phone rang and I answered Rosalie's call. "Skip, where are you? The high school kids worked hard on their floats and the halftime show is in thirty minutes."

"What halftime show?"

"They wanted to surprise you..."

"I need to stop by my apartment, but I'll be there before it's over." I turned back to Vic. "If they have a lion permit, okay. But ask F&W about that poop too. They aren't vegetarians so I'm betting it's not a problem. And they better be in cages! Juan, let's go." I dropped my shoes and socks in a trash can and got in the car.

****

In spite of all our planning, that cricket match pretty much ended the same as last years' as one heck of a party, with two particular exceptions. I learned that lions pee a lot and can aim it at will. Scratch one suit I'll never wear again.

Led by a Chinese clown expertly juggling a handful of cricket balls, the elephants were paraded across the cricket field during the halftime show pooping all the way. The players, guests, and locals were in the same shoe situation as I was. Rosalie promised our residents we'd replace those shoes; those shoes we'd gifted to them for Christmas just three months earlier.

As we surveyed the wreckage of the cricket field I asked, "Where did we go wrong?"

Rosalie responded with, "I have no idea, but would you shower and disinfect yourself before dinner, please," as she sidled away from me.

I felt another talk with Scott coming on.
****

I saw the interviewer as I entered the conference room. He rose and extended his hand. I wondered if I needed to speak up as he wore hearing aids.

"Good morning. Mr. Huang. I am Alan. Please be seated. Would you like anything, a cup of tea perhaps?" A waiter stepped into the room.

"Tea would be appreciated. What do you wish to know?" The waiter took our order.

"I guess first is did you pick number eight, or did Mr. Warren?"

"Neither. It was my high school and college number for basketball and ice hockey. You were probably expecting because it is my lucky kua number, weren't you?"

"Honestly, yes. I understand a Player last year chose his kua number. Hockey moves too fast for me, but I do like basketball," Alan shared.

"Same for me. I'm too old to keep up with the hockey anymore. I did enjoy the cricket game, but I suspect it was the carnival atmosphere more than anything," I confessed.

"Drake's does know how to throw a party," Alan said in agreement. "Why did you come for two weeks?

Besides the Chairs, is there something else that catches your attention?"

"Besides the obvious change in scenery? The chance to drive the winter chill from my bones? What better reasons are there? I have a habit that when I vacation, or get away from it all, I like it to be a different locale or weather as much as possible. If I had my choice, the Chairs would be in December or January. Nothing cures a winter blizzard better that a warm tropical beach and the clicking of a roulette wheel."

"Mr. Huang, what will you do if you lose?"

"I have many relatives. We take care of our elderly. I will spend the rest of my life in a small room overlooking the city, shivering in the winter, too warm in the temperate summer, counting the hours until my next meal tray arrives, or the lights are turned out. I will wonder how many more times my birthday passes without a single visitor or card wishing me a long life or expressing gratitude for their current privileged existence."

"And if you transfer to a different body?"

"I hope and pray for that. If it is a younger physique, I shall enjoy it to the fullest. Wine, women, or men, and song as the bard said, in as many far flung reaches of the world as possible. I can always make money, but I have had very little 'life' in my time. I shall greet death by living life to the fullest. A toast, Alan." We held up our teacups. "As your Union Admiral probably said, 'Damn the torpedoes. Full speed ahead.' " We clinked our cups together and drained them.

###

"Hello, Boss." Beryl said.

"Hello, Beryl. How are Tom and Curtis?...And the

babies? Will you be day tripping this week?...That's great. I have an interesting lady for you to meet. Now, what's up?"

"It's Mr. Huang, Boss. His financials are five star. Absolutely no problems, but I came across something you might find interesting."

"Okay, shoot."

"Mr. Huang and Mr. Lau—yes, that Mr. Lau—are *first* cousins. Not so distant as he said, is it? Be careful. It may be fine; it may not be fine."

"You're right. I'll be careful. See you soon, and thanks."

Did I get suckered? Is Huang looking for revenge for his cousin's horrible death?

****

I put my new sign on the front of my desk: *Ici, on parle français.* We are welcoming a French player for the Chairs. I was told his English is minimal. I figured I could carry on a friendly conversation with my West African French accent.

Yvette walked in with a very suave-looking gentleman who looked to be in his mid-forties. He was the epitome of understated elegance, dressed in hand-tailored tropical attire, perfectly manicured, surrounded by a whiff of the world's most expensive men's cologne: *PourQuoi.* Monsieur Fleury, no doubt.

Yvette glanced around. "Is the Boss in his office?" She had yet to call me Rosalie or Mrs. Abatsong much less start with a civil greeting. "He wanted to meet Monsieur Fleury in person to pick his number."

"Yes, I know. He will—"

Monsieur Fleury noticed some personal items behind me on display. "*Mademoiselle, magnifique,* " he said as he pointed to my African mask.

"Merci beaucoup," I replied. I returned to Yvette, "He should only be a few minutes."

"But I have much to do in the casino. We will have to come back."

"That's not necessary," I said. I looked at the man and pointed to my sign. He saluted me and said words to Yvette who left without as much as a fare-thee-well.

Monsieur Fleury turned his eyes to me, and I was startled. I'd never seen eyes such a dark blue. It was unsettling. It was obvious that his reputation as a lady killer was not over stated.

Chapter 24

Rosalie

"Phibe, I'll be in the Boss's office with our guest, but I know you will be fine."

Leaving the door open, we sat and chatted in French for twenty minutes. He said my accent was charming. He was fascinated by my mask from Cameroon. I told him it had been a wedding gift, hand made by a leading artist from the Fang tribe, a cousin of my late husband's. The face on the mask was mine. I told him about my hunga munga and promised to show it to him later as he was a collector of African art, antiquities, and weapons.

Monsieur Fleury told me about his business dealings in West Africa. After making me promise to have lunch with him today, Gaston left, kissing my hand. It was years since the last man kissed my hand, or even my cheek. I realized how much I missed it.

As I sat down, I saw Skipper leaning on the doorframe.

"Who was that?" he asked.

"Who was who?" I replied, not meeting his eyes.

"That man who was mauling your hand, that's who. What did he want?"

"Really, Mr. Warren. As we say in Texas 'this ain't your first rodeo.' You know perfectly well what he wanted. Don't act coy."

"Yeah, I guess I do. So who was he?"

"Monsieur Alain Gaston Fleury."

"Fleury? Is he coming back? I still had some questions."

"No, I don't think so. I talked to him, and he is playing because he never wanted in the family business, and now no one else will take it over. They all have trust funds to live on if he loses. He definitely does not want to transfer to another body but understands that is a risk involved in this game. If he ends up as a woman, he plans to commit suicide. He wants number six, if it's available. If there's anything else you need to know, I'll ask him at lunch. I'll pass this info on Gaston to your interviewer. Anything else?"

"Since when do you speak French?"

"Since I was married to a man who spoke it as his first language." I went back to my email to Drake's head seamstress as to alterations to the dress I was wearing to the Chairs.

I've had a year to decide, but I only have a few days to make…my…move.

****

I was relieved when Rosalie interviewed Mr. Fleury yesterday. I can't order a croissant much less carry on a conversation in French. My next interviewee speaks English, but with a Brooklyn accent. I heard the doorknob turn.

A man with dark hair graying at the temples entered. "You Alan?"

I recognized him and I was puzzled. The Boss never had anyone from an organized crime family come to Drake's. Why now? *I'll need to be careful with my questions.* "Yes, I'm Alan. Please come in."

He sat down across the table from me and poured

himself a cup of coffee. He pulled a plate over with tiramisu on it and took a fork.

"Mr. Ormanni?"

"Yeah." He took a bite of the Italian dessert, and a "not bad" look crossed his face.

"How are you enjoying the island so far?"

"It's not the Jersey shore, and I can't find a decent pizza anywhere." He smiled as he took another bite.

"Isn't that part of getting away? Here's a hint. Sneak over to the staff snack bar. Pizza straight from New York. They serve an authentic spaghetti and meatballs that I favor."

His mouth was full of tiramisu, but he finally said, "And it's too quiet. I can't sleep." His dark undereye circles proved it.

"I've heard that from other guests. Have the concierge add 'Sounds of the City' to your suite audio collection. You can adjust the sound level to suit yourself, and it will play all night."

"Hey, thanks. I'll try that. Any other ideas?" I hadn't taken any notes yet. *I'll have to check the tape later.*

"What are you doing for fun or exercise?"

"Me exercise? I do like to do a little soft shoe to keep the joints from getting too stiff."

"Perfect. How about a little disco? Call the dance studio and ask for Carrie."

"Hey, thanks again but aren't you *supposed* to interview *me*?"

"Yes sir. I understand you are a retired businessman. What business were you in?"

"Mostly construction, waste management, eco-energy, and real estate."

He even said it with a straight face. I wrote down

'the usual' on my notepad. "Do you have any plans to keep busy in retirement?" His left eyebrow lifted ever so slightly. "I only ask because I interview so many people who don't have a plan, and they die from the boredom."

"Oh, yeah, I guess that could happen if you live that long. I plan to open an antiquarian bookstore. I already found a shop. I'd rather not say anymore until it's ready to open. I have been to a couple of antiquarian book conventions and started to collect my stock and learn the ropes." He finished his cake and helped himself to my untouched piece.

"What caught your attention to that topic? Are you an avid reader?"

"I am. Always have been. I discovered growing up that staying in my room or hiding in the library was the best way to avoid a beating or a stabbing. I didn't grow up in a shady suburb but in a shady section of town. Pawn shops and drug dealers outnumbered the churches and cops.

"I looked white since my dad was Italian and I've always passed for white, and that made me a target even though I was biracial. I have never disclosed that before." He paused and tilted his head. "That actually felt liberating but keep it to yourself.

"Anyway, the average age for Black men in the ghetto is twenty-eight. I planned on raising that average. I made it. You won't put that in the book, will you? I can't divulge it as a part of my divorce agreement. The wife is embarrassed as many bigots are."

"So true. What you divulged is just between us. Did you bring a good book to read?"

He snickered. "No. The juiciest temptation for me here is Ledger's collection of first editions and rare books. I'm usually the only one in there so it's peaceful and quiet. I don't put on any weight by indulging in that."

"Do you have some topics you're more interested in than others?"

"Yeah. I like the work of the early Greeks who were the 'father' or the first to write or do certain things. Euclid was the father of geometry, Aristotle started the work on the scientific method, and Herodotus was a traveler and wrote what he saw like a travel guide and a historian all rolled into one."

"Do you read Greek?"

"I do. I am amazed to see how the basis of so much knowledge, so much politics, and much critical thinking even today traces back to them. More people might better appreciate them if they had worn trousers rather than sheets, though."

I couldn't help but laugh at his fashion declaration. "Will your plan change if you lose?"

"No one cares what a book seller looks like. Even if I have to trade bodies, that's still true. Either way I'll still love books and reading and be as far away from my former 'business interests' as I can."

What better disguise could he have? Much better than witness protection.

"Now let me ask you a question," Bennie the Jet said.

"Sure."

"When that book of yours get published, you will send me a first edition, won't you?"

I stretched out my hand to shake and said, "You can bet on it."

He left and I ducked out through the Maze to find a piece of tiramisu for myself and a strong cup of coffee.

I just shook hands with the infamous mafioso Bennie the Jet and lived to tell about it.

****

Vic commented, "Rosalie, I have to admit, I am looking forward to seeing Beryl today and her husbands, as we call him. I think she ended up with the best of two worlds: Tom's mind in Curtis's body."

I asked, "How is that the best, Vic?"

"Tom was the brains of the brothers, but Curtis was the brawn, if you will, and the heart for that matter. So when the brothers transferred in the Gizmo…"

"I get it. And she was in love with both of them?"

"Yes, without a doubt. She still is even though Curtis was killed in prison."

"I've got my swimsuit on and I'm ready for the beach. The cooler with the lobster salad is in the cart. I can't wait to meet them all."

"Yes, and the champagne. Let's go."

Vic waved as we neared our beach rendezvous location. "Beryl. Curtis. It's good to see you again." Vic gave Beryl a genuine but respectful hug and another to Tom with a handshake.

I stepped forward. "I'm Rosalie Abatsong, I—"

Beryl reached out and took my hand. "We know who you are. Come and get in the shade. You'll burn with that fair skin. Vic, you didn't tell me she was from the south."

Curtis took the cooler from Vic and headed to the table where a small treasure chest sat.

As Beryl and I unloaded the food, the men uncorked the champagne. "None for me," she said. "Just iced tea."

We all took a plate and the food was delicious. We toasted the three of them, "To Beryl, to Curtis, and to

Tom."

I said, "I heard you helped Ledger set up the original accounting systems."

"Yes, I did, and I do the accounting paperwork for the Chairs and Players. Boss has asked me to start planning the systems for the new apparel company Allie and Scott have created."

"That sounds exciting." I noticed she wasn't eating lobster, just nibbling on the crackers. I had a mother's hunch.

Curtis passed around a small photo album of their two children. Vic lingered over their photos. *Maybe he's just an old softie for kids.* The time flew by until Curtis started packing up the picnic. "This was swell, but Beryl wants to take a nap before we snorkel and leave. Thank you both for lunch."

Beryl hugged me as I whispered, "Congratulations on the new baby."

She whispered back, "You're the only one who knows yet, and of course the husbands." She started to turn but said, "I also set up the trusts for you and Allie. I'm happy to put a face to your voice."

Trusts for me and Allie? What? This was news to me. Why haven't I seen it in the budget spreadsheets? Did Allie know about this?

****

Davi Miguel Blanco Moran. That's a lot of names. I was worried he might not show up. He was here for most of the season but spent his time away from the resort. I used my time reviewing his background and the questions I wanted to ask.

Moran was late. The door opened without fanfare and in came a tall dark-haired man graying at the temples who sweated profusely.

"Mr. Moran?" I offered him a glass of water.

He drank it at once and mopped his face and neck. "Yes. I am Moran. Call me Davi." He sat and fanned his face.

"Would you care for some maracuja?"

"You have maracuja?"

I pushed a dish of the Brazilian passionfruit custard towards him. "I sampled it already. It tastes like seconds whatever it is."

"Seconds?"

"Sorry. That means I need a second helping. It tastes like creamy rich grapefruit to me."

"Yes. That is real maracuja." He finished his treat. "Are there seconds?"

"Yes indeed." I spooned more into our bowls and refilled his water.

"Davi, you look like you have been working more than enjoying a vacation."

"Yes, that is right. I hope Mr. Warren told you about our experiment with cupuaçu trees. Its scientific name is *theobroma grandiflorum.* It is native to Amazonian rainforests. We planted twenty acres of saplings in November, and I am here about half of my time. Of course I am here now to play in the Chairs, as I think you know."

"So how is the experiment going? Any results yet?" I took notes as he talked.

"Yes and no. We lost some trees to the storm at Christmas. Trees on the leeward side get more rain but that was expected. In Brazil, the trees grow mixed in with other rainforest trees so we need to plant a few in the natural rainforest, if we can get permission. Since the trees don't produce fruit for five to six years this is still very early in our experiment. I will be here much in the future for the trees."

"I did read up on them. The fruit is versatile as a food, it provides a lot of nutrition, and a fat similar to cocoa butter that can be used in cosmetics and skin products."

"Yes. But surely you didn't ask me here to talk about my trees."

"No sir. I am curious why people take part in the Chairs. It is such an extreme gamble and affects other people, such as spouses and children."

"I cannot say for others but extreme is what I feel I must do. I was born into a very poor family. My father sold me when I was but three. That is extreme, wouldn't you agree?"

I was speechless. That detail was not in the Boss's notes. "Yes, it is." How could a father sell his own son?

"I will not say what happened, but I knew good, and I knew evil. I knew kindness as I also felt pain. I learned all I could to please certain people, and to stay alive, but I also learned what I thought would serve me when I was no longer young and inconsequential.

"The family that purchased me had three nannies who taught me to read and to write, to speak in an educated manner, to do the maths and to take care of myself. But the people who helped me the most were the gardeners."

"Gardeners? How did they help you?"

"You see my owner collected exotic plants from the rainforest. He took me with him, but only for his own diversion. When he was out collecting or sleeping the gardeners took me into the rainforest and taught me all the plants and trees. They showed me the animals and the insects and everything that lived there."

"That sounds great for a kid."

"It was, but they did not stop there. They showed me the place of everything and what it could be used for, how to find and collect the honey from bees, when to collect each fruit or nut. I learned how to protect myself and what to use if I need a treatment. I was never hungry there. I could always make my own shelter if I needed to sleep at night or escape from the rain."

"That must have been a powerful feeling."

"Yes, but the day came that I was turned out into the streets by my owner. I celebrated my freedom. From that point I built up business knowledge until here I am. Very tired. Looking for a simple life again." He looked at his watch. "I am sorry, but I must go. I have another meeting for a vocabulary lesson and lunch."

"Vocabulary? For what?"

"I plan to expand my trees into Africa. Senhora Rosalie is a kind lady I met here who is teaching me words in French and English. For the maracuja I say '*Obrigado.*' In English it means 'Thank you.' " He left as unceremoniously as he came after finishing the remaining maracuja.

That guy was a survivor. He turned a horrendous start in life into a meaningful life and goals. I wished him luck. Did he say "Rosalie?" I forgot to follow up on that comment.

Chapter 25

The Interviewer

"I may be a cupcake, but I'm no pushover, Alan." I was on the defensive with my first question with Leonard Flatz AKA Julian Denzel.

"Julian, I didn't mean to insinuate anything. I was just curious why you want to change your sex but not through surgery."

"The *what* is a fair question, but the *why* is deeply personal. Move on, please."

"Of course. I'm told you are quite gifted. With your intellect, have you ever considered academia? Would a life of research and publishing satisfy you?"

"Who knows what the future may bring? Right now I'm interested in systems in general. How they work and how to make them more efficient."

"Could you give me an example?"

Leonard AKA Julian considered for a moment. "Without further questions on it, I'll give you a personal example. I like to say 'There's always a system. Figure out how it works and then make it work for you.' I spent considerable time investigating the current medical treatments for a sex change. It is a lifetime commitment to medication and care. That's time I'm not willing to spend when I could be doing more meaningful work. Then I found an alternative system: the Chairs. What's the worst that can happen?"

"Offhand I'd say you lose your fortune, and you don't transfer."

"Right. But I can always make money and come back in a couple of years. Try, try again, but no long-term commitment to surgery and pills or injections. I have confidence that if it's not this week, it will be another."

Now that's optimism. "Are you a hands-on type of guy? Are you equally interested in say engineering as well as business systems?"

"I think you'll get a preview of that during the Chairs. I love tinkering in my workshop."

"Will you describe to me your educational background?"

"My father was a military man who deployed abroad in 1988. His death is still classified so I don't know where or why. However, educational funding for the children of men like my father was available. My mom and I used every bit of it we could find. My mother said I walked early, but I wasn't much of a talker, and I'm still not. By college I earned enough scholarships to take me though grad school twice. I'm always taking classes or picking up new skills."

"And what if you win a new fortune?"

"I'll jump right in, what else?"

"Do you have a long-term goal in mind?"

"No. Never have. I figured I would miss a lot of great stuff if I just looked ahead to one thing. I like to enjoy the ride life is giving me to wherever I end up."

'Leonard or Julian, I'd wish you luck, but I think you make your own." I went in search of lunch, and then on to another interview.

****

I had just sat down at the table and retrieved my notebook when the door opened. What now? A middle-aged frowzy looking woman walked in. She took a stance with one hand on the door and the other on her hip. "You're the interviewer, right?"

"Yes, I am just getting ready." I checked my watch. "If you are a maid—"

"I am Leona Bassett Butler," she announced in an authoritative voice.

"Ms. Butler, you are ten minutes early. Could you —"

She shut the door and stood. "I'm here for my convenience, not yours. Get started."

I didn't think anyone on the island would mistake her for part of the staff by the way she was dressed. I've heard of people who bought gently worn clothes at thrift stores to bring on cruises and then left them on board for the crew to wear or send home to their families. The cruisers filled their suitcases with souvenirs and shopping with no extra baggage to check or pay for. Quickly remembering the first requirement for the people I was interviewing was that they were obscenely rich and all that might come with that. Maybe she was feeling charitable. Maybe she was eccentric. Maybe she was just cheap.

I motioned to her chair. "Would you like something to drink or—"

"No." She sat down. Politeness was not her strong suit.

"How are you enjoying Drake's—" She frowned. "I saw you in the casino and—"

She huffed. "Breaking even, and you are taking up my time to change that. Next."

Wow. So that's how it's going to be. "Why are you playing in the Chairs?"

I barely had the question out of my mouth when she said, "Greed. My husband was richer than I was. I want his fortune more than I want mine. I can have his if I lose mine in the Chairs."

"You know the guests bet on the Players on the side, don't you?"

"Not my problem."

"I have heard you could be disqualified if you appear to be losing deliberately."

She perked up. "What does that mean?"

"You lose your up-front costs and half of your bet. They kick you off that night."

"Only half? That's not nearly enough." She stared at me as if she were waiting.

"But if you transfer bodies, what will—"

"I checked with top brain specialists. They believed the Gizmo reprogrammed all the parts of the brains of both people to allow them to continue with the same memories, yada yada, and particularly with the same handwriting, which is what interested me the most.

"With the same memories, such as account locations and numbers and the same signature, I can claim his estate no matter what I look like. With his money I won't give a damn what people think of my looks. In fact, I don't care now. You can be sure I didn't get to where I am now by marrying up."

"Why did you marry at all?"

She paused for an actual moment. "Greed. Yes, I'd say it was greed on both of our parts.

"We met at one of those secret highest-level weekend retreats to strategize how to best control government actions as they affected our industry. Bob, my future husband, was there.

"We had a lot in common. For one, neither of us had a suitable successor or heir we thought would continue towards our desired goals. We kept communicating and four months later we decided to get married and make the other the beneficiary to all we had."

"Sounds like a business take over."

"Yes, it kind of does. I like that. He died. I found out as the will was read that he double-crossed me. I had to divest myself of my fortune entirely to inherit his. Otherwise it all goes to his live-in physical therapist Blondie, the former beauty queen."

"Are you trying to spite him because in a way he threw you over for some one better looking and perhaps younger?"

She laughed. "Not at all. To start with, I am greedier than he ever suspected. Next, I don't take betrayal laying down. And lastly, for your edification, Bob was totally blind. Also, he was creepy. He claimed he needed to touch a woman to get to know her. He'd ask to touch your face or arm or hold his hand within five minutes of meeting you. That's how he came on to me, so I know about it firsthand and up close.

"I never fell for that, and I let him know it before we got married. I had an assistant who was always with me, and it was her job to hold his hand when he thought it was me. I don't think Blondie fell for it either. She always had Bob's valet, or me, or in a pinch, a maid catching up cleaning the windows in the room when she was giving Bob physical therapy.

"I am greedy enough that I won't let him me screw one way *or* another. Time's up. Craps table is calling my name—and don't wish me luck. That's the last thing I want in the Chairs."

I laughed in spite of myself. The lady had a sense of humor.

****

There were three days left until the Chairs. I was rushing to get all the Players interviewed in two days leaving the last day as a contingent in case someone broke their appointment with me.

I'd heard rumors about an attempt on Mr. Warren's life last week. I wondered if Raskolnikov would talk about it since his name was circulating in the rumor mill.

I heard a light rap at the door, and it opened. "Mister Alan?" He pronounced the 'i' more like a long 'e.' Almost a cartoon stereotype accent, but there was nothing cartoonish about him. Well almost nothing.

"Yes, sir. Please come in and sit down. Chai?" I looked closely to find his eyes behind the bush of long hair and flourishing beard. They seemed to be in contention to see which could hide his sight from view first.

"*Пожалуйста*. I mean, thank you." I was able to find his mouth because a fringe of beard under his nose moved in concert with his voice.

"You're welcome." I pushed his tea and a plate of Russian poppyseed rolls his way. He declined the rolls. I hoped he would eat a roll so I could watch his beard move from chewing.

"Mr. Raskolnikov, I understand you are in the oil business. How would you describe it?"

"Dirty. It is a dangerous, dirty, and demanding business…," he offered as he sipped his tea, "…but very profitable." I imagined him trying to shampoo oil and soot out of his hair.

"And yet you are leaving it in a big way for the clergy?"

"The what? I am sorry but…"

I clarified my question. "To be a monk."

Raskolnikov sipped his tea as his eyes looked away. Slowly he said, "*Da.* Monk." His eyes returned to my pitifully naked visage.

"Have you always had an interest in the church?" I was curious to say the least.

"As a young child I sang in the choir." I tried to imagine him as a young boy with an angelic voice and baby face.

"A choirboy? Were you a soprano?"

"We were all sopranos, and in the dark past you stay soprano. Fortunately, times change, and so did my voice. And the girls noticed it. The secular vices of the world captured my attention at early age."

"I imagine that is true for other guests here as well."

"*Da, da.* Pretty girls like pretty things, and they are fickle—is that the correct word?"

"Very much the correct word."

I wondered how pretty girls felt about his not so pretty face now. "Well, poor Russian boys work in oil fields to make money for pretty things. That was me. I work hard; I work long. Now I want to forget. I want others should work hard when I work for God. No more black face, black fingernail, black clothes. Just clean, like Heaven."

I changed tactics. "I understand you have already been here a week. How do you like it? What have you been doing at Drake's?"

"Yes, I come last week but my boat was dirty. I

don't want people should see it so dirty. I go back to sea for few days. My crew clean, clean it all."

"There is a rumor that you were taken hostage by pirates last week. Is that true?"

"Now you sound like paparazzi. A man in my position will always be surrounded by rumors. Has anyone presented any proof of this rumor? A phone video, a May Day call for help, or perhaps a wooden leg or a hook for a hand?" I thought I detected a smile hidden in the bushes.

"Well. Not that I am aware of. Quite right for you to make a joke at my expense. That's quite a long sea voyage. Where did you sail from?"

"Of course, long way. I must go to Black Sea to get on bigger boat to come here. My boat at Poti in Georgia on Black Sea. Then through Bosporus, across Med to Gibraltar, then freedom of the Atlantic Ocean."

I did some quick calculations. "That's almost 7,000 miles, or near 12,000 kilometers. How long did it take?"

"Not so long. I stop in three ports, and I not hurry. Four weeks, I think."

"That's a long trip. Any rough spots?"

"Rough spots? All forgotten now, but in middle of ocean a little trouble."

He's not going to cop to anything. "So now what? One last fling before you become a choir boy again?"

"Fling?" His bushy eyebrows met in a question.

I watched for a reaction. "One last wild party," I said with a leer.

"Party. I see. Yes, that could be. Sadly, it is last time to meet with Ledger. That is hard for me. I have few friends. When I leave it is one less friend."

"I know your plan, but what if you transfer into a

woman's body?"

"If it is God's plan for me, I become nun. Same plan."

"I wish you well. That's not a plan for everyone."

He hesitated. "This fling, is okay. Not a bad thing?"

I wasn't sure what he had in mind. "Yes. It is okay."

"Good." He took two poppyseed rolls as he left the room. Raskolnikov was what I expected: terse when he spoke, closemouthed when he didn't. Win some, lose some.

My next interview was going to be problematic, according to the Boss. I had never interviewed an abuse victim this famous before. I'd need my softest kid gloves.

Boss told me Mrs. Snuggle's husband was a famous pornography king who exploited his child bride for twenty-five years. Boss added he hoped she was able to have some peace and dignity in her life since the pedophile died last year.

I couldn't help but chuckle at Player Three's name: Bunnie Snuggle. I wondered how I would interview her without losing my cool. I saw photos from the magazines, but the woman who opened the door and came in definitely wasn't Bunnie. This was a much younger woman.

"I'm sorry, miss. Are you lost?"

She looked at the number of the door. "Isn't this room C123?"

I answered, "Yes, miss but…"

"Then I'm in the right place. Who are *you*?" She had the most astonishingly open and friendly expression. She was self-contained and confident. She looked at me as if we were two old friends.

"I…I'm Alan. Mrs. Snuggle."

She cracked a grin. She walked towards me as she removed a shawl, and I was shocked. The magazine said she had a 36-H bust, but I quickly surmised that was not the case. Those magazines were obviously photoshopped.

"Uh, Mrs. Snuggle, may I offer my condolences on your husband's recent passing?"

"Well thank you so much. Bless your heart. I miss him every day." She fluffed her hair off her creamy slender neck.

That wasn't the response I expected. "I understand you are originally from Arkansas." She nodded vigorously as her greenest of green eyes widened until I could see white all the way around her irises. "Do you mind if I ask you difficult questions?" My pits were starting to feel damp.

"You go right ahead, sugar. If I don't want to answer, I won't. Okay?"

This was not what I prepared for. "How did you and Mr. Snuggle meet?" I started my shorthand notes so I could keep up with her responses and made sure my hearing aids were on.

"Harold had a cabin on Lake Ouachita—that's capital o-u-a-c-h-i-t-a—and my mama and I would clean, cook, and do the laundry while he was there. I guess you could say I grew up right under his nose. Then one year something happened to me over the winter, and he didn't recognize me."

"It's all right if you don't want to talk about it," I intoned with a politically correct voice.

She bent over laughing and in a tinkling voice said. "Sugar, it wasn't like that. It was just plain old puberty

263

showing up, and Mother Nature gave me a double helping. Of course, Harold, being a man, couldn't take his eyes off me, but neither could most of the men around."

"So what happened?" She was fascinating, and I could not take my eyes off her—nor did I want to.

"Honestly, if Harold could have adopted me, it would have been fine. The law wouldn't allow that, so my mama and he got their heads together and they asked me what I wanted."

"Really? The three of you…decided what exactly?"

"Mama didn't want me to end up doing what she was doing, just scraping by, eating rice and gravy some days, putting up with…well, stuff the police ignored. I didn't want that either and Harold was always good to us, so we got married." I had a disapproving look on my face because Bunnie followed that up with, "It wasn't like you think. He never *ever* touched me. We had separate bedrooms. We sent mama money every month."

I couldn't help myself. "But the pictures, the magazines, the exploitation—"

She cut me off to the quick. "All *my* idea, sugar. Get that part right."

I must have blinked. *Her idea?* That was not what Boss's notes said.

"You must see that Harold was a good writer, but a talented photographer. He did headshots for models, actors, anyone who wanted to look like themselves but better. He made me look like I was twenty when I was fourteen, and fourteen when I was thirty."

I needed to take a breather. Bunnie Snuggle was not what I was prepped for.

Chapter 26

The Interviewer

Bunnie continued our interview much calmer than I was. "It was my idea that we put his writing and his photos together in a magazine for men. We had to sell his cabin to get started. I thought up the name *Southern Comfort.* He authored the articles under six different names, took the photos of me in costumes, and developed the film in our bathroom. I pasted up the page layouts."

"That sounds like a real partnership." I mulled over my next question. "Then why the move to the nudes, the enhanced photos..."

"What enhanced photos?" She had a puzzled look.

I pulled out Bunnie's most famous pinups. You could sit a tray of beers on her breasts. "Like this," I said as I passed the photos over with my face on fire.

She stared at the photos. Then her captivating laugh erupted again. "Those aren't touchups, those are real. Well, as real as we could afford. By the time *Southern Comfort* got noticed we had a lot of competition. Not milk maids in pinafores, but with more skin, more exaggerated proportions, more of everything. I did all that because I had an equal partnership."

"But I heard he always did the talking, the negotiating, the—"

Bunnie broke in. "He did because that's how we

played it, the lecherous old millionaire pimping out his teenage hillbilly wife. All the competition and advertisers were men, the readers men, the subscribers men, they ate it up like the Sunday buffet at Bubba's Boathouse and Bar."

"And now your husband is gone?" I had no idea where her answer would go.

"I had the implants and fillers removed last fall. I'm keeping the Lasik eye surgery—no choice on that one—and the veneers, and the education Harold made sure I got."

"And that golden blonde wavy hair?" that was still gorgeous.

She laughed again. "Natural. Eat your heart out." Then she winked. She was sexier than any of her photos.

I picked up my handwritten notes on Bunnie and the notes and photos Mr. Warren gave me, tore them up, and tossed them in the trashcan. "Bunnie, I owe you a sincere apology." I won't tell her I am her unabashed admirer.

"For what, sugar?"

"You know what." I paused. "So what will you do if you lose?"

"I still can fulfill my dream and teach elementary special ed students."

I hesitated at my last question. "And if you end up in another body?"

"Easy. I've already lived most of my life in what seemed like a foreign body to me. I'll still have my brain. I'll figure it out." I was out of questions. She looked over at me, dropped her eyes, and said, breathlessly, "Don't get up. I'll see myself out."

****

The Chairs is tomorrow night. Last week Chet

installed a new mermaid egg in the Gizmo, and I still didn't have a test to verify if it worked as before. After Lau's death, I was reluctant to suggest two volunteers. Maybe the dog and cat story Dr. Mixon told me might not be so outlandish after all.

I was still awake at 3:35 a.m. when my silent alarm vibrated. Vic was alerting me that someone had breached our security perimeter. My system was comprehensive. I couldn't imagine anyone unfamiliar with it would try a break-in. Four unknowns were in the Gizmo room. I was curious who had that much nerve. My first thought was this was an inside job, but I was at a loss for whomever might try it.

I met Vic outside the Gizmo door with my taser and switchblade. He handed me my loaded .38 Special, my preferred old dependable when the situation was up close and can't miss.

Bad waited outside the Maze door to the Gizmo, his khukuri in hand. He was to enter as we went in the front.

Vic whispered, "It's Xin, Boss, with two armed bodyguards, and a fourth person wearing handcuffs and a black hood. The intruders have flashlights." I signaled Vic to hit the room lights as we stepped in and Bad came in through the rear door.

Xin and his men froze. "Mr. Warren…or are you? I've been a bad boy and trespassed, but my business will soon be over. I hoped to conduct this business and be gone before anyone discovered us, but alas," he said in a simpering voice. He was mighty condescending for a general caught between armed forces blocking his escape.

"What do you want in here?" I demanded. This was my island, and I kowtowed to no one.

His oily smile almost slid off his face when he said, "I've reconsidered and decided to transfer after all."

"You've got the Greek shipping fortune. Time has expired and there is no one to transfer with," I reminded him.

"Well, since I thought that might be the case, I have an alternate solution. You see, my former government *is* accusing me of fomenting a coup to install myself as the emperor of China, so I have 'secured' a volunteer to take my place. Then I will feed this new Xin to the communists, and no one will be any the wiser."

His expression sent a chill down my spine. His man had a gun to the hostage's head. Xin said, "Put down your weapons."

"Come and take them," Vic snarled. He might look like a patsy, but he has the same mind, guts, and nerve he had before he traded bodies.

I was emboldened to add, "I'm not going to transfer you, Xin."

He brayed a pompous laugh. "I don't need *your* help. Stand over there by the door." His hand shooed us back.

We moved without lowering our guns. I knew hidden cameras were recording, but I did not know who was under the hood, perhaps an innocent Drake's employee. Xin walked to the back and flipped the Gizmo power switch on. The hum started and the hair on my neck stood up.

His next move was unexpected. One of his men put handcuffs on Xin. He stepped into one booth, while his other man forced the hostage inside the second. The yellow lights came on and Xin's man pushed the green button.

The hand circling the clock ticked off the seconds. I was furious at Xin's flagrant invasion of my home. I even had a slight concern for Xin's mystery hostage. Ding!

Xin's henchmen opened the doors. Xin stepped out while the hooded man was guided out. The hooded man's handcuffs were removed as he turned his back to us. I heard what sounded like tape being ripped off the man's face. *Ouch!*

"See, Mr. Drake," Xin said as he turned around. "I'm all done. Time to go home." Only thing was, his face and body were Dex. *The dead do come back.*

I looked to Xin's Chinese face but heard Dex's Jersey voice. "I had to do it, Boss. He was gonna throw me over the side wearing concrete shoes."

Now I knew Xin's inside man was Dexter Drake, my former partner. Any concern I had for the hostage was replaced by a double sense of treachery. By calling me Boss, Dex revealed that I indeed was the man Xin had contracted an assassination on.

Vic moved slightly, but I put my hand on his arm. "Now what, Xin?"

"I shall live out a long life in seclusion, with a new face and body, ugly as they are. Come Dexter, or should I say Xin? I'm not done with you yet."

I said," If you step on this island again, I'll have you shot on sight." I looked from Dex to Xin. "Either of you." If Dex had expected me to separate him from Xin, he had just blown that to kingdom come.

Old Xin said, "I'd kill you myself now, exacting the revenge I have demanded for a year, but officials in Beijing would know I was alive. After I arrange for your partner to fall into their hands followed by a swift execution, I must become invisible." Dex, now with Xin's mind, led the way chattering in Mandarin. Dex's mind but with Xin's inscrutable face, was prodded along with a gun in his back. Bad followed them as they boarded their Greek yacht and watched them sail out of sight.

We talked as Vic surveilled the ship by remote camera until the yacht cleared our harbor and coast. I said, "Dex must have given Xin the info to get past the harbormaster."

"I would assume so. I'll have a talk with him about increasing the security for all ships."

"I wonder how long Dex as new Xin will last. He seems to have nine lives."

"Tomorrow, I'll start a new design on all security systems so this can't happen again."

"I'll tell the harbor master I won't need his cat and dog. That would have been embarrassing."

"Yeah. Especially for the cat," Vic intoned.

****

In keeping with our honesty pact, I told Rosalie about Xin and Dex at breakfast. "Vic will have a safe room installed in the closets for the you and Allie's bedrooms. Those will stand up to anything Mother Nature might throw at us."

"I'm glad I slept through everything. Did you say Dex went through the Gizmo again?"

"Yes, I did," I knew where she was headed.

"But you and he traded in May, correct?" She stopped eating.

I nodded again and sipped my brew.

"And you two traded seven years ago the first time?"

Yep. "So old Xin is in a body that's gone through the

Gizmo two—no, three times…"

I looked in her eyes. "…and Dex knew that?"

I nodded and bit into my Saturday cheat French éclair.

"Maybe you should send Allie a photo of Xin and report the situation so they can update their files. Geez, how many others do you supposed there are like that?"

"Like what?"

"Dr. Mixon said one mermaid egg was good for what, fifty transfers? How many other criminals are on the loose in someone else's skin?" *Now that could keep me awake at night.* Then she said, "That's as cold blooded as it gets. Xin has about, maybe two and a half days until…"

I finished her sentence, "…the eggs start scrambling in his brain."

"Well, on the bright side, the ten million is off the table for your scalp."

After we sat and I ate my pastry, she said, "I think maybe you've underestimated Dex. He survived months in captivity, then conned Xin into switching in the Gizmo knowing Xin would die soon and Dex would live. I'd say Dex is capable of betrayal of any kind, wouldn't you?"

I had to add, "Yes, but I'm not sure I wouldn't have done the same if I were in that situation. The survival instinct is strong in certain people." I shook my head for the last time, "But, yes, he's capable of anything." Three days from now, Xin is out of the picture. *Have I forgotten anyone other than Dex? Huang, maybe?*

****

Skip knocked on our door. "Ladies, any time now, please."

Allie stepped out of my room after zipping me up,

"Wow, Mom. Just wow." She turned to her Dad and kissed him on the cheek. "See you. I'm on my way to dance with my fellow."

I opened my door all the way and stepped out. My reception was everything I wished for. Skip was speechless, but his eyes said it all.

After a moment he said, "That dress...that's the dress US Marshal Allie Smith Warren wore last year that made me think she was a ghost of you. That's the dress that brought you back to me. As our daughter just said, 'Wow.' "

I took his hands in mine. "This is our new anniversary then. One year ago we met again for the first time." I put my arms around him. "Happy anniversary," and leaned in for the first real kiss I'd looked forward to in years. That too was everything I wished for. "Let's go."

Allie had seen the Chairs, but I hadn't. Skipper asked Yvette to be my guide.

"*Mesdames*, Boss has a sort of script he uses for the Chairs. First, the introductions."

The Boss stood in a spotlight in the center of eight chairs. Singh stood slightly behind him splendid in his tunic and turban with trim matching the chairs. "Singh," Boss whispered. "This may be our shortest Chairs ever."

The Boss opened with, "Now for our Players for the night. No real names are used. Player One is a retired businessman from New York. He says he loves to watch old movies and read old books. In the Chairs for the first time. Welcome Mr. One!" Boss shook hands with Bennie the Jet who shifted from foot to foot as he stood in front of a chair.

I noticed Yvette ignored me but fixated on Ledger.

Rumor had it she had a fling with Dex last year. Now that Ledger looked like Dex would she make a play for him?

"Player Two is a Brazilian Cosmetics King and an avowed tree hugger. Welcome Senhor Two!" Boss and Davi Moran shook hands as Davi took a place next to Bennie.

Yvette hissed, "I never understand the appeal of this game. It is a waste of time for me."

"Player Three is the owner of a successful publishing franchise. Welcome, Mrs. Three!" Boss smiled kindly at the stunning Bunnie Snuggle as she walked into the circle. The two male Players stepped apart, inviting her to stand between them.

"What could she know about publishing?" Yvette harumphed.

"And yet here she is," I reminded her.

"Player Four is a Pharmaceutical Queen. She's playing for a new prescription in life. Welcome, Ms. Four." Boss didn't quite manage to hide his dismay as Leona tromped impatiently into the circle. He looked at her dress as it trailed on the floor and pursed his lips.

Boss announced, "Player Five is the founder of an Afro-American fragrance and clothing house. Welcome, Mr. Five."

There was silence when no one came forward. Then the crowd parted, and Leonard AKA Julian glided magically, as if on a flying carpet, through the silent room. From his waist up he wore a classic black tuxedo, albeit his shirt was in a shade of purple that changed hue as he moved. Below his waist was a matching billowing skirt that rippled as if alive. Leonard floated up to the Boss, slowly spun in a full circle, and settled into a position next to Bennie, who looked down his nose at the skirt and moved a slight distance away.

The Boss said, "Whatever that fragrance is you are wearing Mr. Five, I want it for my shop next year." The crowd clapped. Boss announced, "Next, we have Player Six who is owner of a famous European house of perfume and fashion. Welcome, Monsieur Six!"

"*Et alors?*" Yvette said. "To be in the same business but to come after Player Five, poor Gaston." She checked her watch.

"Player number Seven is an Oil Baron from Southwest Asia. He says playing in the Chairs is a heavenly calling. Welcome Player Seven!"

Vasily's hair and beard made it impossible to tell who was in his Prada tux. It could have been a yeti for all I knew. After last week's assassination attempt, Boss arranged to speak to every Player earlier.

"And finally, our last Player for tonight. Player Eight is a retired Canadian investment banker and a hockey fan. Welcome Player Eight!" Mr. Huang completed the circle of Players.

"Now may I ask all guests to fill up your glasses and pick a spot. Once we start the music, we ask that you not move around and distract the Players. After all, it's their fortune at stake, not yours."

"Players, all ready." Boss nodded to the orchestra. "At my signal, the orchestra will start playing and continue until I signal to stop at which each Player will sit in the nearest chair. Anyone sitting before the music stops will be disqualified."

Boss said, "Mr. Singh, remove the first chair." Singh took out a chair leaving seven, handed the envelope to the Boss, and placed the chair off to the side.

Meanwhile Yvette mentioned, "The losing Players receive 250,000 dollars, an airplane ticket to any place they wish, and perhaps a new passport. One or two may look very different, of course." She was impatiently tapping her foot.

I'd already seen the result of the Gizmo. *Who in the circle will leave in different circumstances?*

Yvette was obviously antsy. "I wish the Boss would hurry this up. Every minute is money lost to my casino."

The Boss said, "If everyone is comfortable, Players prepare to walk in a clockwise direction. When the music begins, circle until the music stops. No pushing or jostling."

Singh helped Bunnie and Monsieur Fleury to line up properly. The music began and the orchestra played a waltz. The Players' eyes were constantly on the next chair until they were even with it. Then their eyes darted to the new next chair, with the exception of the Player behind Leonard. The ever-changing purple of Leonard's skirt was hard to ignore. *Was that a hazard or a trap?*

Chapter 27

The Chairs

Yvette commented, "The Boss is famous for letting the Players walk for a long—" She was startled when the music stopped. "What happened? I did not see. Was it Monsieur Fleury?"

"No," I said. "Player Three. I think she's not used to wearing high heels. She tripped over her own feet." *Or she might have been distracted by that outlandish skirt in front of her.*

The Boss helped Bunny up while her Escort offered her his arm and led her to a consolation room. Boss signaled Singh who removed another chair and envelope for Boss.

The music continued longer than before. There was one false move by Player One, but he caught himself in time. The crowd became restless and started whispering. The music stopped. The man behind Player Four tripped over her flowing dress and pushed her into a seat. Her face registered anger at Player Two, Davi Moran, whose Escort led him from the chairs.

A tango played next. The tempo resulted in a nervous murmur from the crowd. Player Five executed a 360-degree twirl as he turned a corner, and Player Six waved towards Yvette as she came back into his sight. Unfortunately, it distracted Six just enough to cost him a seat.

Yvette's hands flew to her face as she saw Gaston, the poor man she had recruited, standing alone. His escort offered him her arm and led him to the bar.

The Boss announced, "Ladies and gentlemen, this is the last round for the Chairs. Please respect the silence. After this round we will take a thirty-minute break while I meet with the Players to convey the good news to those who have won. Afterwards I'll return to announce our final winners."

The room was silent: no roulette wheel, no cards, no rattling chips as the tango continued.

I detected a slight whirring sound from Leonard's skirt.

"Finally," Yvette spit out.

The Boss stared at his pocket watch, never looking up. The orchestra started a second tango, never stopping from the first. At the time of four minutes and thirty-five seconds the Boss stopped the music.

There was a desperate rush as the crowd leaned forward. There were gasps as Player Five picked the wrong time to twirl. He overshot and missed the chair completely. Player Five, Leonard AKA Julian, was led from the Chairs by his escort, a rather well-dressed drag queen.

Singh had taken the envelope from each winning Player's chair and handed it to them. They wouldn't know what they'd won until they met with the Boss. "Ladies and gentlemen. Please enjoy yourselves while we conclude the business of the Chairs. The spotlight on the Boss disappeared but the Chairs still sparkled. It was not too late for a souvenir photo.

Allie stopped Yvette, "*Madame*, I believe you are looking at the Chairs in the wrong light. Perhaps it is the accounting you are missing?"

"I am very good at accounting, *Mademoiselle* Warren," Yvette sniffed.

"Obviously but consider this. While you do not collect the assets from the losers on your balance sheet for the casino, it shows up somewhere on Drake's tax return, doesn't it?"

"But of course."

"The house won four fortunes tonight by my reckoning. And how long did it take guests to return to the tables? Mere seconds. Would you prefer the Chairs be held in another part of the resort and your casino stood empty for an hour?"

Yvette recoiled at this suggestion. "I see what you mean. The Boss cannot ignore this because it is a gamble to play here in the casino at any of our games even the Chairs."

Allie smiled. "Perhaps just a small reminder to the Boss…"

Yvette was all smiles. "Yes, I see. *Merci beaucoup, Mademoiselle* Allie, *Madame* Rosalie. I hope I see you next season." She left with a new attitude on her face.

I elbowed Allie. "She actually acknowledged us."

Allie leaned in and asked, "Did I just open Pandora's box?"

****

The losers waited in the consolation room. The winners waited in a separate room where Player Four was livid. Vic brought in Player One into my office. I never could read Bennie's face, and I wondered how the ownership of a significant men's magazine would sit with him. I called him by his given name. "Bernardo, sit."

"What pittance did I win in such a short period of time?" he asked.

"Here's a list of your new assets and instructions for assuming control. You won ownership of *Southern Comfort* magazine, all associated publications, and products—"

"The skin magazine!" He rose halfway out of his chair. His face was angrier than I'd ever seen it. *This may have been a big mistake.* "…and they total to roughly 613 million dollars."

His angry face froze. "Say that again." He slowly resumed sitting.

"I said 613 million." That was almost sixteen times the assets he lost in the game.

"Where do I sign?" and the deal was done. "Anything else?"

"It's your choice to switch into the body of Mrs. Bunny Snuggle, if you choose."

"You mean I win her too. Not too bad—"

"No, not her. By switching bodies you'd be you but in her body."

"A dame?" He thought for a moment. "Naw, I think that's a bridge too far for me. Ledger, if you run into me, act like this never happened. My soon to be ex—"

"I understand. Please go with this lady." His Escort led him to my accounting office.

Next Vic led in a fuming Leona Bassett Butler.

"Mrs. Butler. Please have a seat."

"This is not what I wanted, Ledger, you knew that!"

"You have won a famous French line of fragrances and products worth 478 million."

"What the hell do I do with that? I expected to leave here penniless. You know why—"

"And so you are. Your husband's will only stipulated you had to divest yourself of all your assets 'at the time of his death' and you have. All those earlier assets are mine since they were your bet. There were no stipulations about assets acquired after his death. So you have met the requirements you were aiming for, and honestly, I am glad to say."

As recognition settled in, a crooked smile formed. "Are we done?"

"No. Do you wish to change—"

She cut me off. "You had two Players who had the same bets. You are saying this was the Frenchie's, aren't you?"

"Yes."

"I think not. I'm going back to the States where people know me and fear me. Maybe I can hire Frenchie to run that business for me. Where do I sign?"

Her Escort led her out as Vic showed Vasily Raskolnikov in.

"Vasily, please sit. I'm sorry to tell you that you have won assets of 39 million…"

He looked dejected. "I have failed, then."

I went on "…but it is all in cash." I saw what I assumed were his eyebrows shoot up.

"Ah, not so bad. Cash is much easier to 'move' around. Yes, I think I can make that work. Is there more?"

"Do you wish to switch bodies with—"

He cut me off. "I don't need to know. The answer is 'no' in all cases. Thank you, my friend." He shook my hand and left with his Escort.

My last winner came in, Mr. Harry Huang. "Well, Mr. Warren, I failed."

I waved him to a seat. "No sir, I don't see it that way. You now have 3 billion dollars in assets from the oilman. It includes super yachts, one that is in my harbor. You can leave here for anyplace you want, with anyone you want, for as long as you want, and as warm as you want."

"Since you put it that way… An inscrutable smirk grew on his face. "Does that conclude our business?"

"Do you wish to transfer bodies with him?"

"He is Russian, isn't he? It seems to end badly for Russian oligarchs, doesn't it? So no."

I glanced at Vic standing behind Mr. Huang. "Just one more thing. This last week you seemed to be everywhere I was. I recognized you as the clown at the cricket match. I saw you every night dining in the Starlight and then gambling in the casino. You were in front of me at the fireworks two nights ago. Why was that, sir?"

Huang looked sheepishly at me. "You caught me. Cloak and dagger is not for me, but I felt responsible for my cousin Lau."

"You came here to kill me in revenge for Lau's death? He went through the Gizmo more times than is allowed, and he did so without my knowledge, I didn't even know he was here until—"

"No! I might have known he was lying all along, but I never came to kill you."

"What then?" This was not making any sense.

"Lau didn't know he was sick from the Gizmo. He and his family thought it was some tropical disease he caught here. I feared they would blame you and exact revenge. I came to protect you since I can recognize his family, and you can't."

"Are you saying I think all Chinese look alike?"

Should I be insulted?

"Of course, not. But would you know if someone was speaking Mandarin, Cantonese, *or* Japanese? I know them all on sight as well as their henchmen."

His explanation seemed reasonable. "I thank you for your thoughtfulness. Please go with your Escort. Goodbye, Mr. Huang. Enjoy yourself." He walked out with his Escort on his arm, and a proposition on his lips, I suspected, as I heard her laugh.

I looked over at Vic. "We made it through another…"

"Wait." He opened the door. In came Bunnie, Leonard, and Rosalie.

Now what?"

Leonard spoke. "Ledger, Bunnie and I want to transfer, at no cost, since we both lost."

"Why? That doesn't make any sense."

"It does to us. I approached the women in the Chairs. Mrs. Butler was not interested, but Mrs. Snuggle at least heard me out. We chatted all week. We struck a deal that if we could find a way to transfer we would. This is it. I get what I wanted, to be a natural woman. Bunnie gets a new look that allows her to teach school free from harassment over old magazine centerfolds. The fact that we are changing skin tone does not matter to us."

I considered their request. "On one condition. Leonard, you work for me for two years doing what you did before. Comb through my new assets and make them more efficient, but not at the cost of jobs for good employees. Here or in New York."

"Bunny, what do you want to do?"

"Do you know of a school where I could help special education students?"

"Do you mind living in New York?"

" I don't mind."

"Then I know just the place. Are we all agreed?" Everyone bobbed their heads.

"Vic, lead the way." As we walked, I leaned into Rosalie. "Why are you here?"

"You need to ask? I want to see the dog and cat show for myself."

At the Gizmo, I explained the process to Leonard and Bunnie. They went into the booths, and the next thing I knew it was Ding! and the red light came on.

They exited, held hands, and walked in a circle taking each other in. They seemed so happy, as if *they* were the big winners for the night. Maybe they were.

New Bunnie leaned in and whispered into new Leonard's ear. Leonard tilted back his head, let out an uproarious laugh, and said, "So am I." They laughed and left arm in arm.

I handed Vic his bonus envelope, his usual $250,000. "Your summer plans as usual, I assume. Any farewell comment like last year?"

"Yes, Boss. *Ad meliora.*"

Rosalie snorted and chuckled her approval.

"Vic, let's wrap it up," and we headed back to the casino for final announcements. I'm a*lready worrying about next year's Players.*

****

The next morning, we were saying goodbye before Rosalie, June, and I flew off for a combined business and pleasure trip.

Rosalie hugged her dad. "Keep out of trouble. Reverend Otis might find you something useful to do."

"What comes next, guys?" Allie asked as I hugged

her.

Rosalie hugged her too and said, "The past is the past. We won't focus on what might have been. We're looking forward to what might be."

It was my turn. "Alderich, I think you are a hell of a guy."

"Honestly?" He blushed.

"Yes, I do. I know I'm guilty of kidding you about your leg because…well, it doesn't matter, and I apologize. Since I've gotten to know you better, I worry how do I compete against Inspector Gadget? You're so far ahead in your head than I was at your age, it's scary. Allie. I love you, baby. Take good care of this guy. We'll see you in July at your place."

Rosalie looked at me. "Looking forward, I am calling you Ledger, or maybe Ledge. Skipper is in the past, too but we do need to take one trip back in time."

What did she have in mind now? As my plane cleared the runway I said, "I have complete confidence you can answer three questions for me."

"Shoot," she said.

"What did Vic's Latin message mean?"

"Towards better things."

"Yes indeed. And since you were closer than I was, what did Bunnie say to Leonard?"

Laughing Rosalie answered, "Bunnie said 'I am a virgin.' "

Now it was my turn to laugh. "And so was he. Her statement means I need to re-evaluate her husband's legacy. And lastly, where are we going?"

She raised her eyebrows. "Ready to meet *your* dad?" she asked as she held my hand in hers that still wore my promise ring. I think my eyes said it all again.

A word about the author...

I've been to 85+ countries and territories and around the world twice, once on an aircraft carrier. I am a globe-hopping retired engineering professor who loves to educate people as they read. While I've published other books, I turned to writing novels after retirement. Author page: dtmularkey.com

Thank you for purchasing
this publication of The Wild Rose Press, Inc.

For questions or more information
contact us at
info@thewildrosepress.com.

The Wild Rose Press, Inc.
www.thewildrosepress.com